ALL THINGS FOUND

D.L. BUNCH

strigiform publishing

For my Family

ACKNOWLEDGMENTS

First and foremost, I'd like to thank my family. They've been supportive, helpful, and most of all, patient with me through the process of writing this series. Next, I'd like to thank my editor, Ayden Rails, she's done a fabulous job of pointing me in the right direction on these final drafts. I appreciate everybody who's read some iteration of this along the way and have given their valuable feedback. And last, but definitely not least, thank you to my beta readers, Suzanne Toruk, Jay Logan, and the Taos Toolbox crew. You all are the best!

ALSO BY D.L. BUNCH

The Territory Series

All Things Lost

All Things Hidden

All Things Found

Visit www.dlbunch.com for more information on prizes and deals! You may find a survivalist tip or three as well!

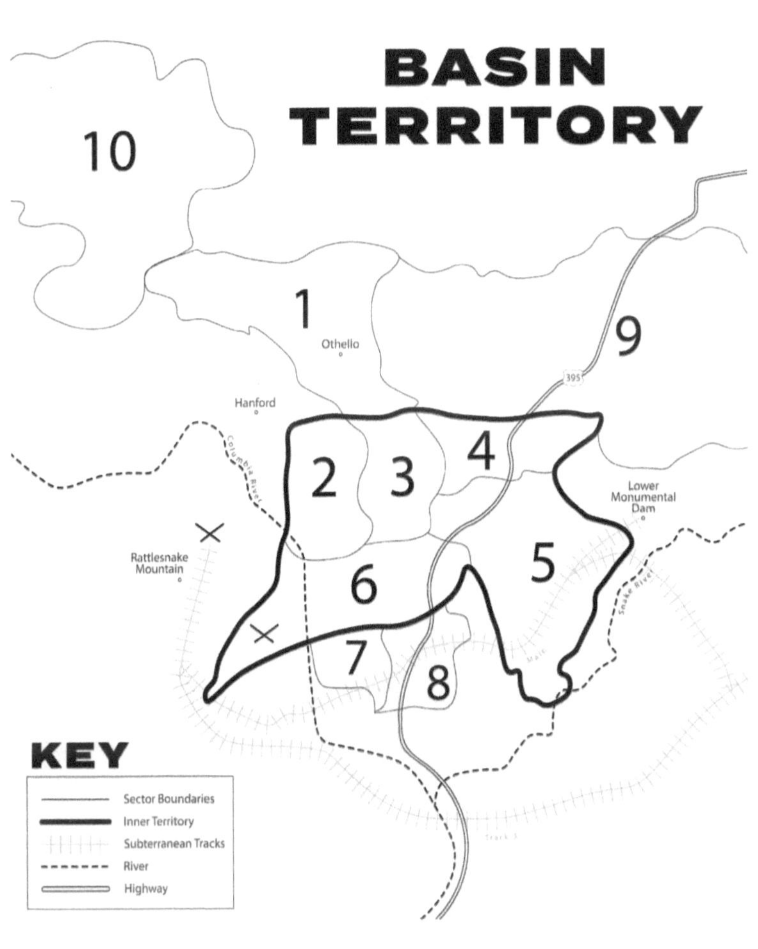

BASIN TERRITORY
10
1
Othello
9
395
Hanford
Columbia River
2
3
4
Lower
Monumental
Dam
Rattlesnake
Mountain
5
6
Snake River
7
8
Male
Track 3
KEY
Sector Boundaries
Inner Territory
Subterranean Tracks
River
Highway

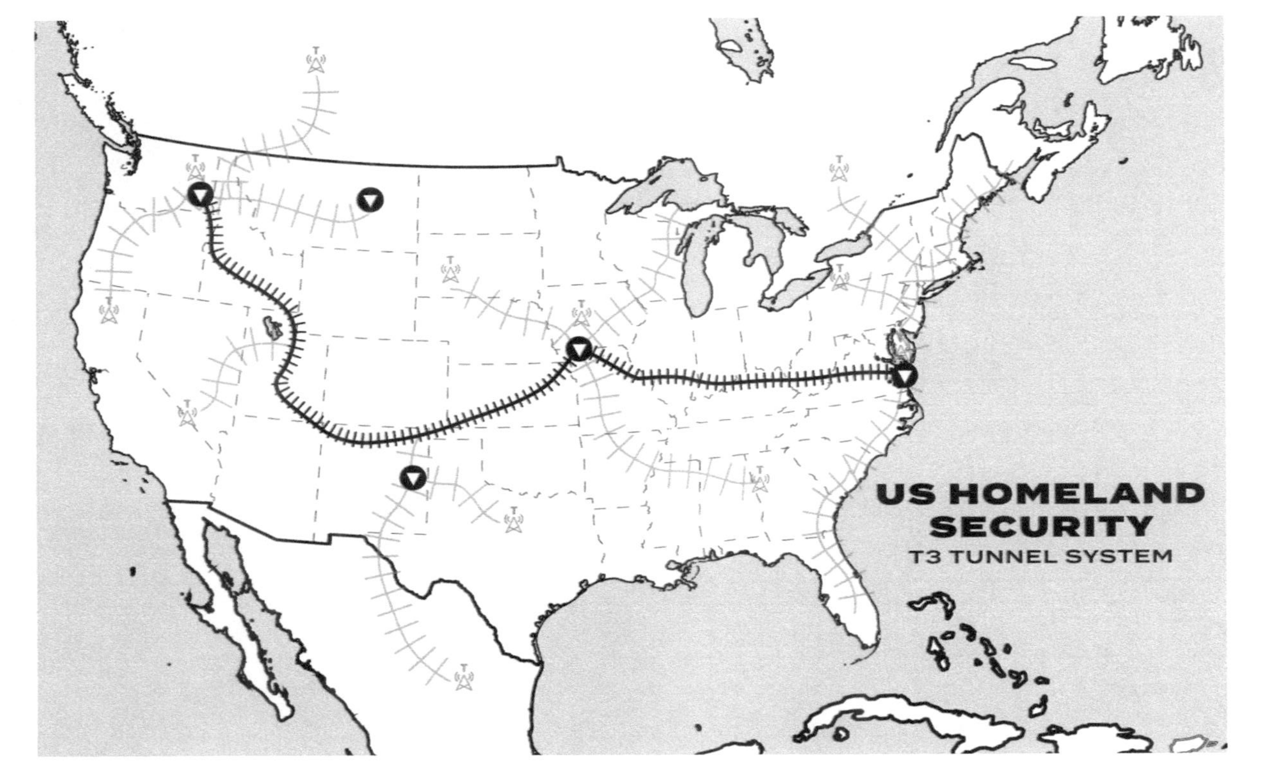

US HOMELAND SECURITY
T3 TUNNEL SYSTEM

PROLOGUE

General Lee Kaspar
September 2054
Ft Belvoir Underground Complex, Virginia

Death never wavered, never relented. It hummed in the shadows, a low, persistent drone ever-present and waiting, piercing through the brightest days or deepest nights. General Lee Kaspar had learned this truth through the brutal lessons of a hardened life. The ever-present images tattooed on his brain of fields soaked in blood, trenches littered with corpses, and stretchers of pustulant bodies and irradiated flesh charred beyond recognition. He'd entered this world shadowed by its spectre, his mother's frail form overwhelmed by the drugs she'd consumed, unable to withstand the ordeal of childbirth. It had been his constant companion, more intimate than any of his three ex-wives, more steadfast than the succession of foster homes that shaped his youth.

It understood him. It made him stronger.

Kaspar's fingers tremored—just a little—over the blackened meteorite enclosed in glass. So beautiful, so alive. A black heart beating just for him. Death at its most intimate. He opened the glass, cradling the icy sample in both hands, the cold so sharp it took his breath away. Something in his blood stirred, oozing through his veins. A part of him wanted—no, needed to curl around the rock and embrace what it would give him: sweet release and homecoming.

Not yet. A voice whispered inside him. *Too soon.*

Another voice, an external annoyance, tickled his ear like a mosquito, coming from the speaker behind him. It could wait. They all could.

The TMRWS device hummed in the adjacent turbine chamber, its absent core making the promise of rain a distant dream. Out of the dozen others scattered around the country, the one here in Ft Belvoir was the largest. Without it, none of the others could form the network of atmospheric control needed to master the weather.

As they stood, the TMRWS were nothing but elaborate energy conductors spinning in their electromagnetic tubes. Daniel Burgess had lied to him and locked away the final design for the organic cores deep within the bowels of the Manhattan Underground Complex, clear across the country.

Resentment clawed at Kaspar like one of the angry beasts he had penned up on the surface. The MUC had been an engineering marvel, blending Columbia Basin geology with modern tech to create twenty sublevels of labs, offices, and living quarters unlike any other. It was *his* by right. *His* inheritance, part of *his* responsibility and command. He'd blown the top levels ten years ago to preserve the treasure inside so that *he* could save the world, and Daniel and that bitch, Eva, had stolen it from him.

Their vision of the future was so narrow. They didn't deserve the place. Why control the weather, when this beautiful gift from space—dare he say, sent from heaven—could gift people with more pure, raw power than any other thing on the planet?

Pain, bright and sharp, knifed through his skull.

Do it. The voice whispered. *It will work.*

"Sir, you shouldn't touch it in its raw form," Dr. Evans' voice pierced the fog of thought and adrenaline, her words tinny through the intercom. Panicked. "It's too volatile to use in this manner."

Kaspar's lip curled. Scientists. Always cowering behind protocol and theory. He swiped at the blood dripping from his nose.

"This rock equals strength, Evans. The Eastern Bloc won't wait for your caution. Neither will I." His voice barked the words like a Master Sergeant he'd once had in basic. It brooked no dissent. Wars were won on audacity, not indecision. It's why he'd injected himself with the Super-Soldier serum the lab here had reinvented from the MUC's unrefined prototype Shield Serum. Raw tellurium enzyme would save their world quicker than the watered-down crap the MUC had been refining.

Shield, even the name sounded weak and defenseless.

If Daniel Burgess and Eva Zapada couldn't give him what he desired, he would start over. The Western Coalition needed their soldiers to be godlike, invincible, if they were going to regain power from the Eastern Bloc. Burgess and Zapada thought they could play him. They sure learned their lesson.

Another agonizing spear of pain gripped his brain. Moisture trickled from his ears. He touched the rock. Relief swept through his body.

Kaspar dismissed Evans on the other side of the observation glass with a wave. He didn't need any scared little doe interfering with what would save them all. His eyes locked on the meteorite in his hand. The rock had warmed and was heavier than it looked, its surface an inky slickness with sparks of life flickering like stars in the night.

He lifted it closer, breathing in the metallic smell, and a jolt seared through him—fire in his veins, clarity in his mind. The lab blurred, then sharpened. He saw everything: the cracks in the concrete, the fear in Evans' eyes through the glass—he'd have to make her follow orders this time—and a vision of the future where he'd crush the Eastern Coalition under his boot, taking control of it all.

It wasn't just tellurium or some inert mineral. It spoke. Not in words, but in urges—sharp, electric, like orders from a higher command. His pulse quickened, a soldier's thrill at a new weapon.

"Please, no." Evans pounded the glass. "There is no Eastern Bloc, sir. The war is over."

"Leave! Now!" His roar shook the room, unnatural, amplified. His skin prickled, black lines spidering across his forearms like tattoos. The rock's voice surged, and he stumbled, catching himself on the control vault. He barely registered his reflection in the glass, which reflected eyes black as oil, the whites all but gone.

Evans fumbled with the alarm. Kaspar laughed, a sound that wasn't his own. "You think alarms can stop this?" He ripped open the conduit box, strength coursing through his veins like electricity in a storm. He inserted the tellurium meteorite into the docking port where Daniel's organic core, infused with a weakened version of the tellurium enzyme, would have fueled the TMRWS for rain, and closed the glass door. His bloody palm smashed the button on the control panel to initialize the system with a surge of energy that crackled throughout the chamber.

The TMRWS's hum transformed into a dull throb boring its way into his bones.

"NO!" Dr. Evans screamed, her ineffectual fists beating on the glass, now leaving bloody smudges in their wake. With a dispassionate tilt of his head, he dismissed her.

The Eastern Bloc and the rest of his enemies would learn this lesson well: those who controlled Death, and all its resources, controlled the world.

Part 1
The Past: 2055
Eva

"The life we lead is our only way of measuring time; the past is always with us, in us, shaping the present."
— John Banville, *The Sea*

CHAPTER 1

September 2055
Leaving Kansas City

The baby howled, a raw, piercing cry that echoed in the train engine's steel belly and burrowed into Eva's soul. Kel, the child's mother, sat hunched against the wall, her mumuu crusted with blood and filth, legs splayed.

The newborn flailed on the floor, umbilical stump oozing around a knotted string, Chet's old shirt kicked aside. Her tiny limbs thrashed, face scarlet with hunger.

Kel clamped her hands over her ears, head sunk into her shoulders like a turtle retreating from the world. Cleaned up, she'd be striking—barely eighteen, with sharp cheekbones and auburn hair underneath all the grime. No wonder Hensley, Kansas City's cult leader, had chosen her to bear his child. His psychopathic grip lingered in her eyes, a shadow of the corrupted enzyme that had twisted his followers.

"This is ridiculous," Tamara muttered, edging toward the wailing infant. She tried to slide him from between the wall and seat, but Kel lashed out—all ragged nails and bared teeth. No one could draw near the girl without risking the child.

I can't blame her. Eva massaged her temples. She'd be feral too, ripped from the only home she knew, even one ruled by a monster. Kidnapping Kel had been a desperate move, but Hensley's cult was a dead end, and her baby deserved better. Besides, a guilty, darker part of her knew the girl made a good hostage.

The train had stopped four miles from St. Louis, where an unknown hostile had slaughtered their clearing crew—all ten dead except for one. The sole survivor, Chloe, lay huddled in a corner, arms wrapped around her knees, watching them all with dull, glassy eyes. Daniel had ordered Chet to establish their perimeter, now bristling with explosives and the portable barricade. The engine, with all of its yummy humans, would be a good trap to lure it out of the shadows. Nothing would pass without being shredded, and the baby's cries were a beacon in the dark. At this point, the noise not necessarily a bad thing if they wanted to capture it.

"Kel, let us help your child." Eva knelt just beyond the girl's reach, voice soft. Her Stranger stirred, restless, drawn to the tellurium meteorite stashed in the train's cargo, its whisper a serpent in her veins. She shoved it down with a weary effort. Her stranger didn't understand words like empathy or compassion, just power. Without the Shield serum running through her veins, she would have succumbed to its effects like the pseudo-humans eating people for breakfast. Daniel called them Aberrants, but she found the word too melodramatic and bulky. Too on the nose, giving the creatures more credence than they deserved.

"You'll steal him!" Kel's hair whipped as she shook her head, eyes wild with a feral light.

"Look around." Eva inched closer, palms open. "He's a newborn. He needs you to nurse him. To feed him."

Kel hissed, a cornered animal.

"Enough." Daniel's voice cut through, cold and unyielding, a commander's order from above and behind Eva. "Pick up that baby and feed her, or I'll have Tamara and Chet hold you down. Clear?"

Tears streaked Kel's face, but Daniel's glare, hard as the tunnel walls surrounding them, broke her defiance. She fumbled for the infant, hesitant.

"Support the neck," Eva said in a gentle but firm voice, the complete opposite of the irritation she felt.

Kel glared, but one glance at Daniel made her comply. She cradled the little girl, wrapping Chet's shirt around her. The baby rooted against the filthy mumu, cries turning to grunts.

Eva winced. The garment was a health hazard. Her Stranger pulsed, urging action, but she kept her hands still.

"I don't know how to feed her," Kel mumbled, brow creased. "It's my first one."

Eva was surprised. In Kansas City's breeding house, girls as young as fourteen nursed infants. Hensley must've kept Kel for himself.

"May I help?" Eva raised her hands, non-threatening.

Kel glanced at Daniel, conditioned to male authority. Eva frowned. Hensley's shadow lingered like a demonic cloud. Only time could heal the lifetime of brainwashing the young woman had suffered. A dose of the stable Shield serum might help the process along, but Eva needed every drop for the organic core they carried with them.

The core, which would slot into a docking port on the Tempered Electromagnetic Resonant Weather System, or TMRWS. With Daniel's enhancements, it would begin reversing the damage caused by the raw enzyme found encased in the tellurium cores of a handful of large meteorites uncovered by the former government.

Like Tolkien's opus, the TMRWS at Ft. Belvoir in Virginia was the one machine to control the rest, at least the atmospheric mechanisms in the energy conductors. If they could install the organic Shield core Daniel had modified, it would at least stabilize the weather on their continent with the added bonus of preventing more people infected with the raw enzyme from turning into monstrous aberrants.

Gah. There was that word again.

Daniel caught the look. "Let Eva help, Kel. She's raised a child."

Kel's lips curled, but she nodded. "Fine."

"And we need you clean," Daniel added, voice calculated, prodding her maternal instinct. "Dirt's dangerous for a newborn."

Eva's dog, Nala, whined, padding closer. Kel flinched, clutching the baby.

"She's harmless. See." Eva stroked Nala's fur.

"Mr. Hensley says dogs are evil. We kill 'em for food." Kel made a strange sign, a looping of her middle fingers and thumb, the baby bobbing. The infant fussed, hungry.

Daniel sighed, glancing skyward for patience, then shot Eva a look—*please handle this*. He muttered something about the perimeter and left, boots echoing.

Nala flopped down, giving Kel her most soulful stare. Eva smirked. The German Shepherd was a bossy creature, but not evil.

"Tamara, wet cloth and water bottle," Eva said. Tamara rummaged and returned, handing them over.

"Your top, Kel. Just us women." Eva kept her voice steady.

Kel grimaced, eyeing Nala, but untied her mumu, revealing skin caked with dirt. The baby wailed louder.

Eva tossed the cloth to her and set the bottle down. "Clean up, then I'll help you nurse."

"You saying I'm dirty?" Kel's voice was sharp, defensive.

"Your baby needs clean skin to feed safely." Eva's tone was calm, despite the stench of unwashed flesh. Water was scarce, but maintaining hygiene was essential for survival.

Kel stared at her breasts, then at Eva. "You do it."

Eva's brows rose, but she complied, cleaning Kel with clinical precision. She guided the baby's mouth to a nipple, and silence fell—blessed, perfect silence. Eva adjusted the latch, then sat back.

Kel hissed at the suction but held the infant closer, a flicker of maternal instinct in her eyes. Thank the heavens.

Eva nodded to Tamara, who stood guard, tense. Time to find Daniel and check the core. With any luck, they'd be able to install it soon—if Kaspar didn't kill them first.

###

The tunnel's steel barrier gleamed under the engine's lights, ten-foot planks propped every five feet, a person-sized gap the only way through. It wouldn't stop a full assault, but it'd slow the hostile that Chloe had described—something mutated for sure. The train hunkered, a false shield against a beast that could peel it open like tinfoil.

Daniel leaned against the wall, rifle cradled, spitting sunflower seed shells. His face was shadowed, but Eva knew every line, every scar. "Chet's supposed to be here."

"He's dodging the baby's cries," Daniel said, voice dry.

She snorted. "He's not the only one."

"Are you sure about this? Bringing her along?" Daniel offered her the seed packet.

"Yeah. We couldn't leave her there, Daniel. Besides, Hensley might think twice about attacking if we have his child." She leaned her back against the wall.

"We could always use her to negotiate our way back around Kansas City, or escape Virginia, especially if the bypass isn't there and we have to travel on the surface." Daniel waggled his eyebrows.

Eva wrinkled her nose in disgust at his suggestion. He was only half-joking. "It's there, even if the map doesn't show the entire thing. The old government loved its contingencies. And I'm not using an innocent person as a pawn, no matter how heinous she is."

Daniel snorted. "If you think that girl's innocent, then you weren't paying attention in Kansas City."

Eva took a few seeds, cracking them, the image of Kel's manic stare and bared teeth embedded into her memory. That kind of crazy, instilled from birth, was nigh on impossible to turn around. "So you saw her in her full glory, huh?"

"Oh, I saw her, even if the view from the pig pit wasn't panoramic. How are you doing? Still have an overwhelming urge toward violence and mayhem?" His eyes studied her face, and her Stranger stirred, languid and hungry. It wanted him for something other than food, she realized.

Eva shivered. Should she tell him the truth? Tell him that she was a hairsbreadth from a complete loss of control and only their mission held her together. "It's loud, but I'm fine."

Daniel paused a beat, either contemplating her answer or devising a way to coax the truth from her. "I'll buy that for now. At the first sign you're not, tell me, don't hold it in, don't try and hide it. What happened back in Kansas City—that can't happen on the train, Eva. If you feel yourself losing control, chaining you up is the only option."

Self-reproach made her snip, "I know."

Daniel's warm hand snagged hers. "I'm not condemning you. Take the emotion out of it. We need firm, sound logic, or all of this is for nothing. At this point, regret will just get us killed."

She closed her eyes and drew in a sharp breath, and jerked her hand away. Every pore and muscle wanted to scream at him, tear him down for his words.

A small voice pushed through the rage and vomit-spewn regions of her brain. *That's the point, isn't it?* Emotions are a luxury ill-afforded at the moment, and the raw tellurium enzyme enhanced every single one. Her shoulders sagged in defeat. He was right. Again.

"We broke the world, Daniel. It's up to us to make it right. As long as I can focus on that, I'm fine." The words clawed out of her throat, ragged edges shearing her vocal cords.

A tense line formed between his brows. "That's where we've always disagreed, isn't it, Eva? We didn't break the world. Others used our research to put the final nail in, but all of humanity had a part in destroying it. We have a chance to fix some of that, a slight chance, but more than what others have." He gripped her face between his hands, resting his forehead against hers in a rare show of affection. All of this talk of controlling emotions, and they rolled off of him like heat from sun-drenched metal. "We're going to do what we need to do and fix what is broken. I promise."

Eva covered both of his hands with hers and squeezed. "You're damn right we will."

He pulled away, his mask returning, fitting into place across his brows and mouth like a puzzle piece. "Reports say Kaspar's unstable, worse than Hensley now. But I knew him, Eva. I might be able to talk him into fixing the TMRWS."

Eva patted his cheek, rough and warm. "If his defenses don't kill us first."

He squeezed her hand. "Trust me. I know his weaknesses."

A scrape echoed in the tunnel, swallowed by darkness. Twin lights glowed, like eyes in the void. It was showtime.

Daniel raised his rifle, swift and sure. "Find Chet, Trae, and your rifle. Now."

CHAPTER 2

The smell of rancid meat and wet fur enveloped Eva, and she gagged. It clung to the air in a dense fog. Whatever lay on the other side of the barrier on the far side of the track was not pleasant.

A deep growl rumbled through the tunnel.

Daniel hadn't fired his gun yet.

She cursed. He was trying to get a closer look.

Eva careened around the end of the train.

"Chet! Go to Daniel, now!"

Chet moved quickly for his muscular bulk, his boots pounding. Eva bounded into the engine, Nala trembling at her side, hackles raised.

Tamara stood, pistol out. "What is it?"

"Fairly sure it's our target. Where is Chloe?"

A whimper emitted from the back of the train near the bathroom.

"One whiff of whatever that smell is, and she freaked. So did the dog." Tamara fingered the safety off on her weapon.

Kel snored on a blanket near the wall where Eva had left her, the baby tucked close, both oblivious.

"Tamara, I'm sending Trae out to help Chet and Daniel. You,

Chloe, Kel, and the baby stay with Nala. If we fail, lock up and take the bypass around Kansas City—possible routes are on the map based on that barricade and side tunnel we found." Eva lifted the lid on a gun case and began to assemble the .50 caliber rifle nestled in its foam padding. "Arm Chloe. It'll steady her."

Tamara's lips thinned to a grim line. "Or she'll shoot one of us. You're leaving me as a babysitter."

Gun put together, Eva shouldered it—thank God Shield made her strong enough—and met Tamara's eyes. "You're not as expendable as I am, and you know our plan with the TMRWS. This world needs engineers right now. It doesn't need geneticists."

Geneticists like her had sparked the Collapse by crafting things best left in the ether of science. Engineers like Tamara built salvation.

Their gazes held for a beat, and Tamara nodded.

Eva exited, nose wrinkling at the stench. She breathed through her mouth.

Daniel had returned, and he, Trae, and Chet had fanned out along the barrier.

Daniel put a finger to his lips.

A flare's red glow bled along the tunnel, a hulking shape lurking at its border. Her Shielded vision might be able to pick up nuances in dim lighting, but even she couldn't make out much detail. Its eyes burned like twin flames, and it didn't move. Just watched. And waited.

Eva dropped to the ground in the space between the barrier and the wall, readied the huge rifle, and aimed.

The crosshairs bobbed in the scope until she steadied. She drew a sharp breath at the sight of the monstrosity on the other end.

An enormous snout erupted from a monstrous round face, sharp canines protruding from its mouth. Brown or black matted fur—it was difficult to tell in the dim light—hung in stringy cords all along its muscular neck. Rounded tufts of ear poked out of the skull and flicked like a feline's, listening. Razor-sharp claws protruded from paws as large as dinner plates. It sat, catlike, mocking them, its bulk radiating power and malice.

"Daniel," she whispered, almost inaudibly.

But he heard.

Dropping down beside her, he traded places and looked through the scope. He froze, gaze glued to the thing on the other end.

"Those insane sonsabitches."

Chet dropped down beside him, whispering. "What is it?"

"It knows where we're at and is on the move," Daniel said in a calm voice that could either mean the world was ending, or he'd like a medium-rare steak. The voice of a leader who had seen it all. He stood. "Eva, man the fifty cal. You get a clear shot, take it. And then put three more in it for good measure. Trae, back her up. Chet and I are going kitty-cat hunting."

Chet eyed Daniel warily.

"That's no cat, Daniel." Eva choked.

"Close enough." He holstered his pistol and brought out the rifle. "We'll try to herd it toward you."

Herd it. Didn't the man know you couldn't herd cats? Eva swallowed hard. "Be careful."

Hunting the mutated, like what they'd done during the Year of Hell, was the worst experience of her life— worse even than getting trapped on the bottom levels of the MUC. The first two were Killian Cooper's mother, Natalie, and her sister Sarah— hunting the latter had been like several knives to the gut twisting in tandem.

Dozens more had succumbed to the effects of the prototype Shield serum, and all had to be killed. Not quite zombies, a term evoking images of crazy dead automatons powered by the desire for flesh, but close enough, she could smell the rotting flesh. Cannibals instead. Alive but craving the blood's iron and the wild tellurium enzyme flowing in the veins of the Shielded.

Science ran amok, the failed serum killing the prefrontal cortex and any empathy.

Her hand tightened on the stock of the rifle. Trae shifted behind her; his breathing amped up, and his entire body vibrating with pent-up energy.

"Easy, Trae." She couldn't blame him. Not really.

The past week had been insane—even by her standards. His being dumped into a hog pen full of pigs that ate human flesh on a daily basis probably hadn't helped his nerves.

"But I can feel it." It was a little more than a whisper.

The hairs on her neck stood on end, and goosebumps traveled their way down her limbs.

Like calling to like.

"Remember your training. Sock those feelings away for now and focus on the problem at hand."

"Yes, ma'am," Trae said. But the response was automatic.

Seconds ticked by.

A crash and a shot echoed down the tunnel, followed by snarls of rage. Then three more shots.

She tightened her clammy hand against the stock of the rifle.

As swiftly as it had disappeared, the creature's shadow reappeared on the walkway just outside the glow.

She lined up the shot.

The cat-creature lunged, bouncing paws off the tunnel wall, then the metal planks of their barrier. Several clattered to the ground.

Holy hell, the thing was long. And fast.

Eva squeezed the trigger.

The round stopped the creature cold for a beat, and it stumbled to the ground. Even more enraged, it regained its footing.

She was about to take another shot when Trae jumped out in front of the barrier and fired his automatic rifle. Erratic shots zinged around the tunnel, some even hitting the creature barreling toward them.

"Get down!"

Too close for the scope now, she lined up the sights at the end of the long, high-powered rifle.

Trae didn't hear her, too pumped up on adrenaline and fear.

The creature swiped at him, knocking him into the barrier with a grunt and a few extra shots into the ceiling.

Eva breathed, the rancid smell of death almost directly above her.

She pulled the trigger just as a giant paw descended from above. The bullet took the giant beast right in the chest, blasting it back.

Eva didn't hesitate; she pulled the trigger again. Reloaded and did it again, her heart pummeling her chest wall.

Daniel and Chet ran into the glow of the flare and fired two more times each into the thick hide of the creature she'd fallen.

At its last twitch, she rolled over onto her back. The tunnel ceiling was arched above her, the vermilion light giving it a theatrical quality. Her pulse slowed, and hands stopped trembling, the aftershock of battle dissipating. This part of the world would always be like putting on a shoe two sizes too small.

I'm a scientist, dammit, not a soldier—an old, worn-out argument at this point.

Daniel's face appeared above her. "What happened to Trae?"

"I think the last two days caught up with him. Is he okay?"

His mouth thinned to a flat line. "He's a soldier."

Like that explained everything.

"He's a teenager with a powerful drug making him stronger, who just watched two of his friends die in gruesome and inhuman ways. One by pig." She pushed to her feet, swatting away Daniel's outstretched hand.

"Leniency won't do him any good."

Eva restrained the sigh.

She walked over to where Chet examined the creature splayed out on the ground. Holy hell, it was huge. Lean with a hump right behind the shoulders like a bear, it had to be at least eight feet long, if not that tall. Riddled with bullet holes, its muscular body seeped deep purple blood in over a dozen wounds. It's ursine stump of a tail twitched.

Chet put another bullet in the creature, and it stopped. He eyed it warily. "We should probably chop off its head."

A troubled look crossed Daniel's face. He stooped to examine one of the wounds.

It was healing.

"Chet, take Trae back to the train and get the fire ax and a blood collection kit. We need to see what we're dealing with." His short, terse statements were even and cold, though his eyes told a different story.

Chet picked up Trae in a fireman's carry and hightailed it around the barrier. Seconds later, Chloe and Nala appeared.

Animal experiments were new and dangerous. Though Nala had to come from somewhere, didn't she?

As if sensing Eva's thoughts, Nala growled, hackles up, eyes luminescing with her own enzyme's glow. *She senses it*, Eva thought, petting her. "Easy, girl."

Chloe braced against the wall. Tears welled up in her eyes. "We hadn't heard anything after the gunfire, and Tamara sent me out to check. Is that thing dead?"

"Mostly," Eva murmured. Tamara had made the girl face her fear. A good human, Tamara.

Daniel shot Eva a look, gun still trained on the beast. "Back to the train, Chloe. Nala, go."

Eva grasped Nala's scruff, guiding them away. The dog obeyed, reluctantly, her growl echoing Eva's Stranger. Wherever Nala had come from, Eva bet it was similar to the place where the dead beast originated—if not the same place.

"Easy, girl. We're taking care of it." Eva petted the dog's wiry fur. She pushed both of them around what remained of the barrier. Nala reluctantly followed Chloe back to the train, indignant at being unable to growl at the creature some more.

Chet walked out with the emergency ax they carried to break down doors, and Eva grabbed the blood collection supplies from him. She curled her nose. This wasn't going to be pleasant.

"Better hurry. She's twitching again." He stood guard over the prone corpse, eyes scanning the track in its macabre glow.

"You think there's another one out there?" Eva stepped back to let Chet do his thing.

"I don't know. Chet and I came across a litter of three… kittens. Cubs? Whatever they are, we put them down." Daniel stood across from Chet.

Eva found herself searching the tunnel's inky black beyond the flare's light. She shuddered. "Where's its mate?"

"Exactly," Daniel said.

Blood and stringy sinew splattered the gravel between the tracks and arced across the cement walkway as Chet hacked at the beast's neck. With the last whack of the ax, the body almost deflated like it had finally gotten the memo that it was dead.

Eva breathed through her mouth so as to minimize the rotting reek of the thing. She stooped to collect blood in a vial from the open neck wound as fast as she could. The syrupy, eggplant-colored liquid filled the tube.

"I dub it Felbeara." She wiped the sweat away with one forearm, taking care not to let her hand touch her face. "Get it? Feline and bear?"

Daniel quirked a brow, but it was Chet who responded. "Nah, too pretty. Maybe, Ursefel?"

Daniel snorted. "You're both way off. It's definitely a Tigursus."

Their grim humor couldn't mask the truth. Another Felbeara prowled out in the dark somewhere, its presence grim evidence that the MUC's research had been used for more than just humans.

CHAPTER 3

va spread the Kansas City maps across a folding card table, its plastic surface lit by an electric lantern. Two camp chairs flanked it. It was a safari scene minus savannah or canvas tent—unless the train engine counted. She reined in her wandering thoughts, sat, and studied the laminated paper, her Stranger stirring, constantly roaming the edges of her consciousness.

The maps were a cartographer's dream, with each square mile section marked with symbols indicating which tracks led where, the endpoints for the TMRWS, the number of cities with hubs, maintenance bays, and guard stations. All scattered across thousands of miles of underground tunnels, along with all of the old government secrets. Tamara and Chet's team had discovered them in Kansas City. In total, there were five maps, none of which were redacted. Except for a small black circle with an inverted white triangle inside, everything was clear and concise.

That symbol. One loomed over the MUC, another in Montana over Butte—her sister Sarah's stomping grounds, hunkering there like a toad in a pond waiting for a fly. The last two hung over Kansas City and Ft. Belvoir like miniature nooses.

Eva scratched at a penned scribble in New Mexico, the outer

edges of a circle still visible. Another one? Or did it mean that it was no longer there? And if so, where was it, now?

The day before, her group had come across the remains of the Basin's clearing crew. Two days had passed, and the place had reeked of death and decaying flesh. They had entombed the ten mangled bodies in an intact maintenance bay, sealing the door with a small blow torch. Her heart hurt. These people deserved better than to be laid to rest so far from home, and in such a manner. Maybe they'd jerry-rig one of the converted mining carts to pull behind the engine on the return trip. Take them back for a proper funeral.

Daniel sat beside her. "We're almost finished with the last of this blockage. Not as shored up as I would like, but nothing we can do about that. The scouts from a few weeks ago said there are only a couple more like this through Indiana and Ohio. We'll need to take it slower from here on out."

She sat back, resting her head and closing her eyes. "That's expected."

Daniel leaned forward, running a finger over the track starting at the MUC and taking the longer route down the western slope of the Rockies and into New Mexico. His hand stopped at the scribbled symbol, and he covered it, his mouth grim.

"There's no label in the key for this one." He pointed to the black-and-white symbol.

"I think it means a portion of the meteorite is at that location. Or maybe even more black sites like the one next to Lower Monumental Dam? Or, guess those would be one and the same if there's a meteorite in a cave like at the dam."

Daniel's frown intensified, and he clenched his fist. "I have something to tell you. Something you're not going to like very much."

She blinked at the speed of his change in topic. "Wouldn't be the first time."

"It needs to happen before we reach General Kaspar, and

now is as good a time as any." Worry lines marred his handsome face. Her Stranger stirred.

"Are you sure you don't want to wait until we're closer. You know, so I'm not angry with you longer."

"I'm serious, Eva. You need to know what we're walking into. What he might try to use against me." He fidgeted with the edge of the map. Daniel never fidgeted.

Eva stilled his hand with her own. "Seriously, it can't be worse than being buried alive at the bottom of a top-secret facility, or being attacked by a genetically modified bear-cat bent on destruction."

"Oh, it might."

She sighed. "Fine. Who knows when the time will be much quieter?"

No babies crying, no surprise attacks, train stopped for a few hours, everybody busy and not bothering them…

"Don't jinx it." He laced his fingers together, thumbs twirling around each other in an even swirl. Oh, it was *that* serious. "So, I met General Kaspar in Alaska. He recruited me after the battle of Diomede. The first nukes fell when we were in New Mexico. That's when things got complicated…."

Daniel
New Mexico
2035
Before the Collapse

The helicopter whirred through the desert sky, its shadow flickering over dunes and cracked hardpan. Roswell, New Mexico. A sun-bleached wasteland that felt like the devil's own backyard.

Daniel Burgess had seen deserts before—Siberia's frozen wastes, Egypt's endless sands—but this place churned his gut like something dead and rotting had taken root there. Maybe it was the history. Or what lay buried beneath. He scowled at the barren expanse as the chopper devoured the miles to its destination.

"Dr. Burgess," the young officer beside him shifted in her seat. "That's the facility. Want a closer look? Hazmat hasn't cleared it for landing, but you can see the damage from here."

Daniel's eyes stayed fixed on the warehouse—a low, sprawling structure, football-field-sized, camouflaged against the desert. A jagged hole the size of a school bus gaped in its roof, debris fanning out below like a scar. Hazmat teams crawled around it, tiny and insect-like.

"I know where it's housed, Lieutenant Young." His voice was clipped. Damn it, this would cost them months. Years, maybe. Time they didn't have, not with the Resource Wars raging and the Eastern Bloc itching for total control of the West Coast. "Is Dr. Soto at the command post?"

"Yes, sir." Her lashes fluttered, rapid and nervous.

He swallowed an impatient sigh. "Initial findings?"

"It… might be intentional. That's all I know, sir." More fidgeting.

Intentional. Like what? Sabotage? An enemy strike? Daniel pinched the bridge of his nose. War and death coiled around the world like vipers, poisoning everything. Fresh water was running out, and desalination plants were unable to keep up with demand. Something was disrupting the planet's water cycle, and no one escaped the fallout. "Lieutenant, you haven't stopped twitching since takeoff. What's the problem?"

She froze, eyes wide. "N-no, sir. It's just… is it true? What you did at Diomede?"

His gaze narrowed. God, she was young. Or he just felt too old even at the ripe age of twenty-seven. "That's classified. You should know better than to ask."

Her cheeks flushed. "Sorry, sir. I've heard… stories."

"Stories." He snorted. More like propaganda. A botched rescue evolved into a myth of one man carving his way through enemy lines to save a dozen with nothing but a machete and gumption. His superiors had turned him into a walking morale poster. War twisted everything, truth most of all. "That's all they are."

"Yes, sir." She stared at her lap.

Daniel unclenched his fists. Not her fault she bought the exaggeration.

The chopper hovered over the breach. Twisted metal and fire-retardant foam coated the wreckage below, steam curling from the shattered husk of the prototype TMRWS device. If this was sabotage, they'd known exactly where to hit. "Is the core intact?"

"Not confirmed," Young said. "It's still too hot to enter."

He nodded. "Pilot, take us to the command post."

The missile came out of nowhere. Later, he would wonder why the pilot hadn't detected it.

A shockwave slammed the helicopter, spinning it like a toy on a string. The world tilted, blurred. Heat scorched Daniel's face. Something sharp tore into his side, pain exploding through his abdomen. He clawed for balance, but the chopper's death spiral mocked his frail human strength.

Lieutenant Young slumped, lifeless. The pilot wrestled with the controls as the gauges screamed. Air roared through the open door, stealing Daniel's breath. His lungs refused to obey amid the panic. Pressure crushed him from all sides.

Metal shrieked as the chopper smashed into the desert. The impact slammed Daniel against his harness, agony igniting every nerve. For a fleeting moment, his mind detached, floating above the chaos like a ghost.

Stay conscious. Pain stabbed his side. He pressed a hand to the wound, blood slicking his fingers. Black spots danced in his vision.

Breathe.

He forced a ragged inhale through the agony, then another. Gulps of air steadied him, reality snapping into sharp focus. An alarm wailed, joined by the crackle of wires and the rotor's dying whine. Acrid smoke flooded the cabin, choking his lungs.

He had to get out.

Blood coated his hand. He fumbled with the harness buckles, but they wouldn't budge. With a grunt, he yanked out his knife and sawed *through the straps. Pain spiked as he collapsed to the floor, something sharp grinding inside him. Broken ribs? Worse?*

No time.

He dragged himself toward the open door, each inch a battle. His right leg was a dead weight. The desert's heat hit him like a furnace as he cleared the wreckage. Vision fading, he collapsed face down in the sand. A mushroom cloud bloomed on the horizon, his final sight before darkness swallowed him.

Bright lights. Voices. Hands. The thrum of rotor blades. Searing agony. Chaos.

Then a return to blessed darkness.

Daniel's eyes cracked open. A scientist loomed above him, her syringe glinting silver as she prepped his IV. Even through the gray fog clouding his mind, he knew that serum.

He swatted her hand away. "No."

"Sir, it's the only way," she said. "You'll die otherwise. General Kaspar's orders—"

"Worse than death," he rasped.

Her brow furrowed. "Worse?"

"Yes."

"It's approved for short-term use," she pressed. "Just to stabilize you. The side effects only last a few days. You're in no condition—"

His hand caught her arm, weaker than he'd like. He struggled to sit, to move, to escape before they turned him into something monstrous.

"Hold him down," General Kaspar's voice boomed from the doorway. "We need him alive and to get him to the MUC in one piece. The knowledge in his head is more valuable than any of your lives. Understand?"

A pair of strong hands pinned his wrists. The needle slid into the IV.

Daniel's world dissolved into nothing.

###

One Year Later

Plop, plop, plop.

Cold water splashed onto Daniel's face, and he woke from his doze with a start. "What the hell?"

Dr. Rani Soto peered down at him, dark eyes narrowed. "You were supposed to be in the lab twenty minutes ago."

Daniel groaned, yanking his wrist up to look at the smart watch through bleary eyes. 0800. Crap. She was right.

Scrubbing his hands over his face, he swung his legs over the bed.

Rani waved her hands out in front of her to stop his forward progress. "Whoa, there, commando. I'll meet you in the lab."

Daniel shook his head and yanked his pants over from the end of the bed. He'd slept for two hours and had not taken the time to shower, let alone put on pajama bottoms. Not that he usually wore them anywhere but in the lab bunks anyway.

Sniffing the army green t-shirt, he wrinkled his nose. It had at least one more day with a good dose of deodorant. He winced when he raised his arm. The IV site from the night before bore a deep purple bruise, a yellow edge to the fist-sized spot. It appeared more healed than it should have been. Hope could be a dangerous thing.

Fluorescent hell blared into his eyes as he made his way down the hallway. The government's gray walls and dark cement floors blended into an enormous natural cavern, where the trappings of surface technology clashed with the natural world. The fact that they were twenty sublevels below ground and had found this place using ground-penetrating radar from the surface spoke to human ingenuity—or corruption. Sometimes the two resembled each other.

The Manhattan Underground Complex. Named not for the city but for the project.

Daniel entered the lab that he'd just left two and a half hours prior. Shining metal countertops gleamed under more fluorescent lighting. Fume hoods dropped from the ceiling, and refrigeration units lined the walls. On a steel island in the center of the room, perched a glass box with gloves sticking inside like the gnarled hands of a spectral jailer. It held a black rock the size of a basketball—the tellurium meteorite.

He ran his hand over the case, patting it before walking to the closet next to decon. It had accompanied them from Roswell to the MUC, along with the TMRWS. The latter, which was now safely installed at Lower Monumental Dam, was a massive undertaking in its own right.

Rani looked him up and down. "That's what you're wearing? You do remember that General Kaspar will be here this morning?"

"I haven't had time to do laundry." He threw on his lab coat and went to the sink to wash his hands.

"That's what assistants are for."

Daniel frowned. "They're here to help with the project, not do our laundry. Or fetch us coffee."

He tossed that last jab out and waited.

"She offered," Rani said indignantly. "And you stink."

"I'm running on two hours of sleep and no caffeine, Rani. Are we going to continue with the tests before the General arrives, or keep lobbing volleys?" He snapped on latex gloves and turned to lean against the counter.

She heaved a sigh, her own gloved hands loose at her sides. Nothing much rattled Rani, even if her bluster said otherwise. "Sit down then."

Daniel sat at the blood collection seat, its arm coming down in front of him. Rani rolled his sleeve up and took out a blood collection kit. The first vial was filled halfway before his skin closed over the needle. Excitement stirred deep in his gut. It was working.

Rani's eyes met his, and she grinned. Yep. All their hard work was paying off. Stabbing the syringe back in his vein, she tried again. He winced but didn't utter a sound. Five stabs later, she'd filled two and a half vials of blood.

"Just what the hell is going on here?" General Lee Kaspar's voice boomed across the lab. Leave it to the man to arrive half an hour early.

Rani flinched, her gaze settling on the floor. She clenched the metal vial holder to her chest.

Daniel hopped down from his elevated perch and rolled down the sleeve of his coat, hiding the pinpricks. He schooled his features to show a lack of concern, even a bit of disgust. "Sir. We were just starting our day. You wanted an update? Why don't we head to the conference room and let Rani get back to work."

The General narrowed his eyes at the deflection. "I don't like being handled, young man. Why was Dr. Soto drawing your blood?"

"Why don't we have that conversation in the conference room, sir?" He moved towards General Kaspar as if to herd him out of the room.

"Negative, Dr. Burgess, I want to know what is going on. Right now." The General crossed his massive arms, looking authoritative and immovable in his service uniform.

Daniel didn't look down, didn't look away. He met the General's eyes and tilted his head. How dare the man question him? How dare he come into Daniel's lab and yell at his assistant?

Daniel's hand clenched into a fist at his side, the anger ping-ponging inside him like a ricocheting bullet.

The General's gaze landed on the aggressive act. He leaned forward, sneering. "Try it. I haven't had a good fight in a long time."

"Dr. Burgess, are you okay?" Rani touched his arm, and he blinked. The blood rushed to his head, and stars danced in his vision. What the hell had just happened? He never lost control.

"I'm fine, Dr. Soto." He wasn't. His insides quaked, scattering his thoughts. Ever since the helicopter crash and initial injection, it had been amping up in increments. A rage unlike any other kindled deep within him. Foreign. Elusive. With a force of will, he focused on the General. "I injected myself with the serum, again, sir. The new one. Before we try it on our soldiers, I wanted to make sure it worked."

Only a small lie by omission.

"It would be damn stupid to take that kind of risk if you're the one refining the stuff, Commander."

Daniel contemplated the other man. It wouldn't matter in the end if the General knew the entire truth. Knew about the cancer. Only Rani knew, its presence manifesting quickly in the months following the first injection—the one without the enzyme from the tellurium meteorite. If he was going to go, it might as well matter doing the research that could save so many.

"You wanted to enhance our soldiers, sir. As fast as possible, and in turn, I could also release the serum through the TMRWS to help strengthen the people of this country. I needed to know the side effects firsthand." Like aggression or anger—all the emotional outcomes indicating that his prefrontal cortex had regressed. He also needed to know if the benefits lasted longer than a few weeks. And the most important result: whether or not the serum had cured his cancer.

"Damn stupid," the general repeated. "I have half a mind to pull you from this project and strip you of your rank, but time is not on our side. The Eastern Bloc is on the move. I have some hotshot geneticist coming on board by the name of Dr. Eva Zapada to help speed up the process of stabilization. You said her work looked promising."

"Yes, but we don't need—"

"You just fucked up, son. Fucked up big time. You have zero say in anything now. I say jump, you say where. Do I make myself clear?" Fury punctuated every word. The older man shoved his face close to Daniel's. "And if you tell anybody about this, I will hamstring you and leave you in a wheelchair for the rest of your life. I don't care what shit you're pumping into your veins."

A fire burned along every sinew, mingling with an ire so foreign that Daniel's throat closed.

He swallowed, choking on the next words. "Yes. Sir."

The General rocked back on his heels. "Good. I'll escort Dr. Zapada down here tomorrow. Prepare a space for her and debrief us both in the morning. Oh, and move that thing upstairs, she doesn't have enough clearance for it, yet."

Daniel's breath came out in hard pants. Delicate fingers of rage twined their way up his spine and settled at the base of his skull. "Yes, sir."

"I want results, Burgess, yesterday." General Kaspar strode through the door, not looking back.

"Dr. Burgess, seriously, are you alright?" Rani's voice was just above a whisper across the room.

He didn't turn. Through clenched teeth, he said, "Run the tests on my blood for enzyme count, ASAP."

2055
St. Louis Stop

Eva stood, maps trembling in her hands, blood dripping from a paper cut. Her Stranger roared to be released, itching to fight, urging her to do damage. If she didn't leave, escape the pain of his deception, she would do just that. "You lied to me. For years."

Daniel leaned back in his chair, his face a mask of calm, emotions locked away. "Kaspar knows, Eva. He'll use it against us—wait, where are you going? We need to talk about this."

Eva folded the maps and put them back in their cases, each step a masterclass of control. She allowed a thread--just a thread--to unravel. "Come near me and I'll rip your face off."

It was the Stranger's voice, its raw, feral influence, but her rage intertwined with its presence, twin flames of hurt and betrayal.

"Eva, please. Let me explain—" His facade cracked, pain rimming his eyes and panic lining his mouth.

Her voice, hoarse and jagged with the weight of her Stranger, rasped, "You pushed me away after the mine explosion. I've suffered trying to control these urges, and you knew. You knew exactly what was happening to me and could've helped. You knew why our daughter's blood does strange things." God, that look he'd given her when she'd told him she was pregnant. And she had thought it pure shock.

"There's a good reason for everything, I promise."

"No, I need space. I can't trust your promises. Not anymore." Another thread of control unraveled. If she didn't leave now, she'd be completely untethered in a matter of seconds.

She walked away, the man behind her a stranger, a caricature of somebody she thought she knew. He didn't say a word, his presence a ball of energy. In the distance, the baby's cry mirrored the storm of emotions tearing through her chest.

CHAPTER 4

Eva sought shelter in a service tunnel not far from where they parked. Nerve endings raw, she paced, trying to shed the excess energy produced by her Stranger. Should she even call it that anymore? It was woven into her very DNA now, a part of her, body and soul. Not a Stranger, but a melding.

Shield was more benign and passive, helping without asking for anything in return. The raw tellurium enzymes were strength and power in their most elemental form. Perfect to create a soldier capable of almost anything.

She choked on a sob and paced. If she screamed, everybody would descend on her in a panicked mob.

Secrets inside of secrets inside of more secrets. That was how Daniel had always operated. The difference, the part that hurt the most, was he'd never done it with her—or so she thought. Was there more? How many hidden nuggets of knowledge was he still hiding? If he could lie about this, what else was he squirreling away?

Eva slumped to the ground, cradling her aching head in her hands.

Boots rattled on the gravel near where she'd sat, back against the wall of the tunnel. The train was still in sight, but even the hundred feet into the dark allowed her some privacy.

"Please, hear me out. Normally, I'd let you have your space, but we don't have a lot of time here." Daniel sat down beside her, drawing his knees up and resting his arms on top.

"Then you should have told me a long time ago." She didn't look at him.

Irritation resounded in his voice. "I may give you more leeway than any other person in my life, including Mia, but that doesn't mean you walk away for good."

"You give me leeway? You give me leeway..." She scrubbed her hands over her face. "Crap, Daniel, I just thought you gave me the respect I deserve after proving repeatedly that we make a great team. That I'm trustworthy. That somewhere inside that rigid exterior, you actually cared. You're my best friend. There is nothing about me you don't know. Nothing."

"I did it to protect you. Protect Mia."

"No, you did it to protect yourself. Can you even compute how enraged I am right now? No, not just enraged, but that you broke my heart? That our entire relationship has been based on a lie? Do you have that emotional capacity?" Eva wiped tears from her face. When had she started crying?

Daniel reached for her hand in the dark, and she scooted over.

He slumped against the wall behind him. "How did you feel with that stone in your gut? How?"

"I don't see how that's relevant."

"It's very relevant. Before you arrived on the scene and stabilized Shield, I watched the soldiers around me, tough men and women, healthy, strong, and courageous, succumb to the effects of the second prototype. Due to the higher dose of raw enzyme, they fell like dominoes, one by one. You thought our trials were brutal, watching most of them degenerate into mindless monsters, then have to put them down...Eva, I waited for that to happen to me, and it didn't. Not in the same way. I don't know if it was that first injection or something in my blood. Everybody reacts differently."

"You still lied to me. It makes me wonder how many other things you're hiding for my own good." She wouldn't give in, not this time. She wouldn't feel sorry for him.

"How did you feel?"

Almost involuntarily, the foreign presence stirred. Anger, unbidden and overwhelming in its intensity, reared its head for a beat before settling, like a slumbering bear disturbed during its hibernation. With the stone, the sample had exacerbated her emotions to the point of incoherence.

Reluctantly, she answered, "The enzyme took over. Consumed me until I was just a passenger in my own body. Intellectually, I know the stabilized Shield counters the reaction —or it should—but any exposure to the raw enzyme seems to agitate even the stabilized serum."

"Don't you see? I didn't feel that with the prototype, not to that extreme."

Like somebody had flipped a switch inside her brain, Eva understood. "Because of the cancer."

"Yes."

Pieces fell into place. Why hadn't she seen it until now? "My sister had meningitis as a child."

"Yes."

"You don't think Sarah was the one eating those people during the Year of Hell; it was all Killian's mother, Natalie."

"But I do think your sister can control the Aberrant somehow. Or like Mia, who can absorb the enzyme without any effect, and Killian, who can utilize the enzymes in Shield to track other enzymes outside his body. Even though neither one of them was sick, they were young when injected. Weaker immune systems. It triggered different reactions." He stood, stretching out a hand, just an outline in the dimness.

Eva hesitated, weary and sad. She grasped it, letting him help her up. "I haven't forgiven you."

"I know."

#

The weeks dragged by as the train inched its way to Virginia. Not that Eva looked forward to confronting the General. She had always seen him as an entitled, pompous ass out for his own political agenda. If he conspired with Sarah and Hensley, then she and Daniel's team were going from a viper nest straight into being crotch deep in crocodiles.

She threw another chunk of concrete onto the walkway next to the track. The clearing crew had cleaned up things a lot neater, but time was limited. They just needed to squeeze through, even if it meant barely scraping by.

Here's to hoping they didn't come across anything as expansive as what was beneath Kansas City.

"Soup's on!" Chet yelled from beside the train.

Wiping a hand across her sweaty brow, Eva made her way to where a meal was laid out. Rations were thin, but several scavenging trips to the surface to supplement the smoked fish and jerked meat supply had been successful. Small green apples and a bowl of berries sat next to a beef barley soup, something Chet had made by rehydrating the jerky.

Kel sat in a camp chair, the baby resting in a plastic container beside her. It brought back memories of the recycling bin Eva had used as a makeshift bassinet for Mia. She marveled at how people before the Collapse would spend fortunes on elaborate cribs and bassinets. Now, you made do with whatever was at hand, and it usually worked just as well.

The teen slurped up the soup, alternating between it and an apple. "Not as good as my mama's."

Eva studied Kel. In the last couple of weeks, she'd allowed her hair to be cut and donned different clothes. In the breeder house, she'd been expected to wear the awful muumuus, or other clothes that were not pants. After Daniel told her they'd take her home on their way back through, she'd quieted and taken advantage of the free food and water. She had relaxed and not tried to run for a week now. Hensley had indeed chosen the smartest one.

"You've never spoken of your mom. Tell me about her." Eva stirred the hot soup before bringing the spoon to her lips.

"She's beautiful. She works in the kitchens and was able to leave the breeder house after she saved Jed's life."

"Jed?"

"Mr. Hensley's war captain. I was supposed to breed for him, but Mr. Hensley saw how smart I am and chose me for hisself. It is an honor to serve him." Kel munched on the apple and seemed oblivious to the sidelong glances around her.

Chloe responded before Eva could even open her mouth. "That's insane. You were going to be given to somebody like a side of beef?"

Kel's face turned red, an angry pout to her lips. "He's our prophet. And I had his child, so now I can get any job I want."

Chloe just stared at the girl, who was at least three years her junior. "If somebody told me I was going to have to spread my legs for some old guy, I'd find a gun and shoot them."

Eva put a hand on Chloe's arm and shook her head slightly. If she had any chance of saving Kel and her child from the devastating brainwashing, she'd need her talking. And calm.

"Your mother sounds lovely." Eva gave up the spoon and used the bowl like a cup, sipping from the rim.

A high-pitched whistle erupted from the depths of the outbound tunnel where they'd erected the barrier. Alec. He and Daniel had called this watch while the rest of them ate. Another trilling whistle followed the first. It was the signal for intruders, but not an emergency. It would have been called a yellow alert on one of the old spaceship dramas on television.

Chet wiped his hands on a towel and picked up the shotgun, jogging to relieve Daniel on the inbound side of the train. Eva set her bowl down and made her way to Alec's position. The rest of their crew loaded onto the train as was their new protocol, with Trae and Tamara guarding the door.

She slowed as she approached the barrier, hand hovering near the butt of her pistol. She didn't want to draw it yet. Who knew if it would escalate a stable situation; people were trigger-happy these days.

Eva slowed and rounded the corner to find a stare-off. A man with electric blue eyes set in a grimy face, hair a wild white halo, and a beard down to his chest stood a car's length away, watching Alec. He wore a filthy bathrobe over pinstriped pajama bottoms, and cracked, faded, hard-soled leather slippers adorned his feet. His arms looped behind his back.

Alec's hand clenched the stock of his rifle, its tip pointed to the ground. His shoulders slumped in relief at Eva's appearance.

"He hasn't moved or talked since coming down the tracks. No flashlight or anything." He moved back to the opening near the wall of the barrier and took up position behind her.

Eva didn't take her eyes off the man in the center of the track, highlighted by the soft glow of two battery-operated lanterns set up across the width of the tunnel.

She raised her hands, showing she was unarmed, and stepped forward so the stranger could see her face in the light.

"Hi. My name's Eva. Where did you come from?" Eva kept her tone low and even.

The stranger blinked, tilting his head, and he grinned, showing a stump of a tongue through broken teeth. He gestured with one hand to follow and walked away.

Daniel stepped into the arc of light beside her. "Guess we better follow. Alec, stay here."

"I go left, you go right?" Eva popped a chemical light and held it out in front of her like a flashlight, its ghoulish glow high-lighting the hollows of Daniel's face.

He eyed her. "You good?"

"I'm fine, not a quiver of enzyme-induced psychosis in weeks." She used the term sarcastically, but it was the best descriptor so far of what she'd experienced in Kansas City after swallowing the small sample of tellurium meteorite.

"That's what has me worried." He hopped down to the tracks to climb onto the other walkway. "You're overdue."

She glared at him but took off at a quick walk along her side of the tracks. Since his big revelation, she'd avoided him. Difficult in the confined space of the train, but not impossible. Some of her ire had dissipated. It was hard to keep up a good mad when the world was shattered. Did he still need to earn back her trust? Absolutely. But she wasn't going to keep beating him over the head with his deception—very much anyway.

The two of them trailed the stranger, keeping well behind in case of a trap.

The dim tunnel swallowed time like a thief. Fifteen minutes seemed an hour before a yellowish glow appeared up ahead. Eva stopped before she would be outlined against the darkness of the tunnel behind her and threw the chem light into the middle of the track. A maintenance bay opened up to her right, the alcoves alongside the track large and looming. A soft glow crept beneath closed doors. Half-filled plates of meat sat on tables, with cookstoves, crates, and old trunks scattered between. Posters had been tacked to the tunnel walls, chairs of all shapes, sizes, and designs huddled around gas-burning fire pits. The space was empty.

The white-haired stranger gestured for her and Daniel to follow.

"It's a settlement," she murmured. With his Shielded ears, he'd be able to hear the words.

"Yes, but how did they find top-secret tunnels, and how many of them are there?" Daniel matched her volume.

The man on the track opened his mouth and made a sound in the back of his throat. Come?

"Well, let's go find out," said Eva.

Not taking her eyes from the stranger, she followed him into the light of the camp.

CHAPTER 5

Armed men and women materialized from other maintenance alcoves along the track. Multiple laser-dots from high-powered rifles covered both Eva and Daniel's hearts like badges. In unison, their hands went up in the surrender position.

She shoved her emotions down. Down, as far as they would go, and put on her game face. Loss of control here would be bad. Very bad.

Two of the people behind her patted them down, divesting them of their pistols and knives. It was a thorough and professional procedure, reminiscent of going through security at the airport. They herded her and Daniel down the walkway and toward a ring of chairs, stopping in front of one of the deep, cathedral-esque maintenance bays.

A tall, dark-skinned man in a ballistic vest and fatigues walked out of the shadows, a pistol in one hand and a toothpick between his teeth. He rolled it to the corner of his mouth.

"Funny thing about strangers these days," he holstered the gun and spun a hard-backed chair around to straddle it. "You never know if they're going to kill you, eat you, or betray you."

Daniel's eyes narrowed at the almost arrogant move, but he

remained calm with his hands in the air. "May I?" He wiggled his fingers.

"By all means." The man flicked a hand, and another red dot appeared on Daniel's forehead. The Stranger stirred in Eva's gut, creating tingling sensations that raised the hair on her neck.

Daniel lowered his hands, letting them hang loose at his side. Non-threatening—unless you knew Daniel. "Her, too?"

"Her, too. What are you doing in my tunnel, strangers? You're coming from the direction of good 'ol KC, but the last time I heard, they didn't use the tunnels. And a working train? Damn fine piece of machinery. Though it begs the question, where'd you get the fuel?" He shifted, the wooden legs looking almost too thin to hold his muscled bulk.

"We're just passing through." Daniel shrugged.

"Right. This dead-ends a couple miles ahead, well beneath Ft Belvoir. And that place is locked down tighter than a penguin's butthole in a snowstorm, besides the fact they're not very kind to intruders. What business do you have there?" The man asked it conversationally, but Eva could see the cold calculation in his eyes. The multiple weapons aimed at them negated the friendliness of the tone.

A frisson of surprise ran through Eva. They were closer to their destination than they thought.

Daniel's lips curled in a humorless smile. "Like I said, we're just exploring."

"Uh-huh. Rumor has it somebody stirred up trouble in KC. Know anything about that?"

"Would it break your heart if there was trouble in KC?" Daniel countered.

"Not particularly. Good riddance in my opinion, but some topside might think differently."

Daniel nodded, the dot moving from his forehead to the bridge of his nose, back and forth in some macabre game of roulette. "Good to know. What should I call you? I'm calling you Asshole in my head, but that's not very polite."

The man snorted. "You have balls, I'll give you that. Zeke will do. And you?"

"Daniel. This is Eva," He answered honestly.

"Nice to meet you, Daniel and Eva." Zeke waved his hand, and the dots disappeared, the muzzles of the guns within Eva's line of sight now pointing to the ground. But not put away. She didn't blame them.

"If I had a white flag, I'd fly it right now, Zeke. We're not looking to start anything, but we will react when threatened."

"Roger that. And ditto. Mind relaying to me what happened in Kansas City? It would go a long way to building a little trust."

Daniel snorted. "Trust is in short supply these days, friend. But I can tell you part of it. Mind if I take a seat and send Eva back to the train to let the others know we're not dead?"

"As long as I can send somebody with her."

"Compromise and say just to the barrier? We have some pretty trigger-happy folks on board that are taught to shoot first and ask questions later."

Zeke contemplated this with a cool detachment, eyes locked with Daniel in some male-to-male silent communication that Eva had never fully understood. Seconds passed, and Zeke finally said, "The other side of that opening you have in the barrier, and your guard stays with her. Afterwards, she comes back here."

"Done. Eva, let them know to keep clearing our side of the barrier until we return, then you get back here."

Zeke offered Daniel a chair, and Eva frowned. "I want you to keep in mind, Zeke, that if anything happens to that man there, I will find you and rip your throat out. And nobody will ever see it coming."

"Eva," Daniel admonished.

Zeke just chuckled. "Understood. And if the guard I send with you ends up dead, I will reciprocate the sentiment."

A red-haired woman, about Eva's age, gestured for her to follow. Eva looked at Daniel one last time. She may be beyond angry with him, but that didn't mean she wanted him dead. His head bobbed, a slight acknowledgement.

The woman behind her wore a headlamp, its beam illuminating the walls of the tunnel and the rails on the track ahead.

No other people had come out of the maintenance rooms or bays farther down the track. Which brought up another question: just how many people did Zeke have in the tunnel? Eva pictured the map in her head. At a quick guess, they were right past the Tennessee border, beneath Virginia, northwest of Ft Belvoir somewhere. If the rest of the track was clear, they could drive right to the Belvoir Underground Complex today. But she could've miscalculated. It was easy to do without GPS.

"My name is Eva, what should I call you?" Eva talked over her shoulder to the shadow following her. At least the woman wasn't holding her rifle, though a pistol was present and accounted for in its holster.

"Stella," she said, not offering anything else up.

Daniel would want Eva to extract as much information as she could from the woman.

Slow and steady won the race.

"Nice to meet you, Stella. We look like we're about the same age." At least Eva looked around thirty-five, the age she was when she took Shield over ten years ago. *Dios,* time moved fast.

Stella hesitated. "I'm thirty-four."

"Thirty-four is a good age. Past your insecure, trying-to-figure-it-out twenties, but not so old that you can't enjoy your newfound wisdom. Though, I guess with the world the way it is, we don't have the privilege of figuring ourselves out slowly, do we?"

Daniel's strategy of get 'em talking before you can get 'em talking had worked numerous times for her before. *Here's to it working again.*

"My twenties sucked."

Well, she was up to three words.

"Mine did too, truth be told. I was separated from my family due to my specialty."

Second strategy, always leave a question to be answered. Curiosity captured most people's attention, unless they were highly trained.

It took Stella less than ten seconds. "What was your specialty?"

Up to four words now.

"I'm a doctor. Though I wasn't quite able to finish my training." It was a partial truth. A doctor of genetics was way too specific for the situation, which led to Daniel's third strategy for getting people to talk: tell as much truth as possible without giving yourself away.

"Oh. Wow. We have a couple of EMTs and a paramedic, but no doctors. We used to have a nurse, but she…she's no longer with us."

Two complete sentences. Not bad. Eva tried not to smile. Damn, Daniel, and always being right.

"It's difficult these days. I've trained several people near home so we don't lose that knowledge. Though with the over-reliance on technology before the Collapse, it's tough to relearn some of those older skills."

Stella was quiet, probably mulling over Eva's words. "Do you think you could train some of us in some basics before you leave? Especially our midwife?"

Eva's heart clenched, and she remembered the complicated and messy birth Kel had gone through. These days, birth was just as much of a threat to the life of women as the monsters.

"I'll have to ask Daniel, but I don't see why I couldn't give some advice and training before we leave." Eva restrained herself from looking behind her to see Stella's reaction. The other woman didn't say much more, and the soft glow of their lanterns along the barrier soon emerged from the shadows.

"Stop right there!" Alec shouted.

"It's me, Alec, and I have somebody with me, hold your fire."

Eva didn't need to yell, Alec being Shielded and all, but she didn't want Stella to get suspicious either.

"What's the word?"

"Kreskin." And now they'd have to come up with a new safe word.

"I'm lowering my weapon, ma'am."

So formal. Probably for their guest.

Eva and Stella walked to Alec's position. Suspicion crossed his brown eyes, but he was well trained, so he stood at attention.

"Stella, here is going to stay with you while I go talk to the others. She has permission to go as far as the other side of the barrier but no further."

"Roger that, ma'am."

He really was on his best behavior.

She met Stella's eyes, the other's brown ones wary but not aggressive. "I will be back in five."

The woman nodded, and Eva turned to pick her way through the concrete from where they'd been clearing the track. Five hundred yards away, their refuge, their home away from home, their means to saving the world, hunkered on the track, sleek and black and beautiful.

Tamara stood by the door. "What's going on? Who's our friend?"

"So far, we have Zeke and Stella and a possible settlement in a maintenance hub. I counted six guards, but Stella is concerned about medical assistance, so I'm sure there are a few more than the eight of them." Eva relayed the rest of what she saw, including the information on how close they were to the fort. Tamara absorbed it, her brows pinched together.

"Zeke is trouble," Kel said behind her.

Eva startled a bit. She hadn't even seen the young woman at the top of the steps, partially hidden by the divider there.

"How do you know, Kel?" Eva said.

"Mr. Hensley said that they were evil and were not God's children. He said every one of them should die a horrible death, and if they were closer, he would make it happen. He said Kaspar should've done something about that rebel scum a long time ago. I wouldn't go back if I were you. Mr. Daniel is probably dead already." She munched on an apple, idly stroking her daughter's head.

Like Chloe had called it down, a loud bang echoed through the air from the direction of the barrier.

CHAPTER 6

Eva made it back to the barrier in record time. Several of the metal planks that made up the foldable wall lay on the ground, scattered in a pile, not as sturdy as they had been before the Felbeara's attack. Alec held a hand to his nose. It was bleeding like a sieve. Stella leaned against the wall, a frown on her face, and her arms crossed.

"What is going on here?" Eva demanded.

"She's just a little jumpy, I'm fine," Alec said through the bloody fingers pinching his nostrils together.

Stella's lips remained in a seamless line.

Eva squared off in front of her. "Stella? We're in a truce, why did you hit my guy?"

Trae joined the mix, his footsteps clattering rock and debris before stopping next to her. "Everything good?"

"Just trying to figure that out," Eva said. Stella's brows drew together even further. She was now outnumbered three to one. Not that Eva was counting.

"I'm good," the other woman said.

Wonderful. Back down to almost monosyllabic answers.

"Alec?"

"She didn't break the truce, Eva. Just a little misunderstanding." He grinned sheepishly.

If she pushed it, it might make things worse. Alec didn't seem too concerned—more embarrassed. Shield had stopped the bleeding, even though he still looked like an extra in an old horror movie. It would take some time to put the barrier back up, but Trae could stay and help.

Eva threw up her hands. Whatever. Nobody was permanently hurt. Who knew, maybe Stella would tell her on the way back. "Fine, if nobody is going to tell me what happened, Stella and I need to get back. Trae, stay and help Alec put the planks back up. Make sure they're better secured this time."

"Yes, ma'am," the two men said in unison.

Eva gestured for Stella to follow, the other woman even more on guard than before.

When they got out of earshot of the others, she slowed until Stella walked beside her.

Stella hesitated but rested her hand on the butt of her pistol and continued walking.

"Why did you hit him?"

"Can you really help train us with medical stuff, or was that a line of shit to get me to trust you?"

Well, that was a complete one-eighty.

Eva mulled over her answer. "Not a line of shit. I will help, but I'm not going to lie, I also want to earn trust with your settlement."

Stella snorted. "Settlement? It's an outpost camp more like."

Eva filed that piece of information away for later and tried again.

"Did Alec try to hit on you, is that it?"

It didn't sound like something the younger man would do in this situation, but the way he was embarrassed told a different story. In her vivid imagination, she could picture Alec making a pass at the attractive Stella and her hitting him in the nose, though that didn't explain the barrier. Those planks didn't fall on their own.

A glow from the camp started to lighten the tunnel. The beam from Stella's headlamp bobbed along, highlighting the cleared tracks and walkways.

The young woman kicked a rock. It skittered along the walkway and fell onto the rail bed. Her shoulders slumped. "Fine. I hit on him, thinking I could get some more information about why ya'll are down here. It startled him so much he tripped over his own feet into that wall, and he knocked his nose into my chin on the way down. Satisfied?"

Eva grinned. "Thank you for telling me, it goes a long way toward building that trust."

"Whatever. At least he can bleed." Stella fell back as they neared the maintenance bays and alcoves.

Before Eva could give much consideration to Stella's final comment, they came upon Daniel and Zeke, an inch apart, looking like they were about ready to kill each other.

Not again. This was getting old.

The old white haired man who'd led them here stood off to the side, giving Daniel and Zeke a wide berth. He flashed Eva a tongueless, toothy grin. A few others had joined the fray, sitting in chairs by the wall, not looking too concerned. Guards and men and women with guns held a perimeter, their barrels pointed at the ground. Nervous hands clenched the stocks, ready to aim at the slightest provocation.

Zeke held his fists in front of him in a boxer's stance.

Somebody had split Daniel's lip. It dripped blood onto his shirt. He licked it and spat a glob of blood at Zeke's boot.

Well, hell.

As if reading each other's minds, she and Stella ran in lockstep, across the side track into the maintenance alcove and up to the wide platform.

Eva inserted herself in front of Daniel, careful not to touch him. He glared, pushing back against her hand hovering near his chest.

"No." She said firmly. His lip was already healing, and nobody around here needed to see that.

Stella got Zeke back to his corner. "What is going on? I thought you were going to talk till we got back."

"We did talk. I had to see if he bleeds."

Again, with the bleeding.

Stella just shook her head. "Men. You know, you could have just asked him to prove it."

"This was faster."

Daniel growled low in his throat.

Not good.

"Let's go for a walk." Eva finally got him turned around and hustled him off the platform.

"I didn't say you could leave yet." Zeke pushed past Stella to intercept her and Daniel.

"Then send Stella with us, at least she's reasonable. You don't want to see him go off. Trust me." Eva shoved Daniel down the stairs and along the track.

"I'm going to slam his head into the wall and see if he bleeds." Anger tensed all the muscles in Daniel's arms and shoulders, his usual tight control gone. He strode forward in the opposite direction of their train, further into the camp.

Zeke nodded to somebody on the other walkway, and the person hopped down, following at a careful distance.

Daniel wiped his mouth with the back of his hand, leaving a patch of blood to cover up the fact that the wound was already a pink line. He kept up the pretense of rage, and they made it to the camp's perimeter, a dark, endless track in front of them.

He leaned over, putting his hands on his knees. Eva rubbed his back and pretended to calm him. Heat from his skin warmed her hand through his shirt.

The guard stayed just out of range, eyeing the tables back at camp like a starving man.

"Did you find out anything useful?" Daniel's mouth barely moved, his voice whisper-thin.

She relayed what little information Stella imparted and the incident with Alec. Then told him what Chloe had said. "If they're rebels, are they rebelling against Kaspar?"

"I don't know, but it's interesting that both of them wanted to see if we bled. Thoughts?"

"Another experiment out of Virginia, maybe?" She shook her head. "If Kaspar was refining the capacity of Shield, he could've found somebody to enhance the ability to coagulate to the point that the Shielded don't bleed. I don't know. My initial project wasn't meant…wasn't meant solely for military application."

"I know," Daniel settled his hand gently over hers where it rested on his shoulder. A tingling sensation coursed through Eva's fingers, and his gaze locked with hers, his eyes deep and shadowed in the faint light. The instinct to withdraw clashed with the profound bond they shared, his recent lies still raw and stinging. He moved closer, his mouth inches away from hers. Part of her wanted his lips on hers, wanted that connection. The slow burn as their bodies intertwined, igniting into a passion she'd never experienced anywhere else. It was the only time his control slipped.

Eva cleared her throat, taking a step back. He couldn't seduce her into forgiveness.

The guard focused on them.

"I'm glad you're feeling better. I do think we need to keep the lines of communication open." Eva said in a normal tone of voice.

Daniel straightened, his stony mask once again in place. "Let's go see what we're up against."

CHAPTER 7

One time, before they were locked down in the MUC during the Collapse, Eva had visited the Belvoir Underground Complex—otherwise known as BUC.

A rather dour scientist by the name of Archie liked to make the half-ass joke that the "BUC stops here." After the fourth time of hearing it, Eva had avoided him as much as possible. He had picked up on her avoidance—Archie wasn't stupid—and had become hostile and critical. Add in Daniel's terse responses, and she'd been glad to leave the place.

The BUC was sterile and gray. Where the MUC was built around natural basalt structures, such as caves and caverns, which naturally bypassed the water table and minimized environmental damage wherever possible, the BUC did not. Blasted straight down into the bedrock beneath the existing Army installation, it was a solid cylindrical shaft, with walls several feet thick, sterile rooms to match its sterile labs and office, and a smaller mess hall. The bunks had been the worst, closed in and more suffocating than the ones at the MUC—if possible—making her claustrophobia swell to phenomenal proportions. To top it off, the emergency exit consisted of fifteen sub-levels of stairs made of metal grating down a narrow tube. Straight up. Straight down.

Eva wasn't looking forward to going back.

These tunnel rats—as she started calling them in her head—were tied to Kaspar and Ft. Belvoir somehow. Rebels. That was what Kel had called them.

Well, the buck may not stop with her, but Eva was used to rolling around in the muck to get what she needed. She snorted to herself, and Daniel glanced in her direction.

"Nothing." She waved him off.

They reached the platform. Zeke and Stella had taken up position by the wall, one of the mechanics' rooms now open. A dozen cots lined the walls. Older adults, pregnant women, and children read, played games, and slept all around the room.

Stella slammed the door shut.

Daniel stalked across the walkway and, before anyone could intervene, swung his fist, striking Zeke in the face.

The man's nose crunched, blood gushing in twin streams down his face.

Rifles ratcheted around them.

Eva sighed.

Daniel stood with his hands on his hips, fixing the other man with a sharp, calculating look. "Now we're even. Just wanted to see if you bleed."

Zeke waved a hand, signaling the others to lower their weapons. Blood seeped through his fingers, staining his hand. "I didn't break anything, though," he protested, voice tinged with indignation.

"Yeah, well, Stella's got a point—you could've asked me to prove it some other way. Enough with the kid stuff. What's the deal here? Why are you holed up in this tunnel? And how'd you even find it?"

Stella tossed Zeke a grimy rag, and he dabbed at his face, wincing as he grazed his nose. He'd be sporting a pair of black eyes soon enough. Lucky for him, Daniel hadn't hit with the full force granted by Shield.

"Why should I trust you?" Zeke shot back. "You're on the run, too, and you admitted to stirring up trouble in Kansas City. Now we'll have to move on because they'll come sniffing around here soon enough."

Daniel shifted his stance. "Not for a while. We bombed the main entrance and some of their supply warehouses."

Zeke gaped. "And what's stopping you from doing the same to us?"

"You haven't threatened us. Not really. And there's no sign of cannibalism, slavery, or psychopathy. I can work with that. How about this, we exchange information. A question for a question."

Zeke ripped the rag and stuffed bits of it up into his nostrils, wincing the entire time. People shuffled around the platform, looking between him and Daniel with wary eyes.

"You have a killer right hook, man." He slumped in the nearest seat and gestured for them to do the same. "Hey, Stells, you mind getting us some of that hooch Dylan made?"

Stella glared at him. "Do I look like your maid?"

Zeke shot her a macabre grin, through a smear of blood. "I'll do your share of dishes for a week."

She rolled her eyes, grumbling as she made her way along the walkway to the farthest door down the track.

A guard came with various mason jars and handed one to each of them. Stella returned and filled them, taking one for herself and sitting beside Zeke.

"Now, a question for a question, huh?" He sipped the cloudy brown liquid.

Eva eyed Daniel before bringing the cup to her mouth. Not their usual whiskey, the fumes were strong and making her eyes water.

She sipped and almost choked on the apple fire burning its way to her stomach. Eyes watering, she eyed Daniel. Not a tear in sight.

"That was my deal." Daniel took another drink. "Decent for homemade."

Zeke nodded. "Stella here thinks it's a waste of water, but sometimes it's nice to have a little something to relax ya, you know?"

Daniel nodded. "That I do. Since we're in your territory, why don't you go first?"

"Where y'all from?" Zeke didn't hesitate, just narrowed his gaze on Daniel, all signs of good humor dissipating.

"Washington State. How long have you been in this tunnel?"

"Eight months. Were you on the Eastern Bloc or Western Coalition side?

"WC. How many people live here with you?"

Zeke glanced at Stella. She sipped her whiskey, her expression stoic. "One hundred twenty-eight? No, nine, Angelica just had her baby. Spread out between this camp and another. Has it rained recently where you're from?"

The softball questions kept flying back and forth between the two men, each one building on the last in rapid-fire succession. Eva and Stella's eyes met, taking each other's measure. Sooner or later, the real questions would be asked —the ones that mattered.

"The entrance we made to the surface is about a mile from here toward the Virginia side. Enough is enough, why you here, man? You can BS with me all day long, but that's really the question. What do you want?"

"Those were two questions." The remaining hooch disappeared down Daniel's throat, his Adam's apple bobbing.

"You know what I mean."

"I'll answer your question if you answer me this: why are you and your people hiding down here?" The glass rolled between Daniel's fingers, back and forth. His eyes never left Zeke's. The door beside them opened with a creak, and a little old lady teetered out, white hair a halo puff around her head.

Sturdy boots clad her feet, and an army jacket, sleeves rolled up, fit her like a dress.

"Go ahead and tell him, Ezekiel. We could use allies, especially ones with trains and the power to run 'em." One of the guards quickly found the woman a seat, and she eased down with a sigh. "My name is Penny."

Unphased, Daniel set the mason jar next to his chair and leaned forward, extending his hand to her. "Nice to meet you, Penny."

"We must have passed your test?" Eva set her still half-full glass down and regarded the older woman. Everybody hovered, protective. One wrong move and she was sure both she and Daniel would be riddled with bullets.

Zeke shifted uncomfortably. "You shouldn't be out here, ma'am. Stells and I can take care of this."

Penny's eyes narrowed to slits. "I ain't dead yet, kid. And we're finally getting to the meat of the situation. Who we are matters. Who they are matters. Maybe they can help. So, go ahead and answer the man's questions."

A frown marred the young man's features, drawing his brows together and turning down the corners of his mouth. "Fine. What I'm about to tell you will sound ridiculous, even fictional, but I swear on my grandmama's grave, it's all true."

Eva leaned forward, wholly focused on Zeke.

"I'm not a praying man, used to go to church as a kid, but after the horrors of the Collapse, I fear I became cynical. What that man is doing to humans, though, is just plain evil, and I've seen a lot of evil things people can do to one another in the past ten years. No, we're down here because we're trying to save people from that man. In the past, during the first Civil War, people often spoke of an underground railroad that helped slaves escape to freedom. Well, this is like that, but we're in a literal underground railroad.

Daniel's gaze intensified on Zeke, and he laced his fingers

together, letting his forearms rest on his thighs as he focused. "Who's doing evil things, Zeke?"

"A man by the name of Kaspar. General Lee Kaspar."

Before Daniel could answer, a ululating cry rang through the tunnel, raising the short hairs on the back of Eva's neck.

"Squalers!" Zeke jumped from his chair. "We're under attack!"

###

Lights flashed. People dodged in and out of the shadows. Penny was shoved back through the door of the mechanic's room with a cursed grunt.

More armed men and women filtered out of the massive maintenance bay alcoves. At least thirty, all heavily armed and armored in a variety of Kevlar SWAT and police vests. These people weren't messing around.

Daniel shoved Eva toward the train. "Get Chet and Alec. Tell the rest to lock themselves in the train."

"What about—" a high screech cut her off.

"Go, now!"

Without another word, she shot down the track, pushing herself and feeling Shield engage her muscles. Mere minutes found her near the barrier, her heart pounding but barely out of breath. The presence inside her stirred, and she let it peek out. She'd need the strength.

After telling Alec what to do, he ran off, and she went to the weapon's stores, yanking out more clips, their rifles, and several K-bar knives.

"What's going on?" Chet careened around the end of the engine.

"Don't know, but they have thirty people to fight it. They're allies, I think. If we help them, I hope they'll help us when we go talk to Kaspar."

"Copy that." Chet started shoving weapons and ammo in his belt and pockets. Alec followed suit.

Tamara closed and locked the engine door, turning off the lights. Eva and the guys would have to depend on their other senses until they got back down the tunnel.

She took off. Back to Daniel and whatever awaited them.

Eva felt the others, like pinpricks of energy running to either side of her. They all ate up ground like it was a walk in the park on a clear summer's day pre-Collapse. Anticipation filled her bones. Her Stranger waking up.

It didn't matter in this moment. She would use it to fight whatever came down that track.

Blood and the acrid smell of gunpowder met her as they neared the maintenance hub.

Eva's heart stuttered, and genuine fear gripped every molecule of her body.

Two creatures, like the felbeara had been joined by half a dozen things she could barely classify as human. Pseudo-human suited them so much better than Aberrant. Like what Sarah had brought to the fight several years ago, but worse, their foreheads had collapsed—complete atrophy of the prefrontal cortex. Extra teeth had grown at odd angles to the point that they couldn't close their mouths. Ocular orbits were expanded, and goggles covered and protected the gaps around their eyeballs. Some individuals had remnants of male features, while others had female features. None of it seemed to affect their strength. Limbs and height had been elongated, making their reach ridiculously long. Instead of muscle upon bulky muscle like Sarah's monsters, these were long and lean. And incredibly quick.

Mere seconds passed as she took in the fray. Bullets barely slowed the human monsters down.

"Blades out and we go after the felbeara's and Aberrant humans."

"Are they even human anymore?" The whites of Alec's eyes showed, but he palmed a combat knife and steadied himself.

Chet gave her a feral grin and yanked out the longest Bowie knife she'd ever seen. "Let's get it done."

And the three of them joined the fray.

CHAPTER 8

Pandemonium swept through the tunnel. Automatic gunfire chattered in short bursts. Panting breath and agonized screams echoed throughout the cavernous maintenance bay as the normal humans fell beneath the manic ferocity of the pseudo-humans.

Eva dodged a clawed hand from a felbeara and streaked across the track to jump onto the platform. One of the pseudo-humans had Stella by the throat, her feet dangling above the ground. In two swipes of her K-bar knife, she severed the tendons in the creature's arm, and Stella dropped to the platform, face purple, throat bruised.

The thing is broken, her Stranger whispered, as if it were conscious. Like it was alive. Words had flashed through her mind before, but never complete sentences.

She ignored its murmurs and plowed ahead, engaging the pseudo-humans.

Nothing but rage gleamed from its eyes. Not only were its arms broken, but its humanity as well. It was what happened when science went awry.

My research contributed to this. Her Stranger squirmed in impatience, urging her to kill it. To cleanse the creature for good.

Its arm dangled to the side, not bleeding, the wound healing in a rapid seam. It whipped its lithe form around as quick as an adder—as quick as other Shielded—and struck out with the uninjured arm.

Someone had filed their nails into sharp points. One finger caught her across the cheek before she could duck.

Chet and Alec formed an attack vector from behind it, the two of them and her now forming a triangle. She dropped to a knee and slammed the knife into the pseudo-human's knee. Alec came for a kidney, and Chet went for the head. Each movement was fast—so fast—and coordinated, just like they had practiced at Camp Chaos so many months ago with Daniel and his Shielded militia.

The thing fell, and with two hard whacks, Chet chopped off its head.

Eva dragged Stella to the side, the woman still alive but half-conscious—no time for much else.

"Next one," she said, her voice hollow even to herself.

The men nodded, already lining up their next target.

They repeated the process two more times, moving swiftly from target to target. Triple cyclones, moving along the tunnel in perfect harmony, the military application of Shield in full effect.

Chest heaving, Eva glanced around at the remaining fighters. Three rebels lay still on the ground, while half a dozen others moaned, bones crushed and sliced skin bleeding. Daniel stood over the body of a felbeara at the end of the platform, knife at hand, dripping with blood. It also splattered his face and clothes in a macabre arc. The other creature lay chopped up across the track on the other platform, a huge man hacking at its head. The furry body twitched with each whack of the long knife. A half dozen other rebels finished off the single remaining pseudo-human, beheading it with swift efficiency like they'd done it before. Hell, they probably had.

Daniel met her gaze across the space. She nodded. His mouth

and eyes softened a minute amount before hardening back into his usual stoic soldier expression.

Footsteps clattered from behind her, but before Eva could fully turn, the cold, hard barrel of a pistol pressed against the side of her temple. She froze.

"You fight like them." Zeke's accusatory voice. His arm wrapped around her throat. Eva grabbed it but didn't wrench. She could break the hold, her reflexes sharper, her muscles stronger than the man behind her. However, they needed the trust of these people—their help and support.

"We're not them," It came out strangled and rough.

"You bleed. How is that possible when you move like them? Are as strong as them?" The chest against her back tensed, and when she concentrated, she could hear Zeke's heartbeat racing a rapid staccato.

"Let her go and we'll tell you." Daniel had dropped the bloody knife, his hands dripping with deep purple blood. He held them up in surrender. "We don't want trouble."

"Tell me now!"

The pistol dented her skin.

"Zeke. No. She saved me." Stella's hand rested on his arm, her voice a rough rasp. Deep, black bruises ringed her neck. She gulped, wincing.

Moans and coughs filled the silence. A man and a woman tended the injured. The rest stood around, hands on weapons, watching uneasily. Maybe the shift from ally to enemy was too swift for them. Out of her peripheral, Chet and Alec were ready to fire, tension along every line of their bodies. Damn, this was a mess.

The door to the mechanic's room opened, and Penny shuffled out. The wide eyes of the non-combatants peered out behind her before she shut the door. She eyed Zeke, Eva, and Stella, then made her way to Daniel.

"What's going on out here?"

"That's what I'm trying to figure out, Penny. They're like

Kaspar's people. Same strength, same speed. I think they're spies. It can't be a coincidence that Kaspar sent the Squalors into the tunnel right after these guys show up." Zeke's grip on the pistol had loosened at Stella's words, though he still hadn't dropped his weapon.

Penny limped toward Daniel, stopping in front of him. "Is that true?"

"We're not spies, ma'am. We didn't get a chance to tell our story before the Aberrant came. I can explain everything."

The two of them gazed at each other, with no other words exchanged, just taking each other's measure. Daniel didn't flinch and didn't look anywhere else but at the tiny, older woman in front of him. Without looking away, she said, "Put your gun down, Zeke. Let's hear these folks out before we do anything else."

"But Pen—"

"Now. If they wanted to kill us, they would have done it during the attack," her tone brooked no argument.

He reluctantly dropped the gun and backed away, taking Stella with him. She collapsed against him, her injuries overwhelming her now that she didn't have to defend Eva.

Zeke helped her to a chair, then sat in one himself. "Then let's get to it."

Eva rubbed her temple, the pain dissipating in a warm wave.

Daniel wiped his hands on his jeans, blood still crusting the half-moons of his fingernails. It would take a good soaking to remove it now. He touched the side of her face, fingers grazing her cheek, wiping something away, and lifting her chin to check the fading bruises.

"Splotch of blood," he said in a low voice. "You good?"

Eva nodded. "Yeah. I'll follow your lead."

He gave her a barely perceptible nod, and they both turned to take the seats they'd vacated during the fight.

The dead had been collected, taken down one of the enormous maintenance bays, and the injured were being transported to the room Penny had come from. If the maintenance storage rooms were like the ones back home, there would be many interconnected corridors and other chambers servicing the bays to either side of them. A reasonably secure place in the grand scheme of things. As long as they could acquire food and water. How long had they been down here?

Daniel contemplated his hands, fingers laced and thumbs twirling around each other. He really *was* agitated. Impatient shifting accompanied the movement until he finally looked up, looking at Penny—and not Zeke—in the eye.

"I worked for General Kaspar before the Collapse. Even before the First Wave, for a year. I entered the military at eighteen, then attended medical school on the GI Bill. Kaspar kept his eye on me. He wanted me for a special project, one that suited my dual careers. Advanced military research. I balked, then the nukes dropped during the First Wave, and I knew I needed to help." He sat back.

Eva digested this information. He never talked about his time before the First Wave. What little she knew could fit in the palm of her hand. The big thing, the thing she was still struggling to reconcile—that he'd been injected twice with prototype Shield and never told her—was only one thing of many. They both had lives before the Collapse, but she often forgot how complicated his was, navigating the sharp corners of military research and multiple wars. She'd never known any different.

"Everybody lost so much then, young man. We all pitched in." Penny said, nodding at him to continue.

Daniel heaved in a breath. "So, I took the job. First in New Mexico and then in Washington State. Two pieces of the same puzzle. You see, they had found something strange—a black rock with characteristics of a meteorite, but with foreign elements they couldn't characterize. After extensive study, we discovered that there were enzymes—or close approximations of enzymes—that could rapidly rebuild and replace the structures of human and animal cells. It needed to be studied for any benefits."

"And military application, like enhancing war fighters," Zeke said bitterly.

"And military application," Daniel nodded, not denying it. "Though we were also trying to attempt a dual outcome: human resiliency in the face of disappearing water stores and a way to control the weather on a massive scale. That's where Eva came in. We created a serum called Shield."

"Human resilience? Like those monstrosities, Kaspar has? That doesn't look too resilient to me, it looks like madness." Zeke had no give.

Daniel massaged the bridge of his nose. "There are earlier, less stable prototypes of Shield utilizing the raw enzyme. Kaspar has to be using an altered or unstable sample under Ft. Belvoir, where our sister lab resides. Except for one vial, all samples are formulated and stored in the bunker in Washington State. That's where we're from."

"You mean to tell me you were doing human experimentation before you got a good sample?" His countenance froze in horrified disbelief.

"Orders. From Kaspar." Daniel continued, "I don't know where he's finding his samples of the serum prototype or whatever he's using. Hell, it could be the raw form of the enzyme for all I know. That is beyond dangerous. It creates psychopathy and the collapse of the prefrontal cortex."

"But you created that shit?" Zeke glared across the space between him and Daniel, his anger palpable.

"Some of it, but I have no idea about the animals or those Aberrant humans. I've seen similar up in our part of the country, but nothing like what we fought here." Daniel shook his head, running a hand through his hair.

"Aberrants? You mean the Squalors?" Zeke asked.

"I prefer pseudo-humans," Eva murmured, quiet until now.

Daniel flashed her an annoyed look, then quirked a brow at Zeke. "Interesting choice of nickname."

He was telling them about the serum but not about the TMRWS. Eva frowned. He probably wouldn't have done that if the rebels hadn't pushed the point. They'd discovered part of her people's secrets inadvertently, but they couldn't afford to give them the rest yet.

"So, dear, you have a super serum that makes you—how did you put it?—resilient. How come you didn't turn crazy like those others?" This time Penny asked the question, quiet until now, letting Zeke take point. The older woman observed it all with a thoughtful look, in stark contrast to her fellow rebel.

"Because we actually have the finished result. Shield is safe and does what it's supposed to. However, there's something wrong with the older versions, and it's spreading, much like a disease. We are heading to Ft. Belvoir to see if we can't reverse the impact of the volatile versions."

A partial truth sprinkled with a dash of lie.

Betrayal sunk its claws in, her Stranger reacting to the heightened emotion. She breathed through the extra shot of adrenaline and took a few deep breaths to calm her heart rate. It would be catastrophic to lose it now.

We're nice monsters, calm and domesticated. She shook her head in disgust.

Maybe Penny sensed something was off because she narrowed her eyes and said, "You're leaving something out. I've been around long enough to tell."

"Yes, but it's not going to affect you or your people, and in the end, it'll probably help them. We need your assistance, Penny, you and your rebels. In the end, maybe we'll end up helping each other. Between Kansas City and those animal Aberrants, we've lost several people. I'm certain that what we need to help stop their creation is under Ft Belvoir in their underground laboratory. If you help, I promise we'll leave you in peace and provide you with directions to the northwest if you'd like to join us. We require hard work, but there's plenty of food and water, and it's relatively safe, much safer than here. Think on it."

"And if we don't help?"

"We'll still leave you in peace, but we can't guarantee your safety. We're going to find what we need and then cave in that entire facility."

And there was the lie Eva had been waiting for. They were not going to cave in the BUC; they needed to keep the TMRWS machine intact. They'd secure the entrances by any means necessary, but they certainly wouldn't destroy the place. Daniel walked a tight, tight rope. How often had he done that with her? Until the trip here to Virginia, she would have believed him incapable of lying to her, but now she questioned all of their conversations, all of their plans.

Betrayal sunk its claws in, her Stranger reacting to the heightened emotion. She breathed through the extra shot of adrenaline and took a few deep breaths to calm her heart rate. It would be catastrophic to lose it now.

We're nice monsters, calm and domesticated. She shook her head in disgust.

Penny regarded Daniel. "I have to discuss it with my people. Return to your train for the night, and we'll talk first thing in the morning."

Daniel nodded, gestured for Chet and Alec to head out, and offered Eva a hand. She took it, the dried blood on it rough against her skin.

"See you in the morning. And Penny? We're not the enemy, but if I know Kaspar, he has plans for you all, he just hasn't executed them yet. I think we can help each other."

She regarded him, an inscrutable look on her worn face. "We'll talk in the morning."

CHAPTER 9

Morning came to the sound of a squalling baby. Eva jerked awake, the three hours of sleep leaving her groggy--even with Shield. Good grief, that baby had a fantastic set of lungs.

She rolled over to find that Daniel had placed his bedroll not two feet away from hers. There was a time when they'd sleep so close together you couldn't tell where one person stopped and the other started. That's what secrets and paranoia did: they drove a wedge between love and goodwill.

Eva sat up and discovered Daniel's eyes on her. Her heart skipped a beat at the intensity, just as it had in the old days. The moment passed almost like it never existed, and he leaned his head on a bent arm. "What's going on with Kel and the baby?"

Good question.

"I'm about ready to find that out." Eva stood, stepping over her bedroll to make her way to the door of the train.

The rest of the camp was stirring; the cries were so loud that they were probably also waking the rebels a mile down the track. It could be colic or any number of things.

She boarded the train and discovered Tamara on the floor, with a bloody gash on her head. Chloe and Kel were nowhere to be seen, and the baby lay there in her box, arms and legs flailing, face red.

"Tamara," Eva shook her friend. "Tamara, are you okay?"

Shield would repair most of the damage. Already, the wound was healing, the blood making it look worse than it was.

Eva tried again, patting each side of the woman's face this time. Tamara groaned, hand coming up to shove Eva away.

"Stop that." The words were slurred and groggy. Major concussion. Shield would heal it, but it would take a couple of hours. Anything with the brain seemed to take longer.

"Where's Kel and Chloe, Tamara? What happened?"

"Bitch clocked me, took Chloe as a hostage. She didn't take Talia?" Tamara sat up, leaning against the engine wall.

So Chloe and Tamara had finally talked Kel into naming the infant. A step in the right direction. Leaving her here was several steps back.

"Apparently not."

Tamara cursed. "At least there's that. She became increasingly agitated being this close to the rebel group. Kept saying how they were the pathway to sin and instant hell or some crap like that. I guess after the fight last night, she really freaked. She couldn't have gone far."

"Maybe. She is wily, no matter how uneducated." Eva swaddled and picked up baby Talia. She instantly nuzzled Eva's chest, looking for something to eat. Uh oh. "We need to find her. We have nothing to feed an infant."

"Think we could try the rebels? From what you said, they had civilians there." Tamara massaged her temples.

"Let's talk to Daniel. Kel couldn't have taken Chloe too far."

Talia scrunched her tiny face, her little mouth seeking. Eva handed her to Tamara, washed her hands, then snuggled the baby close, sticking a pinky finger in her mouth. The baby sucked on her finger vigorously. It wouldn't last long.

Tamara rose to her feet on wobbly legs, both hands going to her head. "I'm good. Just need a sec."

"Meet me outside."

Daniel met her at the door as she exited the train. "I heard. I've have already sent Alec to the camp to see if there's anyone there nursing who wouldn't mind another mouth to feed temporarily. I'm going to go talk to Chet."

Eva joined, working out how Kel could've escaped. "Kel's clever, Daniel. She must've planned this. But how could she leave her baby? I had a hard enough time handing Mia to you right after birth."

Chet waited by the barrier, a sheepish look on his face. He put his hands up like he was surrendering. "She said she needed to use the facilities, and the damn train was closing in around her. Chloe was going along as a lookout. I never thought she'd leave without the little one, I swear."

"Chloe didn't say anything?" Daniel asked.

"No, sir. She's had that frightened mouse thing going since she found us. I didn't think anything of it. I was just about ready to go looking for them when the baby started crying. Am I in trouble?" Anxiety took the place of sheepishness, and Chet dropped his hands, waiting for the hammer to fall.

"Punishing you won't help now, Chet," Eva said to both men. Daniel didn't meet her gaze, his one eye twitching in anger. He didn't contradict her, though. There was that.

Footsteps clattered across the gravel, and Alec appeared, stopping next to them. "They have a mother willing to feed the baby until you find Kel."

Daniel nodded, already arming himself from the locked box in the welded storage compartment beneath the train. "Perfect. Eva, you and Alec go back to the rebels. Alec, I want you to go search down the tunnel toward Ft Belvoir. One mile, no farther. Make sure Kel didn't take Chloe that direction. Eva, let the baby eat with our milk donor, then bring her back."

"Tamara can do it. I'm coming with you." Eva jiggled the frustrated baby, squirming in her swaddle, the finger no longer quieting her.

"You've talked to them, though. They know you," he insisted.

"Well, now they can meet Tamara. Alec can introduce her to the group." Eva wouldn't let Daniel sideline her. The Stranger inside her was somewhat under control, even during yesterday's fight.

He frowned but relented. "Fine. But we're running."

"Like that's ever stopped me." Eva handed the infant to Tamara and armed herself.

Daniel took off without a backward glance.

Eva followed silently at a steady clip.

###

Eva and Daniel's relationship—they had never put a label on it—had started over a couple of glasses of whiskey and developed beneath the pressures of a world gone mad. Eva often wondered if they would have become what they were now in the relative normalcy before the First Wave. Would he have allowed himself that much loss of control? Especially with somebody under his command?

The two of them had discussed so much in the dark of night, lying entwined on his bunk and later on their bed. Did he hold himself back because deep down, he knew? He knew that their connection was situational rather than organic. It ate at her when she let it, that thought. Now, armed with the knowledge of his deception, she had to rethink everything, including her feelings.

Arms and legs burning after the third mile along the track, she pushed herself harder, trying to escape the press of emotions weighing on her soul. Love was a multi-faceted torture chamber, she concluded, and she stepped up her pace on the walkway. Daniel ran in between the tracks, his bootsteps hitting every other railroad tie in their mad dash to find Chloe and Kel.

Another mile ticked by before there was any indication of somebody passing by on foot, and he halted mid-stride, light from his rifle shining on the ground. She followed suit, hands on her knees, gulping in breath.

"Three sets of tracks," Daniel murmured.

"Kel had help." Eva kept her voice just as low.

"How did this person approach the camp without Chet noticing?" Daniel walked along the mess of tracks. There appeared to have been a scuffle. Or, something else.

About ten feet further, Daniel frowned and turned around, scouting along the other side. "They're gone."

"The tracks?"

"Go see if there's any sign up there on the walkway."

Eva shone the light along the cement path, up along the wall, and back down the edge, stopping by Daniel.

She peered down at him. "Nothing."

He gave a frustrated curse and backed up to the scuffle marks. "They must have been able to salvage one of the maintenance handcars back in Kansas City. That's the most likely explanation."

"Could it have been Kaspar and his people?"

If it had, they'd just lost the element of surprise.

"I don't know. The last entrance to the top inbound was the one we scouted in Tennessee about a hundred miles back."

"What about Chloe? We need to go back and get her."

"And compromise the current mission? We're so close, we can't do that, Eva, no matter how much I want to."

"Damn it, Daniel. That's not right. We don't leave people behind."

"What do you expect me to do? Load everybody up and head back the way we came? Let me lay it out for you. By the time we made it back, we would be out of fuel, the rebels would all be dead, and Kaspar would be aware of our interest-so many things that could go wrong, all for one girl. I can't do it. I like Chloe as much as you do, but we stay on mission. We'll look for her on the way back."

"And what, let them rape and torture her? No, with the

engine, we could overtake them within a day." Eva turned back toward camp.

Daniel grabbed her arm. "The hell you will. I will lock you in that damn train if I have to."

"Let me go. Killian was right, you are going too far."

A blue luminescence appeared in Daniel's eyes, and Eva shivered. She'd thought it a trick of the light before. Now she knew. Something was behind that light.

He gritted his teeth. "That's the price of being a leader, Eva. The hard choices."

"When was saving a human life, even just one, a hard choice? Seems pretty damn easy to me." She jerked her arm out of his grip and strode off once again back toward the train.

In one leap, Daniel stood in front of her, frustration and agony playing out in equal measure along the lines of his face. "I thought you, of all people, would understand."

"Me, of all people?" A horrible knot formed in her gut, the pressure of that foreign presence threatening to push its way to the surface.

"Yes. That decision you made during the Year of Hell saved so many, including our daughter, and yet we had to sacrifice two of our own."

Eva blanched. "That was different. Sarah and Natalie were irretrievably compromised. And Sarah ended up escaping."

"Yes, but after Natalie healed after being shot, we could have injected her with the new version of Shield. Why didn't you decide to do it? Or your sister?"

Tears formed in the corners of her eyes. "Because we wouldn't have enough samples for everybody else, and there was a risk of it not working on Sarah and Natalie."

"Exactly. Hard decisions."

Guilt and shame gnawed at her insides, but she still jutted her chin out and fired back. "But this isn't the same thing. Chloe isn't compromised. She's one of us, one of our people—a resident of the Basin. Jack would go back. No question."

Daniel took a step back. "You're seriously going to bring him up now?"

"Isn't he one of your biggest insecurities? That he's a better human than you?"

"Now you're just making things up in your head."

But she'd hit a nerve, she could tell by the tic in his jaw, highlighted by the minuscule light from their rifles. Loved ones always knew where to hit the hardest.

"No. You don't know what it's like being a woman. Those are some bad men, hyped up on meteorite rock. You didn't see the young girls in the breeding house, and that's where Chloe's going. She won't be recruited as a soldier. One, she's from an enemy settlement, but two, Chloe may be strong, but she doesn't have what it takes to kill somebody, not like you and me. They will rape her, then torture her, then give her to some freak with a black rock, thinking himself a god, and she will be used over and over. Now put your daughter in her place and tell me we can't go back and get her." By this time, the tears flowed freely, running down her cheeks and soaking into the top of her shirt. "This isn't the same thing as my decisions in the MUC. Not by a mile."

At the mention of Mia, Daniel leaned forward, his brows pulling together. "But—"

"And you owe me after not telling me about your history with the prototype Shield."

Tension thrummed between them. So much water under the bridge, so much knowledge of how the other reacted, thought, and cared. If she knew anything about this man, it was this: he would do anything for his daughter.

Another long minute unraveled, feeling more like an hour. She knew the second his emotions engaged, and relief flooded her entire being. Cold, logical Daniel was gone. Human Daniel present and accounted for, the brisk change from one to another making more sense now than it ever had.

"Fine. But we're leaving Tamara and the baby here with the rebels."

He jumped off the platform and, without waiting, took off down the track back toward the engine.

Eva followed at a slower pace, allowing the distance to widen.

The sheer force of love, anger, and hate wove themselves into a tangled knot, blending each thread until it became indistinguishable and multifaceted—a perfect descriptor for her and Daniel.

CHAPTER 10

Chet shifted the engine in reverse, and they flew down the track.

Every one of Eva's muscles tensed. Why hadn't the Kansas City fighters attacked the rebels once they'd caught up to them? Why not sneak into her and Daniel's camp and take them all out? Those KC psychos didn't understand restraint or fear.

A nagging feeling stirred where her Stranger lurked, that inner voice hardened by war and pain, whispering that something was wrong with this entire setup. It screamed trap. But it didn't matter. Chloe was one of their own, and they'd bring her back, no matter what.

Before departing, Tamara had figured out the speed of the modified handcar used by the Basin's clearing team and realized the train could outpace it by a wide margin. It infuriated her that the enemy had gotten their hands on one of her creations at all. The fact that it had survived the Kansas City cave-in only added to the engineer's frustration. If Tamara's math held up, the Basin crew would catch up to those who kidnapped Chloe in a matter of hours and not burn as much fuel as Daniel had feared.

Daniel hadn't talked to her since they'd gathered everybody, including Stella and two other rebel fighters who had wanted to join, the woman's neck one massive bruise.

He brooded in a seat in the back, arms crossed, looking out the window, his face a stony mask. Anybody else would see stoic Daniel, contemplating strategy and deployment of fighters. He could hide it better than anybody else, but he was not happy about her standing up to him.

Well, too bad.

Chloe needed saving, and the baby, Talia, needed a mother. What would be the point of saving humanity if they lost what made them human in the first place? They didn't leave innocent people with monsters. And in the long run, a few extra hours weren't going to make a difference. At least, that was what she told herself. What bothered Eva more was how and why Kel had left her baby all alone without a mother.

The tiny infant was strong and healthy, and she was sure Hensley would want his child back if he were still alive. Not to mention, Kel had shown a mothering instinct. No mother in her right mind would leave a newborn all alone, especially without the easy availability of a bottle or alternative food source. The entire situation rankled like a bitter taste lingering on her tongue.

"They're up ahead!" Chet hollered from his position in the engineer's seat.

Daniel swayed as he made his way to the front, leaning a hand on the wall and bending to peer into the darkness ahead, his face illuminated by the bright light mounted on the roof outside. A faint glow beyond the border of darkness and brightness was the only indication anybody else was out there.

"Two carts. Dammit. That's possibly five people each, minus Chloe and Kel, which leaves maybe eight fighters with those black rocks. Too close of a match." Daniel repeated their assignments, still not looking at Eva. She narrowed her eyes at him. Not that he noticed.

After they had stopped everybody, her job was to take Stella and the rebel fighters to circle to the back of the train, using it as cover, while Daniel, Chet, and Trae would attempt a frontal assault. Alec would snipe from the roof and guard the engine. They were down Tamara, who guarded the baby back at the rebel camp. In the long run, her absence could really hurt them.

Rifles ratcheted bullets into chambers.

"A rub or a ram?" Chet asked.

"Tap them first, just enough to push them into the other cart. If that doesn't stop them, we'll go a little harder." Daniel gripped the pole near the door to keep from fumbling forward after they bumped the cart in front of them.

Eva gripped the arm of her seat a bit harder.

"Roger that," Chet replied.

The engine sped up. Soon, the back cart was visible in the harsh glow of their light, as big as a pick-up.

"A little bit more…more. Now."

As soon as they made contact with the back of the cart, it plunged off the track, skittering over the rocks. Billowing dust fogged the windows, and the screech of metal on metal pierced the air as the two machines scraped past each other in the narrow tunnel. Everybody slammed their hands over their ears.

Out of the corner of her eye, she saw hands and feet and bodies fly out of the cart. She hoped Chloe hadn't been in that one.

The dust cleared. The other cart was twenty feet in front of them, attempting to pull away. Chet pushed the throttle forward.

"This time, maybe just nick it," Daniel said mildly.

Chet glanced at Daniel. "That was a nick."

Daniel's lips compressed. "Do your best."

"Yessir."

Movement skittered around the cart, and soon a bullet pinged against the window. Spiderwebs shot through the train glass from the point of impact but didn't penetrate. Bulletproof.

Ten feet away.

Five feet.

"Easy."

"I got it, sir."

Thud.

Eva jerked forward at the impact. This time, the rear end of the cart left the track but slammed back down without being derailed. It slowed.

Another gunshot cratered the window in a starburst pattern.

"One more like that, Chet." Daniel indicated, with an intense look, squinting his eyes and furrowing his brow.

"Yessir." Sweat popped out on Chet's brow. He eased the throttle forward.

More bullets pockmarked the front window. Eva could make out shadowy figures blurring in and out of the beam of light.

Whump.

This time, the rear of the cart wouldn't disengage from the front of the engine. Sparks shot out from the railway wheels as the engine continued to fly down the track.

Chet eased the throttle, engaged the brakes, and the train shuddered to a stop. Without a word, the group dispersed to their assigned positions, moving with practiced precision.

Eva gestured for Stella and the rebel fighters to follow her through the rear hatch onto the tracks. Stella nodded, leading her two companions to the right, their boots crunching faintly on the gravel. Eva swung left, the sound of their footsteps on the opposite side confirming they were in position.

Alec scrambled up the ladder from the back door, taking his perch on the engine's roof, crouched low like a predator. Ahead, the grunts and thuds of combat erupted—Daniel, Chet, and Trae had engaged the enemy.

A figure stumbled across the tracks, slamming into the tunnel wall. Not one of theirs. Eva raised her rifle, sighted, and fired. The man's startled eyes locked with hers as he crumpled, blood pooling beneath him. Her stomach twisted, but she pressed forward, shoving the guilt aside.

The Kansas City fighters had somehow crammed six men

onto a handcar, its rusted frame barely visible in the dim light. Eva's jaw tightened. With that many, plus whatever reinforcements rode the second-hand car they'd salvaged, and the black meteorite rock fueling their Shield-like strength, they could've overwhelmed her group and the rebels if they'd stopped both together. Yet here they were, sloppy and exposed.

Another fighter staggered back, thrown by Daniel's fist or Chet's boot. Eva lined up her shot and dropped him before he could recover. Stella and her rebels mirrored her on the right, picking off stragglers with ruthless efficiency.

Six bodies stained the gravel with their blood. One rebel clutched a shallow gash on his arm, but he waved off help. Not bad for a plan hastily put together at the last minute.

The smell of super-heated metal thickened in the air. Eva ran to the cart.

Chloe lay at the bottom of it, hands over her head, trembling.

"Chloe, they're gone," Eva said.

The young woman didn't look up.

"Chloe," she tried again.

A tear-stained face looked up at her, and at the sight of Eva, Chloe launched herself up. She hugged Eva with a ferocity she hadn't experienced since Mia was a tiny girl.

"Shh, it's all right."

"You came back." More tears.

"Of course we did."

"You shouldn't have. They wanted you to follow for some reason." The young woman pulled away.

A chill shivered up Eva's spine at Chloe's words.

Eva helped her down and escorted her over the uneven ground back to the train. Chloe curled up in one of the seats, arms wrapped around her knees, wild, teary eyes flicking from the bullet holes to the injured rebel in the seat across from her.

Eva went out to help the others haul the cart off the front of the engine.

Lump in her throat, they all heaved the tail end, and it slammed back down to the rail.

"We need to talk," Eva rubbed her hands against her jeans, the thin abrasions from the metal of the cart healing almost instantly.

"Not now," Daniel clipped the words.

"Yes, now. Chloe said something to me, I think you should hear."

Daniel frowned but indicated down the track away from the Shielded ears that would hear everything.

"What?"

"I think this was a diversion of some kind. Chloe said that these guys wanted us to follow. It can only mean a bigger attack on the rebel camp. It's the only thing I can think of that makes sense."

Daniel cursed, walking a few steps away, his back toward her. He remained in place for mere seconds that felt like a lifetime, his entire body tense.

When he finally turned around, a blank mask met her stare. "Load up."

Irritation warred with disappointment. *She* was the one who was supposed to be angry.

Daniel gave a loud, harsh whistle—the signal for an emergency exit—and the others hightailed it to the engine. It wasn't the time to push his buttons, so she followed suit, plopping down into the seat beside Chloe.

Daniel hopped on, Chet taking his place in the engineer's seat. "Trae, you're on the back hatch. Make sure we don't run into that other cart on the way by. Kel's made her choice. We need to return to camp. There's another possible attack."

"Yes, sir." Trae picked up his rifle and made his way to the back end out of sight.

Daniel turned and met her gaze. "I need to talk to Chloe."

Without a word, she sat in the second row beside Alec, who raised a quizzical eyebrow. Eva shook her head and pointed to the two in front of them. Daniel was pissed. Eva didn't regret coming back for Chloe. In her mind, there was no other choice. But if it led to the death of others, it would eat at her heart and soul until the day she died. What kind of world did they live in where the decision to save one could mean the death of many? Human life should mean more.

"What did they say, exactly?" Daniel asked the girl.

Chloe blinked back the never-ending flow of tears. "They told me what they would do to me when we stopped for the night, and then two of them started saying how Mr. Hensley was going to reward them for the girl. The one didn't want a squalling baby on board, so they wouldn't let Kel go back for her. Kel said Mr. Hensley wouldn't like it, and the guy said it wouldn't matter in a couple of hours anyway. One of the other guards told him to shut his mouth. It sounds like Kel's talked to them somehow in the last couple of days."

"What else?"

"They wanted to bring Tamara, but there wasn't any room left. The one driving said we needed to go slow enough so you would follow, and that's all, I swear, Dr. Burgess."

Daniel nodded, his head resting against the back of the seat.

Eva frowned. They had a missed a spy so close to their camp, Kel was communicating with them.

As they went past the other cart, a few people scattered, though Eva couldn't tell how many. She felt sorry for Kel, for her circumstances. Was the girl too far gone? It was hard to know in the short time since she'd joined them. Somebody so brainwashed she'd leave her baby…yeah, it was tough to tell.

The time passed in tense silence. As they finally approached the camp's border, stopping the engine right next to the outer edge, smoke filled the air.

Daniel ordered everybody else to remain on the train and gestured for her to follow. "Grab your gun."

And they strode off into the abyss.

CHAPTER 11

The first body was less than a hundred feet from the main camp. Mangled and twisted, somebody—or something—had broken every bone in the woman's body—limbs like spaghetti noodles skewed at odd angles, unnatural and bloody. The next one wasn't much better. Dust and smoke filled the air, and each dead body appeared like a wraith from the mist.

Then it cleared.

"*Dios mío*," Eva breathed.

Daniel cursed.

Two bodies were nailed to the wall in a spread-eagled mess of gore and flesh. Both were headless.

Eva covered her mouth with her hand to keep from vomiting. Not much elicited that response these days, but seeing somebody she knew—even for a short time—so violated made the gorge rise in her throat.

Past that, a row of the rebels had been lined up against the backdrop of rubble and concrete, skeletal arms of rebar poking through in spots, and been shot. Their corpses served as a strong warning.

Beyond the bodies was more madness. The tunnel had been

strategically caved in, and the brick arches had been blasted, leaving half-piles of debris across the openings. Overturned chairs, tents, camp gear, cooking stoves, barrels storing food and water, all of it lay scattered, broken, torn, and destroyed in the aftermath of the sneak attack. No train was betting by that anytime soon.

If she and the other Shielded had been here, they could have stopped this. At the very least, they could have prevented some of the deaths.

Guilt compressed her chest, making it hard to breathe. They wouldn't be able to use the tunnel now to get to Ft Belvoir. They'd have to travel on the surface.

The soft wail of an infant pierced the air. Daniel and Eva looked at each other and moved forward. Survivors.

The metallic mechanic's bay doors were dented and caved in but unbreached. The cry came from there.

Without words, she and Daniel pushed against the door, putting all of their Shielded strength behind it. The door scraped against the floor, an alluvial furrow marring the cement floor.

A rifle met them on the other side.

Penny.

"Good to see you, friend." Daniel raised his hands beside his head, eyes focused on the face behind the barrel.

The older woman's shoulders slumped forward. "Oh, thank God."

Further into the room, sat a half dozen others, plus a woman holding a baby. No Tamara. No Talia.

"What happened?" Daniel asked.

Penny shuffled to where she and Daniel stood in the doorway, tears filling her eyes. "Kaspar, that's what happened. Shoulda hid when the scouts came down here. Dammit, we shoulda hid instead of fightin' 'em."

"Where's Tamara and the baby?" He placed a hand on the older woman's shoulder in a rare show of sympathy.

"Gone. He took them and my Zeke." The woman's voice trembled, but she was surprisingly stoic.

A long, painful wail echoed through the tunnel. Eva glimpsed Stella running down the tracks toward them. She side-stepped to intercept the distraught woman.

"Let me go! Where's Zeke?" Stella tried to bypass the firm arm Eva extended in front of her.

"Kaspar has him and our people. There are only a few survivors left down here." Eva gripped both of her shoulders. The other woman jerked out of Eva's grasp. If she'd wanted to, Eva could have kept her there, not let her see the total devastation in the tunnel and on the wall.

Daniel touched her arm and shook his head. It was like his words whispered through her brain. *Better to rip the band-aid off.*

Was there any good way to be presented with the death of your loved ones?

Stella collapsed to her knees at the massacre spread before her on the tracks. Her friends. Her family. All gone in an instant. Sobs wracked the woman's body. "No, no, no. This can't be. No. I can't."

"Stella, dear, you need to come with me." Penny crouched beside the crying woman, rubbing her back.

Stella pushed her away, but Penny held firm, wrapping her arms around the other woman.

Long minutes passed as the two women whispered their comfort and grief into the dim light.

"Penny, you should all come with us on the train. You can't stay here now, it isn't safe," Eva murmured, hesitant to interrupt the two.

"No place is safe. Not as long as that man is in the world." Grief etched Penny's face. "We'll find the other half of our people on the surface and lick our wounds. We still have work to do getting folks out of Virginia and down to Florida, away from Kaspar and his monsters."

Daniel stopped beside her, his mouth a grim line. "It would

take us months to clear out that tunnel, maybe longer if they collapsed the tunnel even further along the track. Is there another way out? Around to the Fort?"

"We have another exit. One we made back in that maintenance bay," Penny pointed to an alcove across the track. "It's hidden in the ceiling. You'll need to use a ladder to access it and apply oil or lubrication to open it. We haven't disturbed it in years. It's an emergency exit. Bring us back our Zeke and the others, and we'll do anything we can for you."

Stella scrambled to her feet. "I'm coming."

"You just suffered a horrifying loss—" Eva started to say.

"That man will pay. He'll pay dearly for what he did." She strode off into the dark toward the hidden entrance.

Eva couldn't argue with that.

The survivors laid their dead to rest and collected whatever supplies could be salvaged. They rolled food rations and water barrels down the tracks to the engine. Despite all efforts to convince them, Penny and the others were unwavering, determined to track down the rest of their rebel group, rumored to be southeast, working to free captives at Kaspar's other slave camps across Virginia.

"We need to come up with a different way to access the lab now that we've lost the element of surprise," Eva stated the obvious. Daniel had to talk to her sometime. The accumulated death in the tunnel was on her, but even if she could rewind and make a different decision, she wouldn't. Guilt would gnaw on her for years due to that decision, but saving even one soul from a nightmare worse than death was worth it. It had to be.

Daniel opened one eye from where he'd been dozing in the seat next to her. So close, yet so far away. "Kaspar is communicating with Kansas City somehow. I need to get him alone. Distract him while you try to install the core."

"Then what are we going to do? Just mosy right on out?" Unease settled low in her gut. Why Daniel wasn't raging troubled her. The eerie calm was almost worse, as if he were resigned to some decision she wouldn't like.

A loud whistle pierced the air outside the train. Chet. Eva shot out of her seat and ran toward the door, Daniel and Alec hot on her heels.

He trailed behind Kel, rifle pointed between her shoulder blades. Bloody clothes hung on her thin figure, and a bruise marred the side of her face.

"Where are the rest of them?" Daniel asked.

"Dead. I killed them. I want my baby back." A trail of blood smeared across her jutting chin, and she placed her hands on her hips.

"That's not—" Eva started, but Daniel threw a hand up to halt her words.

"We're not just going to give you an infant to take back to that madman you call a prophet. You can stay here or go with the rebels. Otherwise, the baby remains with us."

Kel glared. "It's my baby. I can do with her as I please."

"She's not a piece of property, Kel, she's a human being." Eva spat the words.

The young woman's narrowed eyes landed on Eva. "I grew her, I keep her."

"Then I guess you're joining us," Daniel stated matter-of-factly. "Because Kasper has her."

Defiance and fear flashed in Kel's eyes, and a tense silence fell over the group. Chet shifted, the gravel grating under his boot. Nobody moved.

Kel's lips finally twisted into a sneer. "He's chosen by God, he has the black rock too. I want her to be protected by somebody strong. He won't hurt my child."

"Aren't we strong? We were able to escape Kansas City and prevent your people from harming us. We have plenty of food and water, Kel. You'll both be safe with us. Your baby won't be safe with General Kasper. He enslaves and uses people. For sex, for food, as fodder for his war machine. He'd throw Talia to the literal wolves if they needed food." Eva took a careful step forward, nice and easy.

A range of emotions washed over Kel's face: anger, sadness, and confusion, all jumbled together. Tears started dribbling through the dirt and blood on the young woman's face, and she brought her hands to cover her eyes, burying her face into Eva's shoulder. Either hormones or a fundamental change was starting in the young woman, but only time would tell. Chet lifted startled eyes to her and Daniel.

"I knew she'd finally come to her senses." Chloe's quiet voice said from behind them.

Daniel just shook his head. Chloe's assessment was optimistic. More likely, Kel was trying to manipulate them.

"I guess we have another passenger. Handcuff her to the seat. She'll stay here." He let loose with a shrill whistle. "Everybody, load up, we have a lot of work to do."

Yes, we do, Daniel, yes we do. Exhaustion settled over Eva like a cloak.

CHAPTER 12

Eva surfaced from the hidden hatch buried deep in the Virginia woods, its rusted frame buried layers deep beneath desiccated ivy and the crackling leaves of red maple and oak.

Nestled near the ocean's edge, the region still welcomed some rainfall throughout the year. Green vegetation thrust through the cracked earth in patches around rusted, skeletal cars, boarded-up houses, and a desolate strip mall, its empty window frames gaping like hollow, haunted eyes. Nature was already doing its best to reclaim what it had lost.

The underbrush parted, the air thick with the scent of the ocean and the faint, acrid smell of smoke. Something burst through the leaves above her, and she went for her gun. A solitary crow croaked its disapproval as it took flight, and Eva pressed a hand to her racing heart—damn bird. She cleared away from the rough-hewn hatch so the others could join her and got her first good look at the skyline.

"Holy hell," she breathed. The sky above Ft Belvoir raged and pulsed with steely clouds so heavy that she could almost reach out and touch the rain inside. The rain and clouds swirled in a slow, angry vortex, yet, less than two miles away, clear, cerulean blue sky, the sun bright and hot, blazed above her.

"He somehow got the weather system online," Daniel murmured, checking his rifle. It was the first words he'd said to her directly in hours.

"I thought that couldn't happen without the core?" She stood shoulder to shoulder with him, a position so familiar it made her ache.

A muscle twitched in Daniel's jaw. "Kaspar must have jerry-rigged one together, and recently, but it's not working correctly. See? Those clouds should be dispersing and not holding onto the moisture. Without the other TMRWS to help stabilize air pressure, the clouds just swirl in place. I haven't sent a scout here in several years, so whatever he's doing is recent. He must have a functioning desalination plant nearby to be getting that amount of water to use in the seeding process."

The rest of their group climbed out of the hatch, grim determination on every face. All of them had changed into the rags and filthy clothes most often found in Ft. Belvoir. Eva itched the dirt on her face. "What happens if there's any more accumulation and all the rain falls at the same time?"

Daniel's hard gaze connected with hers. "What do you think?"

Eva's Stranger stirred in anger, and Daniel's eyes narrowed. "You good?"

She must have a tell, like him, and his luminescing eyes. Who knew? Maybe hers did the same. "Yep."

Daniel regarded her, all of his intensity focused and worried. She narrowed her eyes at him. He turned to the group, ignoring the look, his face grim. "Chet, take Trae, Stella, and her two folks and go find our people. Head southeast. That's where Penny said the slave pens are located. There's a rough service entrance they use with some of the residents. Eva and I are going to find Kaspar. Wait for the signal before blowing anything up."

"Copy that. Good luck, sir." Chet adjusted his gear and waited for the others to join him.

Eva startled. "I thought I was leading the search?"

"Plans change. I think we'll do better together. We're a good team, remember?" Daniel didn't wait for her response, just signaled for everyone to head out.

He'd used her own words against her. Ass. She glared at his back. Not that it'd help, and it certainly wouldn't change his mind. After forcing the issue with Chloe's rescue, it would take a lot to do that for a while.

Trae and the rebels—Joss and Milo, wiry men with hollow eyes—hoisted their packs. Milo was doing so gingerly, his arm patched and sore from the earlier fight. They trailed Chet and Stella with a wary vigilance.

Eva heaved an internal sigh—and her rifle—and did the same with Daniel in the opposite direction.

"What's the plan, now?" Eva murmured, catching up with Daniel.

An abandoned airfield and desolation stretched between them and the wall of corrugated metal roofing and barbed wire surrounding what remained of Ft Belvoir. Beyond, the jagged stumps of buildings and threads of smoke crept above the makeshift barrier.

Plain arrogance that he hadn't built a sturdier defense.

Who needs defense when you have mindless monsters to keep everyone in line? Eva hunched her shoulders. She doubted very much that anybody in the area had the balls—or ovaries—to confront Kaspar in open conflict. Even the rebels worked in the shadows.

"We find a good place to set a fire in the woods, far enough away that they can't reach it in time, but close enough for Kaspar to come inspect. Then we'll slip in during the chaos, follow him to wherever he's holed up once he comes back, and then we have a discussion with him." He skirted the old airfield with practiced grace, his steps silent on the ground, neither crunching nor slowing.

Eva gaped, stepping where he stepped and working hard not to sound like an elephant over dry twigs. "That won't work. Somebody will see us. Penny said security is tighter since their last rescue."

As they neared the fort's boundary, the remains of the past disappeared. No houses or buildings remained, no shells of abandoned vehicles or anything that could be used for shelter inhabited the area. It was like Kaspar had erased anything that offered even a glimpse of times gone by.

"It'll work. Unlike Penny's people, we have Shield and can climb the back side of the wall between patrols with no problem as long as there is a distraction. We'll cut the razor wire at the top and over we go." Daniel scanned the distant fenceline and the surrounding area. "Kaspar is too arrogant. Nobody around here offers him a true challenge." His thoughts reflected her earlier ones.

Scorched earth, like somebody had burned all the dead brush and life in one fell swoop, created a field of fire around the entire wall. The cleared expanse, stripped of brush and life, dared them to cross its barren waste.

The fort stood in brutal contrast to the Territory's wall back home, where Eva and Daniel had carved something efficient and protective out of the desert to shield their people from the worst of this new world.

"I'm ready when you are," she murmured.

"Once we set the fire, we need to run. Assume everybody in that compound is Shielded—or the equivalent. We'll sneak in and wait for Kaspar to appear. He'll check the fire or show himself to give orders to his people. Then we track him down and have that talk."

The two of them moved farther back into the woods.

Eva grimaced. "I don't like it."

This plan was unlike Daniel. His usually methodical ideas washed away in the last-ditch effort to attain their ultimate objective.

"Without the tunnel entrance, it's all we got. That service entrance the residents use is too close to the gate and too far away from the BUC." He didn't offer any more of his thought process, and she didn't push. It really was the best they could do with the limited time they had.

She prayed it wouldn't get them killed—or worse—captured.

Daniel shouldered a slim pack with the hard case holding the organic core. It lay tight against his body and barely made a hump beneath the settler's rags they'd donned to blend in with the people taken as slaves in Ft Belvoir once they were over the wall. He lowered his voice and gripped Eva's arm, firm and insistent. "Wait a second. Please."

Eva finished dressing in her own torn jeans and a tattered t-shirt, topped with a zipped hoodie, her pack holding explosives hidden beneath. She hesitated but relaxed under his grip. "Make it quick."

"I'm sorry."

She froze. "We don't have time for this, Daniel. We can talk later."

"We both know later often doesn't come. You were right about Chloe and about not telling you about the prototype. Like I've said, I thought I was protecting you and Mia. Doing what needed to be done."

Eva clenched her lips together, the air moving between her lips stale and sticky. She looked up. "I don't know what to tell you. How to make it right. But if we're going to be better than the monsters we fight, we have to be honest with each other."

Daniel cupped her cheek, a move so foreign, Eva covered his hand with her own before her brain fully engaged. "If something happens, Eva, know that I love you. I know I don't say the words, but I've loved you since the first night of lockdown with the glass of whiskey and you wearing those fuzzy slippers. None of this—none of it—is your fault. It's mine. It always has been."

His eyes held hers for a fleeting heartbeat, carrying the weight of years—the love made and promises broken, lives lost and saved, and the curse of everything they'd created—all wrapped up in one glance.

She expelled all of it on a breath. He'd said it with such finality. Her chest tightened as memories cascaded through her brain like a slideshow. Before she could form words, his hand dropped, and he slipped into the twisted woods and broken suburbia, his silhouette swallowed by gnarled branches and ash-dusted debris.

The air thickened, heavy with the sting of woodsmoke as he lit the fire. It intermingled with the fort's acrid reek. Distant flames crackled.

Eva's pulse hammered, Daniel's words searing her mind as the fortress loomed, its razor wire-topped walls daring them to come closer.

"I love you, too," she whispered.

CHAPTER 13

The woods roared with a hunger Eva hadn't anticipated. Flames, sparked by Daniel's forest fire gambit, devoured the dry brush, a wall of orange and black clawing toward Ft. Belvoir's scorched perimeter. Above, heavy clouds churned, dark and bloated, though slivers of blue sky peeked at the horizon.

She crouched beside Daniel behind a charred tree, the heat prickling her skin, her pulse hammering as the fire's crackle drowned out any other noise.

"Too fast," Daniel muttered, his eyes scanning the fort's perimeter. The corrugated metal wall loomed ahead, barely visible through the growing smoke. "We need to move. Now."

Eva nodded, her throat tight with the acrid stench of burning wood. Shouts erupted from the fort as soldiers and ragged settlers spilled out, their silhouettes frantic against the firelight.

Buckets sloshed, axes hacked at smoldering trees, and the Aberrant's—ugh, pseudo-humans' hulking forms lumbered among them. To make sure nobody escaped or to help was difficult to tell. The chaos was their chance.

Daniel darted forward, Eva on his heels, their boots silent on the ash-dusted earth. The back wall, less guarded but still formidable, rose before them, its metal dented and patched with plates of scavenged steel.

A lone soldier patrolled above, his back to them, facing the fire. Daniel gestured sharply with a raised fist—*wait*—and scaled the wall with practiced ease due to Shield, sussing out jagged seams as handholds. As soon as he cut the razor wire, it coiling in springy defiance from being stretched, Eva followed.

Her fingers scraped rust, the tips burning at the minute edges she found to haul herself up.

Heart pounding, she reached the breach in the wire. Daniel had leaped over the top to take out the soldier on the other side.

The man, who had moved down the rough wooden plank lining the top of the wall, opened his mouth to shout, but Daniel was too swift. A muffled grunt, a crack of the neck, and Daniel eased the limp body down.

They descended creaky stairs to cracked pavement and flickering shadows. The two of them slid behind a pile of rubble and crouched.

Inside, Fort Belvoir was a decaying labyrinth of old office buildings and apartment barracks, their windows shattered, walls streaked with soot and bullet scars. Paved streets, fractured by time and neglect, buzzed with fear. Kaspar's slaves scuttled between buildings, heads bowed, their clothes tattered and eyes hollow, all streaming in the same direction: the gate.

Among them roamed pseudo-humans like ones she'd seen in the tunnels attacking Penny's camp. Dozens of them, spread out among the residents of Ft Belvoir. An awful version of crowd control if there ever was one. What had Kaspar done? How had he twisted her serum to such an extent? Eva's stomach churned as one sniffed the air like an animal catching a scent, but it shuffled past, distracted by the fire's distant roar and stench.

Daniel pulled up his hood, his face half-hidden, and Eva did the same. They waited until the last of the creatures had passed, then shuffled behind the final cluster of residents. Heads down, they mimicked the defeated slump of the fort's captives. Eva's gun pressed against her thigh, a cold comfort as they weaved toward the heart of the settlement.

In the central plaza, General Kaspar stood atop a makeshift platform, his voice an enraged bark as he issued orders. His uniform hung loose on his gaunt frame, edges frayed. Tufts of steel-gray hair stuck out like porcupine quills all over his head. Once a giant of a man, he was all hard edges and concave cheekbones. He hadn't eaten for a while. Easy to do with Shield, but a body still required fuel to operate efficiently, though the serum reduced the frequency. He'd be a walking skeleton before too long.

"Get your ass down there and increase the output. We'll douse the damn thing and water the crops later." Spittle flew from his mouth. "I want that fire dead before it reaches the wheat!"

Beside him, a scientist in a tattered white coat—her face pale, hands trembling—argued in low, urgent tones. "General, the cloud seeding…the air's saturated. It'll—"

Kaspar's hand cracked across her face, silencing her. "I don't care. Do it, or I'll give you to my men."

Eva's fists clenched, but Daniel's subtle nudge kept her moving. The crowd shifted, and they tracked Kaspar as he stormed toward a hulking central building, its concrete facade cracked but imposing. Guards flanked its entrance, and an elevator hummed within, its doors gleaming unnaturally in the gloom through the open glass doors. Kaspar dragged the woman through the foyer.

"He's going down," Daniel whispered, his voice barely audible. "I know this place. That's the main entrance to the BUC. There's an emergency stairwell on the east side. Let's go." Eva nodded, her mind focusing on details so she could find her way back to the exit.

Unlike back home, where the MUC hid beneath an unpopulated desert, the Belvoir Underground Complex had developed amidst civilization.

Camouflaged against the base of a mountain, very few had known about the MUC's emergency exit after the First Wave. Here, the door had been installed on the side of the main building—hidden in plain sight. Three armed guards, alert and most likely Shielded in one way or another, stood between them and the door.

She and Daniel circled wide, sticking to shadows, darting between two buildings to exit the crowd and reevaluate. Daniel took the first guard, a silent blur of motion, knife flashing across the soldier's throat. Eva tackled the second, her arm locking around his neck and twisting until he slumped to the ground. Her Stranger reveled in the act. It just made her sick.

The third guard turned from his place at the corner of the building. Before he could shout, Daniel's boot met his skull with a sickening crunch. In total, it took them seconds to take out the guards, their actions swift and coordinated.

She and Daniel dragged the bodies behind the building. A card scanner and a touch screen, hung by wires, were cracked and broken next to the door. Daniel turned the knob. It opened on a squeal. He quirked a brow in her direction. Yeah, either it was Kaspar's arrogance, or he was expecting them.

They slipped into the stairwell. The air grew colder and heavier as they descended, the hum of machinery and a faint, unnatural pulse seeping through the walls.

At the door to the second sublevel where the control room was located, they came across their first real barrier. The thick fire door lay flush with the wall, no handle or hinges visible. There was also no security panel to wire or retinal scanner to override, and blowing these types of doors was tricky at best.

"Up or down?" Eva murmured.

"Up. I don't want to get too deep into the facility. First sublevel had a handle." Daniel did a one-eighty and climbed the stairs two or three at a time.

"That's sure convenient."

"Isn't it, though?"

They retraced their steps to the first sublevel door. Daniel stationed himself to one side, pistol trained on the entrance. With a nod, he signaled Eva, who eased the door open slowly to avoid any creaks. It wasn't locked.

Daniel slipped around the jamb, scanned for threats across his field of view, and proceeded along the hall. Eva positioned herself at his back and to the right, close, but not too close, her gun aimed past his shoulder. A lone exit light above the door behind them cast a long, shadowy glow over the hallway. Just enough for the two of them to navigate with their Shield-enhanced vision. The doorless walls created an almost tunnel-like atmosphere, oppressive and claustrophobic.

At the end, the corridor opened into a vast office space, filled with crumbling cubicle dividers, their thin, decayed panels sagging over dented metal desks and broken office chairs. A dozen or so doors lined the cavernous, rectangular room, the high-pitched whine of the TMRWS muffled by the thick concrete walls. On the opposite side, another door glowed beneath a dim exit sign, a hallway branching off to the left of it.

Without a word, Eva veered right to move counterclockwise toward the other side, checking each of the offices and storage rooms as she passed. She could sense Daniel's presence moving clockwise, doing the same thing.

They converged in front of the hallway and the second exit.

Daniel tested the handle. It turned smoothly. He released without opening it and contemplated the hallway.

"Which trap is going to have the biggest dragon?" he whispered.

Eva snorted. "Where does the hallway lead? I was always on the tenth sublevel when we were here."

"If I remember correctly, it connects to a service ramp from an observation deck at the top of the TMRWS turbine shaft and then drops down to the second-floor control room. This door leads to the second sub-level offices, with access to an antechamber outside the control room."

"So, same difference."

He shrugged. "More cover with an extra room between us and the control vault."

"If they don't come down those stairs." She pointed to the hallway.

"Yeah."

The whine from the TMRWS increased, sounding like a jet engine about to accelerate for take-off.

"That can't be good, " she murmured.

Daniel's lips compressed into a thin line. "Some things never change."

"How's that?"

Daniel glanced down at her. "Kaspar not listening to his people."

He eased the door open, revealing a shadowed stairwell that ascended and descended in a spiral of concrete and steel, flanked by an elevator shaft. Exposed cables dangled in the dark void, their faint metallic groan echoing in the stillness. Steel beams with remnants of concrete walls to encase the shaft hung from exposed rebar. Rusted handrails framed the open landing, offering an unobstructed view above and below. A dim light flickered somewhere below them.

Daniel led the way down the stairs with deliberate steps, scanning for tripwires and hidden traps. Kaspar might not blow the shaft, but she wouldn't put it past him to rig a shotgun or another surprise to slow them down.

Without the insulating effects of the concrete on the other side of the door, the sound of the TMRWS was thunderous. Minus the noise, this trek into the abyss triggered another memory of such a venture. That trip, into the depths of the unknown beneath Lower Monumental Dam, had almost ended in both of their deaths.

Either picking up on her thoughts or having the same ones, Daniel reached behind him with one of his hands. She gripped it, squeezing once, then resumed following him to the second sub-level.

The door was propped open.

Before either of them could be framed in the doorway for long, they took up positions on either side.

Daniel raised his hand in the sign for halt and took a swift look into the brightly lit office room on the other side of the entrance. It may have been the same size as the one on the level above, but someone had cleared it of office furniture, except one desk and a couple of old chairs.

"I see you out there, Danny, my boy. Better come in for a chat." Kaspar's voice was genial and friendly. Opposite of the crazy he'd been spewing on the surface not minutes earlier.

"I can hear you fine from out here, sir." Daniel put his back against the wall beside the door and tilted his head so one of his ears pointed like a satellite antenna toward the other room. He closed his eyes.

Eva kept hers wide open.

"It's quieter in here, son. This room is insulated like a bunker built to withstand a nuke. We'll call a truce, even though you're trespassing in my territory." The words were clipped and hard, like those of a commanding officer speaking to a subordinate.

Eva gripped the butt of her pistol, her hands sweaty and slick.

Daniel didn't twitch. "What was it you taught me, sir? Always have an exit? We'll stay right here."

"Who do you have out there with you? That sweet piece of ass, Dr. Zapada, I bet. I can't believe you knocked that girl up while on the job. Sloppy, son. Downright disgraceful. Now, get your ass in here before I do something crazy, like tell my people on the landing below you to start shooting."

A frisson of terror rocketed through her, and she eased to the railing to look down. True to his word, a half-dozen Aberrants, at least, waited on the stairwell below them, frozen like statues.

Daniel's eyes were open when she glanced at him. She nodded once, her heart pounding.

He blew out a resigned breath, unstrapping the backpack from beneath his loose, ragged sweatshirt, eyes not leaving hers the entire time. He placed it on the floor. "Eva stays on the landing. I'll come in for that chat."

The glance stretched to forever. All of the things she'd left unsaid tangled together with the regret forever residing in her heart. *He plans to sacrifice himself,* a voice deep inside of her said, sadly. *So you can fix it.*

Resolve hardened her spine like steel. If he thought he'd die for them, he was mistaken—Eva wasn't about to let that happen.

CHAPTER 14

f possible, the sound of the TMRWS rose an octave higher once Daniel entered the room. Whatever Kaspar was doing, it was reaching the limit of the machine's capacity and risked blowing the control panel. Without the other TMRWS networked to communicate air pressure boundaries, the entire gaseous, cloudy state of the water above the fort would instantly turn to liquid.

The impact on one targeted area, especially if the scientist they'd seen with Kaspar had increased production, would be devastating. The Shielded, Aberrant, and meteorite carriers would most likely survive, but their slaves and food sources would be gone.

Eva shuddered at the thought, nausea clenching her gut. Sometimes, the enslaved people were their food sources.

All Eva could see was Daniel's back, tense as he held a pistol on Kaspar.

"You wanted to talk. So talk." All hollow signs of respect with the "sirs" were gone, Daniel's take-no-shit-from-anyone voice, cold and hard.

Eva darted across the open doorway, flinging the ragged sweatshirt to the side to retrieve the second pack hidden beneath. This might be her only chance to plant a charge on the elevator shaft wall.

Below, the soldiers stood rigid and at attention, like puppets waiting for some signal before manifesting into real boys. Not one glanced up at her.

Working quickly, she set the timer to detonate in forty minutes. Surely that would be enough time? Her finger hesitated over the final button, and she clenched her fist. It would have to be enough. The placement wasn't ideal, but anywhere else might force the guards below to act, and she had no desire for that.

Two more charges remained in the secure box, and she stuffed them into Daniel's backpack with the TMRWS organic core, stuffing her old sweatshirt between the cases for padding.

Kaspar's voice cut through the air like a machete. "You'll show respect. As far as I see, I'm still your commanding officer."

With that pronouncement, Daniel laughed. Not one of his fake, trying to fit in chuckles, but a surprised, deep roll, with a whistle at the end. "Society collapsed a long time ago, Lee, and most of the world's governments right along with it, as far as I can tell. Nobody's come knocking from overseas, so it's probably a fairly good assumption. No government, no chain of command. I no longer take orders from you. But nice try. Now, I'll try pleading with the man I used to know, if he's still in that husk of flesh you call a body. Turn off the weather mechanism in that machine. Without the other TMRWS networked to stabilize air pressure, you'll cause a flash flood on the surface with that much water, right over Ft Belvoir and kill all of your unShielded."

At that, she tightened the straps to fit her more petite frame and unholstered her pistol yet again. Daniel wouldn't be able to keep Kaspar distracted for much longer. She zipped back to her original position and kicked the hastily placed doorstopper from the floor. Daniel and Kaspar's voices echoed in the confined space of the room.

Her Stranger struggled against her consciousness, wanting to rip the General limb from limb. If she let that feral power rage through her body, consume her to nothing but war and fighting, she'd be no better than the General in the next room. Everything she and Daniel had built back in the Basin Territory would be gone in this shattered world. The Stranger would be all she was, her sole focus and goal: to subdue and dominate to create perfect order, no matter what the cost.

She'd developed Shield to build resiliency, to help provide better lives in the face of drought and looming famine. She never wanted it to be used like this, as a means of subjugation and pain. A means of war. Eva bit her lip until it bled—*it's good you can bleed*—the sharp pain anchoring her to her vow. Shield was for hope, not for what General Kaspar—or her sister, Sarah, for that matter—had become.

"You should have thought of that before setting the woods on fire, son. Their deaths are the cost of your actions. Now, why did you come here? I told your spy years ago that the BUC was off limits, and I would kill any intruders." Eva couldn't see Kaspar's face from where she waited by the door, but the ugliness, the utter contempt in every word, told its own story.

Daniel went with honesty. At this point, there was nothing to lose by telling the truth. "The weather system component of TMRWS. We aim to make it operational and integrate it with the other systems across the country. The satellites are still functioning. If I initialize the entire network, we can reboot the weather. Your TMRWS is the key, the central control. Ultimately, having standard weather patterns again would benefit you as well, sir.

"Back to 'sir' when you want something, is it?" Kaspar's voice dripped with disdain. "I already brought the weather system online without you. It's working how I want."

"Eventually, killing most of your people is what you want?" Daniel's voice filled with contempt.

"That's not what I'm doing, boy. You just wait and see."

Eva was so focused on their exchange that she missed the faint thud of footsteps climbing the stairs below until a booted foot flashed in her peripheral vision. Crap. Unwilling to face an Aberrant alone—let alone half a dozen of them—she lunged into the office space and slammed the door shut, bending the pull handle down with a groan.

Daniel's body stiffened. "You good?"

"His soldiers are on the stairs," she murmured.

Kaspar's spooky, black gaze narrowed on her. Inky stripes stretched across both cheeks like tattoos—or like the enzyme in the prototype Shield had replicated to the point of excreting out of his pores. He toyed with a Bowie knife, flipping it end over end with eerie nonchalance, as if his hand were disconnected from his body.

Eva drew her gun.

He arched a brow. "Breaking the door won't stop them for long, sweet cheeks. And I can't let you pass. Hand over that backpack, you're both guarding like gold."

At this point, it didn't matter how he'd figured out the backpack was essential. Her and Daniel's rough plan was dissolving by the minute. Partly, because she wasn't going to use the man she loved as a distraction while he fought Kaspar, and she slipped by. *Idiots. Both of us are idiots.* You'd think geniuses would know better, yet here they were, running on pure emotion. *Time to come up with a different plan—if there's still time.*

Eva tilted her head and furrowed her brow in mock confusion. "What do you mean?"

The knife streaked past her face, embedding itself into the concrete wall with a thud, buried to the hilt with terrifying force. "Enough talking," Kaspar snarled.

Daniel stepped forward and to the left, the barrel of his gun never wavering. His voice growled, low and unyielding. "You're making a mistake, Lee. That backpack's not your concern. Let us fix the machine, or I will act, and you won't like the result." His eyes flicked to Eva, a silent check-in.

She nodded, her finger so close to pulling the trigger that she could taste it. But part of their plan was to use Kaspar to get out of here, just as they'd used Hensley in Kansas City. She and Daniel couldn't kill him, not yet, and that put them at a disadvantage.

A relentless, rhythmic pounding reverberated through the thick metal door, each thunderous impact delivered with superhuman precision. The steel groaned under the strain, warping at shoulder height where a bulging dent emerged.

Kasper sneered and yanked out two twelve-inch, double-edged blades from sheaths at his belt. Their polished edges caught the bright fluorescent lights in the hollowed-out room. "Time to play, Danny-boy. I've been waiting a long time to wipe that arrogant, smug look off your face."

Daniel's gun stayed level, his eyes narrowing as he shifted his weight, ready to move. "You're unhinged, Lee. Always were. Put those down before you hurt yourself."

Eva's heart hammered, her Stranger twisting and roiling in the need to fight, to protect. She eased to Daniel's right, forming a better attack vector, and retreating from the door. The TMRWS's high-pitched whine spiked.

Kaspar lunged, his twin blades slicing through the air in a deadly arc, and aimed for Daniel's chest. Daniel sidestepped, the gun barking once. No blood oozed from the wound through Kaspar's shirt.

Saturated. The man was almost completely saturated with raw enzyme.

The General twisted with unnatural speed, the stripes on his cheeks pulsing like living shadows. He aimed a knife at Daniel's thighbone. Daniel leaped back, his boot catching one of the rusted chairs, sending it clattering across the floor. Kaspar dodged, a blur of motion. Daniel fired again. The shot punched a hole in the wall by the door to the antechamber. Concrete exploded into the air.

Eva's breath caught as she darted to the side. Daniel never missed. Wait. He was playing with Kaspar, distracting him.

Conflict waged inside of her. Help Daniel, or try for the control room?

Fight. Her Stranger insisted. Eva's arm aimed the gun at Lee Kaspar of its own volition. If she let the Stranger win, they would all lose.

The noise at the door intensified, the door screeching in metallic death. Kaspar would soon have backup, and she had seconds to regain control of her body.

She and Daniel were always out of time.

Every molecule of Shield and raw enzyme inside her screamed to take Kaspar out, bathe in his blood. By this point, her lower lip was a tender, blood-streaked ruin, Shield struggling to mend the damage. *It would heal faster if you let it*, her Stranger called, its urges closer than ever.

Both hands shook on the butt of the pistol, and she backed up until her shoulder blades met the wall. Its solidity focused her, and she eased around its border, heading toward the door to the antechamber on the other side of the room. If she moved too fast, Kaspar's predatory instincts would give chase, regardless of the fight.

Daniel rolled, diving behind the now toppled desk as Kaspar's blades whistled past. One nicked his forearm, blood welling through his sleeve. Kaspar howled, an inhuman indulation of sound that knifed through Eva's soul. He jerked his head toward Eva as she moved, his second blade slashing toward Daniel's neck as an afterthought. God, the man's speed and coordination were incredible. Daniel ducked, the blade grazing his collar, and countered with a swift kick to Kaspar's knee, forcing the General to stumble for the first time, effectively bringing Kaspar's attention back to him.

Eva seized the moment and picked up the pace. She had to do this. For Daniel, for Mia, and most importantly, for all of the survivors scattered around the continent.

Almost there.

The hum of the TMRWS was deafening, the air thick with humidity this close to the antechamber.

Another screech of metal from the door. Dammit, the soldiers in the stairwell had peeled the top corner down, massive hands reaching into the gap, bending and tearing it further.

A few more feet.

Daniel had fully engaged by now, limbs moving quicker than any normal eye could see. He'd drawn his Bowie knife, gun skittering across the floor. He took parries from Kaspar's blades.

The General roared in frustration, each movement meant for death. Daniel's knife sliced Kaspar's forearm, a black gaping wound opening in a macabre grin, bloodless even at that depth. The two men crashed into a side wall, the concrete cracking with the impact.

Did Kaspar still have blood in his veins, or was the enzyme healing it so rapidly that no blood could escape?

A question for another time, Eva, she scolded herself.

She reached for the antechamber's door handle, back to the room, and a powerful fist grabbed her throat from behind, lifting her from her feet. Shock zinged through her body, and her tenuous grip on the Stranger's presence broke wide open. To hell with keeping the man alive. They would just fight their way free.

Adrenaline and power washed over her. She twisted, not caring about the crushing pressure at her neck, and fired an entire clip into Kaspar's body. He stumbled back, breaking his hold.

Insect. Weak. She stalked after him.

His mouth turned up in a wild grin. "What do we have here?"

"Eva?" Daniel's voice.

She blinked.

No. Crush the bug and sort things out later.

"Somebody showed up to play. My, my. She's not as pure as you thought, eh, Danny-boy?"

Daniel appeared at an angle, messing with her line of sight. Streaks of blood and a shredded shirt hung from his muscular frame. Blood dripped from the wounds in a slow pattern. "Out of the way, Daniel. Nobody messes with my people. He doesn't deserve to live."

"That may be so, but we still need him as a hostage. Remember what we practiced. Get it under control and find your purpose." He snapped out the last words.

Her Stranger fought the command. Her purpose was to kill the man in front of her, eviscerate him for what he'd done.

"I don't think she likes what you have to say, son. Come and get it, sweet cheeks, this will be fun." Kaspar waved her forward with both hands, one still holding a blade.

"Eva. Please," Daniel pleaded.

At that moment, the door finally gave way, and all hell broke loose.

CHAPTER 15

The instant the door burst open, Kaspar took advantage of the distraction and snapped a brutal kick that sent Eva reeling backward. A knife sliced at her throat, and she scrambled back.

Daniel pile-drived the man, and Kaspar stumbled. In a fleeting heartbeat, a mere second, her gaze snapped to Daniel's; his eyes luminescing in blue fire, and the world paused, a silent communication sparking between them and whatever resided inside them—enzymes, Shield, or hell, maybe even an alien presence.

Dawning realization washed through in shocking technicolor. Daniel hadn't conquered the presence in his blood; he'd woven it into his very being. Something shifted inside of her, fell into place. An understanding of sorts with the Stranger residing in her blood, her flesh. It wasn't a Stranger. She and it were not separate, but kindred, likely fused since her near-death ordeal in the cavern beneath Lower Monumental Dam.

Daniel had retrieved his pistol and fired it at Kaspar and the monsters now stalking through the door. She ducked the ricochets. The bullets wouldn't stop Kaspar and his men, but they would distract all of them long enough for the next move.

Kaspar charged. She braced against the antechamber door and swung both legs up in a powerful kick, driving them into his center mass. He may have been inhumanly fast, but he couldn't overcome the laws of physics. The energy of her kick collided with that of his forward momentum. Her energy was more, and he lost his balance, flying to crash into one of his soldiers.

"Hurry," her voice was low and rough. She yanked the antechamber door open, and Daniel didn't argue.

She bent the handle on the other side as she closed it. If it worked once...."We don't have much time."

"Eva? Is it you?"

She met his concerned gaze. Lord knew what hers looked like. "It has always been me, Daniel. I just figured that out and stopped fighting it. Let's get this done. Talk later."

The banging started on the other side of the door. This one wouldn't hold for long, its composition much weaker than the one in the stairwell.

Daniel sheathed the knife and put a new clip in his gun, his fingers sticky with blood. He glanced at the door behind her, frowning, "If you can't control—"

"I've got it now. Promise. Let's go." She didn't miss the flash of concern—and maybe a touch of fear—in his eyes.

Later. The word flowed through her brain like warm honey, and she blinked. It didn't come from her, or her—Stranger didn't feel appropriate anymore. *It's just me.*

The antechamber resembled the one outside the control room of the Basin TMRWS. A thick glass observation window looked out over a metal grate platform, the turbine spinning in its electromagnetic shaft. The utility vault, housing the control panel and computer, was nestled next to the conduit box for the weather system's organic core.

Steam rolled off the turbine like smoke, and red lights blinked in a furious panic next to the panel. Whatever Kaspar was doing with it, the machine wasn't meant for this kind of use.

A woman with a shotgun held at her hip stood in the open pneumatic door of the control chamber, a ratty, filthy lab jacket buttoned like a dress. "I can't let you do this."

Weak. No power.

Eva shushed the voice. *I need to listen.*

"Marie? Dr. Marie Evans? Is that you?" Daniel shifted, moving closer to the woman.

"Dr. Burgess, you can't do this." The barrel dipped, and she tightened her grip.

"But a lot of people will die," Eva intoned.

"No, you don't understand. You *can't* fix it."

The emphasis gave Eva pause, and she frowned. Can't was a pretty strong word, one she'd constantly challenged. "Let us be the judge of that."

"Come on, Dr. Evans, lower the gun. Dr. Zapada and I helped develop these machines, maybe there's something we can do." He reached out one of his hands, inches away from the end of the barrel.

"If you release it, we're all dead. I tried to stop him, I promise I did, but I wasn't strong enough." A single tear slipped down the woman's cheek.

See, weak. Eva hushed the voice again.

The banging continued behind them. Not long now. Eva didn't look back to see what kind of progress had been made.

"We don't have much time. Please." Daniel softened his voice, pleading.

Dr. Evans looked between them, brow furrowed, cheeks wet with moisture. She lowered the gun. Daniel grabbed the barrel gently and shooed her back.

Eva closed the thick pneumatic door behind them, securing them inside the control chamber with a whoosh of air. A solid kerchunk indicated the locks engaging with the steel frame. The whine of the TMRWS receded inside the sealed room.

On the other side of the door, about ten feet away, the metal staircase wound to the observation deck above them. Another pneumatic door would be on that level, and Kaspar could come from there after he'd disengaged whatever trap he'd set. It was an assumption he'd set traps near that access point, but it was probably a pretty accurate one.

"Daniel, the staircase."

He glanced at it and nodded. "I don't want you near it. He probably rigged it somehow. Just keep an eye on it. Okay, Marie, show me what you mean."

Dr. Evans walked him to the conduit box next to the vault, thick cables snaking out of it into the floor below. "See? If you open it...." Her voice trailed off.

Daniel's entire body froze, and she shifted her gaze from the deck above to peer closer at the microwave-sized box. Besides cables and a docking port, it should have been empty without the organic core she carried in the backpack.

It was not.

"*Dios mío*," she whispered. The other part of her retreated. It was scared.

Swirls of black meteorite dust surrounded a chunk of jagged rock the size of a volleyball. Tentacles of the accumulated enzyme snaked throughout the compartment, growing into the conduit line and covering the walls of the box. An inch of space remained behind the thick glass cover, a fragile barrier against the encroaching growth, its surface fogged with condensation and streaked with scratches from its futile attempts to break free.

Horror spread across Daniel's face. "It's pumping raw enzyme straight into the outtake pump. That entire cloud is full of it, isn't it?"

Dr. Evans nodded.

Months ago, she and Daniel had descended into a black site near Lower Monumental Dam. There were underground offices above an enormous hole that the government researchers must have been mining before the Collapse. At the bottom of that hole was an enormous chunk of the tellurium meteorite. Particles of the raw enzyme had attacked them and almost killed both her and Daniel. It was a minor miracle they'd made it out of there alive. Not long after, her Stranger had appeared.

The raw enzyme found in the meteorite—which, when refined and stabilized, fueled Shield and the organic cores for the TMRWS—self-replicated. If raw form was pumped into the air at the molecular level….

"We need to reverse the seeding and shut it down, Daniel. We need to do it now." She urged, almost frantic, mostly in reaction to her Other.

"All of those people exposed? That man is insane." Daniel rubbed tired hands over a weary face. "We won't be able to install the organic core. Not now."

Eva had a shallow understanding of the TMRWS mechanical functions. The machines had been Daniel's babies, his life's work.

"Isn't there a way to contain the sample outside the conduit box?" Eva asked.

Dr. Evans crossed her arms, hugging herself tightly. "Once we open it, the particles will burrow into our flesh. Even hazmat is tricky. It takes specialized equipment we don't have here anymore."

Eva shuddered, the dust accumulating on her flesh and boring into her skin still fresh in her mind.

"And the cooling-off period for the machine is a nightmare." He shook his head. "We just ran out of time." Daniel opened the doors on the lower half of the control vault, tearing them from their hinges. Anger radiated off of him in waves. "Eva, keep an eye on the stairs. Marie, help me."

"What are you going to do?" Eva did as he asked. She didn't argue. The lab was her specialty, not hardware.

Dr. Evans's eyes widened as he rearranged the contents and exposed wiring inside the control vault's undercompartment. "You're using the turbine to create a micro-EMP pulse. It could work."

"It's the fastest way for the emergency override to take over. It'll suck most of the cloud back into the reservoir, then the fail-safe will initialize and lock everything down. If we blow the entrances, nobody is getting down here for years." He rummaged beneath the vault, the lights on different panels blinking in tandem.

Soldiers appeared behind the glass of the pneumatic door. Eyes black and watching, forehead concave. One tried prying it open, but the control room was as secure as it could get. One, two...four soldiers stood on the other side. It meant Kaspar had the other two with him.

Speak of the Devil and he shall appear.

"Can't let you do that, boy. Step away from the vault." Kaspar's rough growl echoed from the metal staircase above. A shot zinged from one of the soldiers' rifles, its ricochet only cratering one of the glass panels. Bulletproof. Dr. Evans cowered behind Daniel.

Eva bolted to the base of the metal staircase and fired a single round upward. The bullet sparked against the metal grating. She ducked low and darted to the side, her pistol steady as she sought cover beneath the railing's edge. Bullets from Kaspar's men rained down, pinging against the steel steps. With a swift pivot, she fired again, the shots slicing through the air. Daniel and Dr. Evans just needed a bit more time.

One impacted, and somebody grunted from above. Hollow, dead eyes stared back at her from the top of the staircase. The woman fired again, and Eva crouched. Air moved as the bullet streaked by her face and caught Daniel in the back.

Black flooded the edges of her vision, and she dashed up the stairs. Something like fly bites nipped her arm and side, but nothing else mattered. They had shot Daniel.

Before the creature in front of her could reload, she drew her boot knife and sliced its throat, then plunged the blade right between its eyes and twisted, riding its body to the floor. Kaspar came at her, knife in a striking position. She rolled, coming up to her knees, and swiped, impaling his foot with the knife clear through the boot. He bellowed, striking down where her body had just been.

Eva was smaller than Kaspar, quicker too, even though they were both Shielded. Tactics flooded her brain in a dozen different scenarios to apply to the situation, her Other trying to help. Before she could choose one, thick arms grabbed her from behind in a full Nelson—the other guard.

"I got your woman, Daniel. I'd hold off on what you are doing unless you want her throat ripped out." Kaspar led them down the stairs, her arms dangling from the large man's hold. She palmed her knife; the men were too focused on Daniel to disarm her.

Eva waited. She'd have to time this just right.

Daniel held a small black box in his hands, blood leaking from a bullet wound in his side. Dr. Evans still hid behind him, her hand hovering over a button on the control panel.

"Why don't we do it this way. You release her, or I'll have Marie here push the button." Daniel stood motionless.

"Standoffs never end well, kid."

"Who said we were in a standoff?" Daniel smirked.

And Eva relaxed her entire body, one of her shoulders popping out of its socket on her way to the ground. She jerked back up, arm sliding into place, and did the same slice and plunge to the guard behind her, following his body to the ground and rolling to the side.

Dr. Evans slammed her palm down onto the button, and the TMRWS whooshed and groaned, reversing direction in the shaft. The entire room shuddered.

The massive panel doors high above parted like the Red Sea, their hydraulic arms groaning from disuse. A murderous sky came into view, the vortex of cloud and rain heavy and menacing. A pulse of energy surged upward, and electricity zipped across the clouds. Like a drain had been pulled, the mass swirled, the enormous turbine swallowing the liquid and gaseous matter back into its depths in a tornado of cloud and water. Droplets of rain coated the glass of the control room in a mist.

The energy plume plummeted back down the shaft, a shockwave of sound and energy flattening them all to the floor. The room plunged into darkness. Seconds passed, then a buzz of sound and red emergency lighting indicated an insulated generator somewhere had survived.

Blood poured out of Eva's nose before Shield could staunch it, and she clapped her hands over her ears, the warmth of her blood there as well. She lay prone on the floor, unable to move, every muscle aching. Dr. Evans was the only one still standing. *She's unShielded.* The micro-EMP must have affected the enzyme in some way. She glanced at the conduit box through bleary eyes. The particles inside writhed, slamming themselves against the glass panel. They had been insulated against the pulse.

Kaspar was the first to recover, lurching up the stairs to the observation deck and out through the door to the first sublevel. Not even a goodbye.

An automated voice crackled through the control room. "Mandatory evacuation initiated. Proceed to the emergency stairwell. Ten minutes remain until lockdown. All personnel must evacuate."

Daniel rolled to his knees, a black box held firm to his chest. Dr. Evans helped him to his feet.

"Eva?" He crouched to touch her face, his own covered in blood. "You with us?"

"The bastard got away," she croaked.

"Not for long. We need to leave. Now." He reached out a hand, and she grabbed it, hauling herself to her feet.

Buried alive. She wouldn't survive another round of that. She shook out her limbs, prepared to run. "How much exposure? I mean from any leftover rain."

"It'll be hard to tell until the roof seals." Shield's effects slowly flooded her system, its warmth spreading throughout her body.

The automated evacuation order once again came over the

speaker. "Mandatory evacuation initiated. Proceed to the emergency stairwell. Nine minutes remain until lockdown. All personnel must evacuate."

The goons on the other side of the pneumatic door had collapsed to the floor, twitching in reaction to the pulse from TMRWS, and had not recovered. Eva looked between the glass of the door and the meteorite in its cage within the conduit box. Why wasn't the meteorite behind the glass affected if it was the same material as the door?

Leave now, think later.

She seized Dr. Evans's shotgun, its weight steadying her resolve, and took the lead up the metal stairs toward the observation deck. Dr. Evans followed close behind, her steps quick but cautious, while Daniel brought up the rear, wincing as he favored the side where the bullet had struck. In one hand, he gripped his pistol, its barrel glinting faintly in the dim light, while the other clutched the black box of the hard drive.

Here's hoping Kaspar didn't rig his traps again—more words like honey in her brain. Eva shot Daniel a sharp glance, and he winked. Pins and needles rushed through her bloodstream.

The trip to the surface held no surprises, the stairwell a blur of concrete and shadow. The sloppy setting of the last of the explosive charges was unavoidable due to the time constraints. It would have to do. One at the entrance to the first sub-level and one at the surface. The one she'd set in the elevator shaft below would still be counting down—Lord knew how long they had left on that one.

Two soldiers blocked the top, rifles raised, but Eva's knife found one's throat, and Daniel's fist crushed the other's windpipe. They burst into the open, the fort a maelstrom of chaos. The wildfire still raged beyond the wall, its roar mingling with the screams of people rushing the gates. Droplets of moisture sprinkled the air in a fine mist over the buildings. Soldiers fired wildly, their black eyes cold and hard.

Eva scanned the area, seeking out any sight of Kaspar. Or

their people. Nothing stood out, though the absence of mutated beasts offered a glimmer of hope that those creatures remained contained at least.

"Can you climb?" Daniel asked Dr. Evans.

The woman shivered, hands clutching her elbows. "I hope so."

They retreated away from the crowds, back towards where they'd climbed over the wall, senses seeking any anomalies, any signs of attack. Nothing came for them, the mayhem at the gates and beyond was enough of a distraction. It ate at her that Kaspar had disappeared. As long as he was out in the world, it didn't bode well for the future.

As if reading her mind, Daniel murmured, "We'll get him. Even if it's not today."

They jogged as fast as Dr. Evans could manage and reached the wall. Daniel had picked up a length of cord along the way to help Dr. Evans on the descending climb.

"I can lower her." Eva held out the shotgun to Daniel. "You're shot."

"So are you." He nodded at her arm and side. Eva blinked in surprise. She hadn't even felt them. Raw wounds, half closed in healing, looked back at her when she lifted her shirt to examine them. Well, crap.

"I must have gotten them at the stairwell."

Daniel arched an eyebrow but didn't say anything. He tied the cord around Dr. Evans' waist and the other end around his, wincing as it grazed his half-healed wound.

They all made it to the other side of the wall, the wind blowing smoke and ash into eddies of dust around them. Dr. Evans panted, eyes wide with fear, but taking direction without a word.

Daniel, Eva, and the scientist plunged into the woods, the fort's alarms and chaos fading behind them. An explosion shook the earth. Minutes later, two more rumbled the ground, making them stumble.

A building behind the wall crumbled to the ground. Several smaller blasts from the southeast indicated that their people had also succeeded in their mission, and the sound of something crashing followed the detonations.

Branches clawed exposed skin, and dust billowed around their boots, back toward the relative safety of the entrance to the tunnel. Dr. Evans puffed behind her, and she slowed the pace.

The old airfield loomed ahead, its ruins a ghost of a bygone era. They collapsed behind a tree, gasping, the air filled with smoke and debris. Droplets misted over them, remnants of the cloud above the TMRWS. A few sharp stings bit into her skin, and she brushed the tiny black particles away. Dr. Evans hunched over, huddling beneath the branches to keep it from touching her.

Eva clutched Daniel's hand. He squeezed, not releasing it. "We'll come back," she whispered, more to herself than him. "We'll fix it."

Daniel stood resolute, facing the havoc that was Ft. Belvoir on fire. "Not for a while. It's a band-aid at best, and once Kaspar regroups....I don't know if we're leaving the place better off at all. We still need that machine to network with the others after we fix them."

She rested her head for a brief moment on his shoulder. "Then we'll proceed with your original plan and get the other ones operational first. Then we'll come back."

The rest of their group staggered from the treeline, a haggard Zeke and Tamara, bloody and bruised, being half carried between Stella's people.

Daniel rose. "The baby?"

Chet opened his coat. In it, the baby snuggled like a kangaroo in a pouch. They'd need to feed her soon before she became dehydrated.

"What about all the enslaved people? What happened with them?"

Stella showed her teeth in what was probably supposed to be

a satisfied smile. "We got as many as we could running to the next stop on the railroad."

A weight she didn't know she'd been carrying lifted from Eva's shoulders. "That's great news. I wish we could've done more for them."

"You did more for them than we could have done throughout the next year." Stella slapped her on the shoulder. "That rain hurts, let's get out of here."

Her people opened the hatch and started helping the others down the rickety ladder.

Eva pulled Daniel aside, waiting for their people to enter the tunnels first. "Wait a second."

The tips of his lips quirked in an exhausted smile. "Whatever argument you're about ready to pose, you win."

"It's not all your fault, Daniel. I think we've been running so hard and so fast for over a decade that we can't see the past clearly anymore. You tried to fix it. We both did--are. It'll take me a while to get over you not telling me things you should have, but Daniel, I love you, too. And I would even if it wasn't the end of the world. Life is too short to stay angry for long." Eva squeezed his arm and turned, but not before he spun her around, his lips finding hers in a searing kiss, seeking, questioning. Her fingers threaded through his hair in answer, pulling him closer.

They lingered in each other's embrace, the sweat, blood, and fear melting away as their bodies pressed together, the familiar hum of desire snapping into place—a solace of strength from an unbroken bond they'd had since the lockdown.

Chet cleared his throat. "Umm, ma'am? Sir? Everybody's in the tunnel."

Daniel pulled away, his face still inches away from her, eyes closed. "Thank you, Chet."

Eva brought her hands to either side of his face. "Let's go home."

The fire's glow flickered through the trees, a reminder of

what she and Daniel had started—and what they'd have to finish. For right now, though, it was a problem for the future.

PART 2

THE FUTURE

2072

"We are products of our past, but we don't have to be prisoners
of it."
— Rick Warren, *The Purpose Driven Life*

CHAPTER 1

MIA

Summer 2057
Mia's Dream

As sundown approached, shadows drifted over the low hills of the Columbia Basin. The craggy hollows and basalt peaks, bare and ancient, spoke of prehistoric and otherworldly places.

Just a step away from the wild.

Mia shivered. She was reading *A Wrinkle in Time*, again, and it made her jumpy being out here beyond the wall, surrounded by the thin places, like she'd be pulled into the past by some errant use of the tesseract and be consumed by the untamed world around her.

She turned another page, barely able to see the words through her tears. The book wasn't helping. She couldn't stay there anymore—at the market, with her snarky, mean, once-upon-a-time friends. She'd had enough of them. She couldn't help who her parents were, and she didn't think she was better than anyone else. Things came easily to her—that was all, even compared to the other Shielded. All she wanted was to fade into the background, be equal and unassuming.

Slapping the pages of the book together, she set it on her lap. The shade of the massive wall was a comfort—and a relief. The hollowed-out section of sandy soil beneath a dented dryer was the perfect fit for her body. A hidey-hole even somebody at the top of the wall couldn't see.

Mia plopped another strawberry into her mouth and chewed, closing her eyes. The sweet juice coated her mouth, making up for the bitterness she felt. Another hour and the sun would be down, and she'd make her way home and face the music with her parents. It wasn't her fault her "private tutor" couldn't keep up when she decided to use all the power coursing through her veins to run away.

"You know, with your eyes closed like that, some wild thing could come eat your face off before you could even move."

She jerked to standing in one smooth motion. The book flew out of her lap and thudded to the ground. The owner of the male voice just smiled grimly and remained well out of reach. In a show of just how little of a threat he found her, he put his hands in his pockets and rocked forward on the balls of his feet. With sandy hair and deep brown eyes, he was familiar, though maybe five or six years older.

"It would have to be pretty fast to get me."

"Like me sneaking up on you? Pretty sloppy, Mia." He stooped to pick up her book. He whispered the title as if it required a great deal of mental effort to read the words.

She shot her hand out toward him. "That's mine, give it back."

He cocked his head to the side and raised one eyebrow. "You're a spoiled little thing, aren't you?"

Mia scowled. The voices of her old friends mirrored what he just said. She crossed her arms. "What are you even doing here? Aren't you one of my father's soldiers? Shouldn't you be at Camp Chaos learning how to kill people?"

The guy flinched but schooled his features. "You really don't remember me? I guess it has been a while. I lived with you and your parents when you were a toddler, and then Rani before moving out to the camp. Your dad and Jack have kept me busy, and I don't get into town much."

"Really?" She racked her brain. A name came to the forefront from her short time at Camp Chaos, and she blurted, "Killian."

"Call me Cooper. I like my last name better." His eyes smiled, though the rest of his face was troubled. She could tell because of the worry lines etched into his forehead. Too deep for somebody so young. Well, older than her anyway. "Now, let's head back. They're concerned about you. Your father has everybody at the camp out looking."

Mia sat back down and picked out another strawberry from the carton. "No."

It was a little girl move, but the thought of returning to her parents, to that market and the bitchface Gabby, made her stomach tie in knots.

Cooper raised his eyes to the sky and heaved a heavy sigh. He picked his way over the rocks and sat down next to her, but not too close, and handed her the book.

"Thank you." She hugged the book to her chest.

"So, what happened with the girl?"

"She stole my strawberries."

"Seriously? That was enough to break her nose?"

It was Mia's turn to sigh. "Why do you even care?"

"Maybe I'm just curious what would send the little princess out beyond the wall by herself."

Idiot. She threw a rock at him. "Don't call me that. I'm not a princess."

"Ahh. I think I understand. Is that what the girl called you?"

Mia frowned. "Something like that. None of my friends want to be around me anymore. It's not my fault they're all training out at the camp, but I'm stuck with a tutor. If my dad hadn't gotten it into his mind that I needed different training, it would be fine. Everything could go back to normal."

"You're what? Eleven? Twelve?"

"Twelve," she mumbled reluctantly. She wanted this older boy not to see her as a kid, though she supposed that couldn't be helped with the way she'd been acting.

"Twelve. Yeah, everything seems huge and painful when you're twelve. Trust me, there are a lot bigger things out there. A lot worse situations to deal with." Cooper tossed a rock into the distance. It clacked against another one, and a little poof of dust blew away in the breeze. The worry lines around his eyes and mouth deepened.

"Easy for you to say."

"Not really," he murmured. Another rock flew through the air. *Crack.* "Tell you what. If you read to me, we don't have to go back right away. I've never heard of that book. It sounds interesting."

Mia studied his profile. So serious. And really cute. A little flutter swooshed around her stomach. "It's my favorite."

Cooper nodded.

Mia opened the book to the best part and began to read. After a while, the sun sank behind the distant horizon, and even her Shielded eyes had a difficult time picking out the tiny print. When she couldn't read another word, she closed the book and looked over at the silent boy by her side.

Cooper's head rested against the wall, the front end of some beat-up car, and his eyes closed. "Thank you, Mia."

"For what?" Confused, she stood up and brushed the dust off her backside.

He just shook his head with a sad, troubled smile playing across his lips. "For reading to me, of course. Now let's get going before your parents start sending out bigger search parties."

Mia shuddered at the thought. Wouldn't that be embarrassing? "And thank you."

Him this time. "For what?"

"For not forcing me to go right away."

Cooper nodded. "Anytime."

He kept a firm distance between them as they walked toward her parents' house. The night sky shone brightly above, like the thin places had opened and sprinkled stardust in their wake.

September 2072

Mia shot up off her cot, the dream stark and clean in her mind. When she and Cooper had touched for the first time on Track Three, the memory had been fleeting. This time, it had been clear as a bell.

She scrubbed at her face and listened to the distant sound of tractor motors as they cleared the rubble away from the North Gate. If she hadn't seen the source of the explosion—well below ground in one of the north tunnels—she would have thought the group of itinerant refugees she'd allowed to camp next to the wall had blown it up. As it stood, those people were now within the fenced-in Sector One in temporary housing. They wouldn't be able to move around much there, and there were plenty of people to watch them.

Two days. It had been two days since the gate was blasted. Two more days she wasn't out looking for Cooper or the antidote for her father. If they didn't get him out of cryo soon, even Shield and the cure combined wouldn't be enough to save him.

Her mother had initially shown some interest in finding the lost people beneath the blown-apart cars, trucks, washing machines, rusted farming implements, semi-trucks, and other metallic debris that made up the inner wall of the Territory. However, after half a day, she had drifted back to her house to sleep—Shield still fighting the poison ravaging her body. It would take them weeks to fix the wall, and her mother. Both needed to be finished sooner.

Sweat soaked the neck of her tank. Mia poured herself a glass of water and gulped it down, then opened the door to her tent. Outside, bright emergency lights on their wheels spotlighted people in long sleeves and gloves neatly stacking the remnants from the wall. She'd pulled two of the combines from harvest, knowing what it cost to do so. It would cost even more if Montana arrived and the wall was breached.

The weight of responsibility settled more firmly on her shoulders. Should she send somebody else on the hidden train far beneath them on Track Three? Entrust somebody else to infiltrate the top-secret lab buried beneath Ft. Belvoir in Virginia? Her father and Jack had trained many Shielded militia. Anyone could lead the mission. Couldn't they?

Giving up on ever going back to sleep, she shoved her feet into her boots and slipped on a thin flannel to keep the dust off. She stalked off into the dark toward the night shift supervisor. The man stood, leaning against a shovel, and ensured the workers sorted the piles of debris correctly. Some could be reused to patch the giant hole in the wall, while the rest would be shipped to Sector One for recycling.

"How're things going, Jack?"

The man leveled his best *what the hell are you doing out here* gaze at her. "Go back to bed, Mia. Even you need more than two hours of sleep after three days."

"I've been thinking about something."

"Uh-oh."

"I think you need to stay here with Mom, and let me take the train, first to rescue Cooper from Aunt Sarah's monster camp in Montana, then to take the bypass track to Ft. Belvoir. I've been studying Mom's notes and the old maps—"

"Your father would kill me." Jack swept his free hand in front of him, negating her entire statement. "And if your mother felt better, so would she."

"That's my point, Jack. Someone needs to stay with her, fortify the boundary, and prepare for an attack. I need to go. I need to do this. I feel it clear to my bones." Mia implored the older man. Jack may have been sixty-five, but due to the Shield serum, he still looked thirty-five. She didn't let his youthful appearance sway her. "They've overprotected me for too long. Aunt Sarah already got a sample of my blood. The worst has happened."

A week ago, her Aunt Sarah had kidnapped, used traitors from Sector Nine of their territory to hold her down, and half drained her. For what, she didn't really know, though it freaked her mom and Rani out. Her blood could absorb the raw enzyme without any adverse effects. This could be weaponized, and both women thought that was what Sarah wanted it for. Psychotic her aunt may be, but she was as brilliant a scientist as either of her parents or Rani.

"Not by a long shot, kid." Jack tapped his hand on the wooden handle of the shovel, gazing off into the distance. "If Kaspar gets his hands on you, it's over. Your parents have installed cores in all of the TMRWS except for the one at Ft. Belvoir. It's the key that'll reverse the drought. Nobody's been able to infiltrate the place in seventeen years, not since your parents blew up the place. And everybody Shielded with knowledge of Belvoir, who we thought we could trust, has been infected with whatever Sarah injected them with—almost like it was done on purpose, if you catch my drift. I don't even know who I'd send with you."

Mia smirked. "Then you have thought about it."

"Of course I have, darlin'." Crickets sounded in counterpoint to the tractors, and Jack let a minute slide by before finishing. "Take your mom. She knows the ins and outs of that tunnel system. She's been traveling it for years. Take Talia and the Colville kid, Jorge. Only Talia is Shielded, but they're both trustworthy. Plus, Jorge still wants justice for his grandfather's death. It'll keep him focused."

"We could always inject him."

Jack's face blanched, his hand clenching the shovel until his knuckles were white. "You do know what you're exposing them to? They could go cannibal if there's even one particle of raw enzyme nearby. And anyway, you'd have to get it out of your mom where your dad has the vials stashed. He keeps that more secret than a snowflake in a blizzard."

"Not many have turned cannibal from the Territory. My mother's notes don't seem to explain it very well, but it has something to do with our version of Shield. They should be good —I hope. And I know where he keeps it. Cooper found it before Sarah trashed the MUC."

The MUC—Manhattan Underground Complex—named for the Manhattan Project during World War II was the sister laboratory to the one under Ft Belvoir in Virginia. Top-secret before the Collapse, the two labs still survived, hoarding their secrets beneath mountains of misery like Smaug on his mountains of gold. The biggest difference between her father, Dr. Daniel Burgess, here in the Pacific Northwest, and General Lee Kaspar in Virginia? Her father wasn't psychotic due to ingesting raw tellurium enzymes and had stopped using humans as guinea pigs for defunct old-government projects.

Jack's face hardened. "You have to give him full disclosure and get his permission, Mia. If I had known about all the side effects, I would have never injected myself with that crap."

Mia believed him. His ex-wife, Petra, had left him once she started aging, and he hadn't.

"I wouldn't do that to anybody, Jack. They'll get the full story." She'd never had a choice. Not that her parents necessarily did either. It was either be injected with Shield and save themselves after being buried alive on the twentieth sublevel of the MUC, or die.

They'd perfected the serum on desperate people—volunteers, yes, but it still hadn't been anywhere near being a choice. Daniel and Eva injected the serum into over two hundred survivors and themselves. Most had survived—the majority with the final dose of the serum. Some had not. Guilt still ate at them, heart and soul, even if they saved one hundred and seventy-two people the year it took for them to escape.

He massaged the bridge of his nose and finally nodded. "It looks like you're going to need Rani to hurry up on those train repairs, then, huh?"

Mia just smiled.

CHAPTER 2

COOPER

2072

Dead branches slapped Cooper in the face. Shield-fueled adrenaline pumped through his blood, making his legs fly in a blur across the sandy surface of the eastern Montana soil. A bullet whizzed past his head. He zigzagged around the skeletal remains of pine trees, and another shot thudded into the wood by his head.

He accelerated.

Exhilaration filled him. It always had when he pushed the bounds of his strength. He'd been six when Drs. Daniel Burgess and Eva Zapada had injected him. He could barely remember a time Shield didn't run in his veins, making him stronger, faster, and more resilient. It had saved his life in the MUC. It had saved his life too many times to count.

Earlier samples had killed his parents when they were used like rats in a lab, but not him. Oh no, he was the experiment materialized and fully developed.

Cooper swerved around the burned-out skeleton of a car, its tires rotted to powder where they met the road and zipped across the crumbled asphalt.

The car exploded behind him.

Sweat beaded on his forehead, and his heart rate increased, a sure sign that after five miles, he was finally starting to push the limits of his body's abilities.

Heat blazed across his back, there and gone. A piece of shrapnel from the car. Or a bullet. Shield healed it before it became an issue. Soon, though, even his advanced healing would slow down.

Another mile. Motors in the distance this time. Air puffed out of his lungs like bellows, and he leaped over a log, muscles burning. Just one more mile. That was all he needed. He lifted a silent prayer and sprinted toward his goal: a derelict barn in the distance with ramshackle boards at odd angles and the roof caving in. At one time, it had been red. Now it was just a rusted burnt orange, rotting into nothing like everything else post-Collapse.

A bullet clipped him in the leg, and he stumbled.

At the last minute, he caught his footing and cursed as he darted the last hundred yards through the doors of the barn.

Collapsing on the ground, he heaved in great gulps of air and examined the bullet wound in his calf. It had already started to pucker around the edges. He pinched the sides to squeeze the bullet out, but it had lodged into the muscle.

Cooper groaned as the bullet finally squished out of his flesh after a few seconds of squeezing, bloody and warm. The coppery smell of his blood mixed with the scent of old farming implements and body odor. He sprawled atop the remnants of old farm animals and the grease of many tractors. The rafter above him crisscrossed in a gray monotone that housed spiderwebs drifting in the breeze. Everything came back into focus as his heart steadied.

A severe female face, black hair scraped back into a braid, peered down at him. "Twenty-one minutes, seven seconds. You need to get that shit under twenty or we're not getting in. Get up, you're doing it again."

Cooper glared up at her. Sarah had never been subtle. A tyrant to the *nth* degree, that was Sarah. "Even you can't be that stupid. I got shot and just used all my reserves to run your ridiculous obstacle course. Why twenty minutes, why not five? Or ten? Hell, Sarah, it'll only take me three to run the mile to the door and a quarter mile to disarm the gas."

"Twenty builds stamina." She barked. "Not that I owe you an explanation."

Cooper sighed. "It'll take me at least a couple of hours to recover."

Sarah tapped her foot impatiently. "You have one."

"God, you're a bitch." Cooper heaved to his feet and invaded the shorter woman's space. A total power move, but he didn't care. "Where are the rations? And water?"

Ever since he'd been forced to agree to Sarah's conditions for his daughter's release in that cave, she'd gone full steam ahead with this plan to infiltrate the remnants of the Western Coalition, grab everything they had, find a counteragent for the effects of the meteorite—what they all called black rock—and blow the entire place with General Lee Kaspar inside.

Cooper balked at the audacity. Kaspar was a real sonofabitch, and if Sarah Zapada was difficult to kill, that man was even worse. And from all accounts, Ft. Belvoir had been impenetrable since Daniel and Eva's infiltration years prior. Now, the elevator and narrow passage from the cleared underground Track Three were the only ways into the BUC. If breached, it would fill with a gas that would knock out even the Shielded and kill any unShielded.

Sarah's plan was simple: she'd distract Kaspar with some diplomacy bullshit, Cooper'd break into their secret underground tunnel, grab what she wanted, plant the bombs, and get out through the top after Sarah and her gang of mindless cannibals butchered the opposition.

At this point, he followed along because he wanted to. Somebody finally needed to put a stop to Kaspar's craziness. He'd given in to Sarah's demands at first because she held his daughter's life over his head. Now, Claire was safely behind Basin Territory's borders. Well, as safe as anybody got these days.

Sarah's nose wrinkled, not backing down. "In the packs on the Jeep."

He shoulder-checked her as he limped by. Getting shot sucked, even if he healed fast.

She tripped his foot with a snarl, and he almost fell before catching himself and continuing to the rig. It wasn't worth another confrontation with miss crazy.

The dried pork jerky and fruit strips barely satisfied his hunger after the sprint and subsequent bullet wound, but he choked them down. Sitting in the front seat of the Jeep with its top off, he surveyed the temporary camp they had erected on their way to the East Coast.

Canvas tents were interspersed with the domed nylon variety. Dirty beige, blues, and neon orange fabrics inhabited by feral-looking humans roamed around and prepared the electric-operated trucks. Wires connected to solar panels mounted on top of each truck cab snaked down the middle of the windshield to the engine block. How Sarah had acquired them was anybody's guess; she certainly hadn't had them when he'd been a part of her forced labor less than a year ago.

The truck beds carried six tall cages. Inside the cages were her not-so-secret weapons. The mindless monsters that were the product of early Shield experimentation. They were unstoppable killing machines that lacked a prefrontal cortex to control their urges, and Sarah cared for them like pets. Daresay they were the closest thing to zombies the government ever produced.

Cooper gnawed on the jerky and contemplated it all with a quiet rage. He should just leave, but something pulled him forward on this suicide mission, and there was no turning back.

###

Cooper shaved twenty seconds off his second practice run.

"I can hold my breath when I'm in the passage with the override lever." He placed his hands on his knees and coughed, trying to catch his breath.

"While running? I think not. We'll practice again before we leave." Sarah escorted him to his tent.

"Nobody has ever breached Ft. Belvoir since Daniel and Eva. Not Kansas City, not even Daniel and Eva again. You're crazy if you think this will work."

A psychotic snarl tipped the edges of Sarah's mouth. "I've never had reason even to attempt it, and Daniel and my sister gave up. Cowards. Saving people instead of ending this misery of a drought for all of us. They should have just shot themselves in the head back then, saved me from having to do it later."

"Then why didn't you do it when you were down in the lab? You had every opportunity to kill us all, but you didn't." It was better to be blunt with Sarah.

"Didn't I try?"

"Screw that. If you wanted the MUC's autodestruct to take all of us out, you would have shot Rani. You knew she'd get it shut down." There was no doubt in Cooper's mind about that last statement. None at all.

"Maybe. Maybe not. I really don't care about those bleeding hearts wanting to save the world out of some twisted sense of redemption. My sister has always been self-righteous. I take what I desire and leave the rest. I'll get what I want from them eventually." Sarah opened the flap to his canvas tent, which contained his cot and blanket. She gestured for him to go in, and a guard came to stand next to him. He ignored the hulking man.

"What about the black rock down in the cave?"

Her blank expression met his gaze. "What about it?"

"I think you want to be free from it all, the burning rage, the violent urges. Why not team up with Eva and Daniel? Together, there is no doubt you all could fight Kaspar, get the supply of tainted Shield and whatever else he has down there, and destroy him and his experiments."

The fist came out of nowhere, totally unexpected. His head snapped back, and blood gushed from his nose.

"What the hell?!"

"I will never work with those worthless pieces of shit. They made me what I am, killed those I loved, and did it without remorse, you *hijo de puta*. I will not work with the enemy. I don't want to have to be looking for the knife. You do anything to betray me, and I will burn the entire world down to get to your daughter and slit her throat. You understand?"

The blood had already stopped, though his entire face was wet with it. He wiped at it with the back of his arm. "Screw you, Sarah. Whatever happened to the enemy of my enemy is my friend?"

"Eva and Daniel will never be my friends," she snarled.

"Well, I hope you're not setting us all up to die," he said. The guard next to him shoved him through the tent door.

"Just don't stab me in the back, Cooper. Remember what I told you in the cave. You know what's at stake."

And she left him contemplating the canvas flap of the tent.

The Cave
8 Days Ago

There it was—a cavern, monstrous, enormous. Stalactites clung to the ceiling like daggers pointed at the earth. And in the center, a jet-black stone knifed through the air, as large as a car. A sturdy wooden walkway surrounded it, the planks rough-hewn and worn, as if someone had paced around it.

Energy coursed through him. He took a step forward, drawn to it like a magnet.

"I wouldn't do that if I were you. It exacts a price."

Cooper swung around, drawing his pistol. Sarah sat on the ground in the shadows, back against the granite wall, legs crossed at the ankles, stretched before her. Only her eyes glittered in the dim light.

She smiled, a slight, evil grin. "That won't work in here, even if you take me in the head."

"How did you get back here so quickly?"

"Oh, just like you, I have my ways. Tell me, Killian Cooper, what do you feel standing here next to it?" She didn't stand up, didn't even look worried, just eyed the rock in the middle of the room with an inscrutable expression. Naked. Hungry.

"Sunshine and lemonade, lady. That's what I feel." Dread gripped him in its maw and wouldn't let go. He wouldn't make it if he ran back down the tunnel.

She met his eyes head-on, this time a bit of focused curiosity peeking out. "Funny. I feel fury and pain."

He cocked the hammer back on the pistol, taking a page out of Mia's book. It really wasn't necessary with most semi-automatics. "Where are the rest of your goons?"

Sarah clucked her tongue. "You think I'd let them see that? You're more of a fool than I thought."

He blinked. "Are you saying you let me see this?"

She held up a small device, her voice vile but resolute. "I've been tracking you all along, Killian. I let you save your daughter. I safeguard my resources."

Claire.

Sarah continued. "I'm saying you're going to help me."

"No." Simple. Effective. He wouldn't be controlled by this woman again.

She cocked her head to the side and gestured to the rock thrumming in the center of the room. "Move closer."

"Are you hard of hearing? I said no. I don't take orders from you anymore." So cliche, but so true.

Sarah held up a fob, slightly larger than the tracking device, with a switch at the top. "I push this, and that side-by-side you rode in on with the skinny runt of a kid, ugly mutt, and your daughter will just disintegrate. Poof. Now, move closer to the damn rock."

Violent rage colored his vision. He stepped toward her. He could move faster than she could flip the switch; he knew he could. The anger—no, wrath—swirled through his brain, coursed through his body, and settled in his limbs. He flexed his fingers, rocking onto the balls of his feet.

Sarah dropped the fob in her lap with a satisfied thump. "Ahh, there it is. You feel it now, too."

Breath puffed from his lungs. His need to strangle her, rip her throat out, and leave her in a pool of her own entrails was crushing.

No.

He closed his eyes. The rage began to dissipate gradually. He forced the images from his head. Only once had he felt this out of control. Each puff of breath came quick and hard. Something foreign slid along his consciousness, looking for a way in.

No.

"There are many black rocks around the world, some closer to the surface than others. All of them date back to the last Ice Age before the Collapse. This one speaks to me, calls to my blood. There are enzymes—or something that looks like enzymes—inside these rocks that Daniel and Eva used to make Shield. Other people used them for other things as well. I have an idea they used my niece to stabilize it, poor clueless girl. Let all that rage soak into you. Thatta boy."

He stopped the rapid breathing and opened his eyes, clarity returning in a rush. "No."

A sly smile spread over her mouth, and she slow-clapped. "I knew it. How old were you when you were injected with Shield? Five? Six? It's so much a part of you now, you don't know any different. If you're able to fight it, your blood might be able to stabilize the effects of the meteorite, too, with a little help. Eva and Daniel hid Shield well enough in the MUC that I couldn't find it in time. But there's something else I need more. Something they stole from me a long time ago."

"I'm not helping you."

She held up the detonator switch. "Boom."

Long moments passed in which he glared at her, and she smiled at him. She had him by the *cajónes* and knew it.

"Why don't you just try to work with them?" he tried again.

"Because they're Infected, and if you're not careful, you'll be too."

CHAPTER 3

MIA

Two more days passed. One for Mia to talk to her fellow travelers and convince Jorge not only to come, but also to be injected with a serum that would change his life forever. The other day was eaten up with Rani finishing the modifications and repairs on the train.

Now, Rani's lab in the MUC had been transformed into a hospital room. The stainless-steel counters, full of medical equipment, gleamed in the fluorescent lights filtering in from the hallway. A cot lined the walls, its occupant miserable atop the sheets.

"How are you feeling?" Mia asked Jorge. The young man was still pale after the infusion.

"Still lightheaded, and everything is so intense. The lights, all the sounds. And God, the smells. How do you live with all of it?" At the moment, Jorge had two wads of cloth stuffed up his nostrils, earplugs in his ears, and the veins in his face and forehead pulsed against his dark complexion.

Mia paused her preparations of the medical supplies they'd need for the trip. She'd never thought about it before, how enhanced senses became with Shield. She'd always had them and knew no different. "You'll get used to it, and your brain will just filter it after a while, so it won't all be so overwhelming. Or so I'm told."

Jorge groaned. "It would help if the world would stop spinning."

"It should get better by tomorrow. I promise. Now, I need to talk to my mom. Don't move from this room, or Rani will have a fit."

Jorge lay back down and closed his eyes. "No problem there."

Her mother was in a room down the hall. Sleeping. Most Shielded still required sleep, but only a few hours a day. Lately, her mother had slept all the time. Jack and Rani thought it was only partly the fault of Sarah's poison. They both thought it had more to do with depression from the necessity of Daniel being in cryo, but Mia wasn't so sure. She also wasn't sure that bringing Eva along across the country at this time was the best thing for her.

Mia walked through the towering central basalt cavern that had been built around the bottommost sublevel, with different hallways branching off like giant wormholes. As a teen, she'd lie in the middle of the room and stare up at the fusion of technology and nature and wonder at what it took to build such a place. The engineering, the desire for someplace so secret that the people doing it burrowed into the very depths of the earth.

She opened a door to what had been an old office. Her mother lay curled on her side, back to the door, heart rate and breathing steady, though slower than usual, like they had been since Daniel had gone into cryo. What did it feel like to be so attached to somebody, love them so much, you'd literally wither away without them in the world? It was difficult for Mia to fathom that she ever wanted to be that dependent on another.

"Mom?" She touched her mother's shoulder to wake her.

Eva awoke with a jerk, hand going to Mia's throat, eyes blazing in unrecognizable rage. In a startled panic, Mia tried to break the hold with a sweeping arm under her mother's outstretched elbow, stumbling back across the room, but it didn't work. Her back hit the wall, Eva's hand firmly cutting off Mia's air supply.

Black spots flooded her vision.

"Mmm—" she tried again, but Eva's face didn't reflect an ounce of recognition or emotion other than pure, unadulterated anger.

Mia slammed a foot into her mother's knee without success. If she didn't break the older woman's hold, she didn't know if she'd survive this.

"Where is he?" It was her mom's voice, but it sounded like someone was trying to impersonate her.

The fingers around Mia's throat tightened, and the black spots intensified to a brilliant white. She tried to pry them away with both hands, but steel infused those digits.

With everything she had, Mia slammed her fist into Eva's face. Once. Twice. With the third hit, she weakened, consciousness fading from her limbs like water from a pitcher.

As quickly as her mother had grabbed her throat, she let go with a choked cry, hands covering her mouth. Eva backed up until she could sink onto the bed, her back to the wall. "I'm...I'm so sorry."

Mia slid down to sit on the floor, heart slamming against her rib cage, and throat burning. "What was that?" She rasped.

"It hasn't happened for a long time." Eva covered her face with both hands, trembling.

"But what was it?" She wouldn't let her mother skate past this one. Not this time.

"If I'm not careful, it's like the enzyme can take over my body. I have control now. I promise. I must be weaker than I thought." The pained look in Eva's eyes, her voice, made Mia's heart ache. But now she had even more reason for Eva to stay here.

"I don't think you should go on the mission. I didn't think so before, I certainly don't think so now."

Eva's eyes narrowed. "You don't get to make that call, *mija.*"

"It's my mission, and you're obviously in no shape to come along. You'd be a liability. What if this happens again?" Her throat ached, the words gravelly.

"It won't."

"How can you be so sure, Mom? Damn it, you almost ripped my throat out." The pain was receding, but the memory of that uncompromising wrath was still very fresh. Whoever that person had been, it wasn't her mother.

"You don't understand." Pain, raw and unfiltered, dripped from her mother's voice.

"Then make me understand."

Eva heaved in a breath and let it out in a slow, steady stream of air. "Kaspar is brutal, and if he finds out about you—your blood—he'll stop at nothing to use you until you're drained dry. I need to finish this. He's the last one. He has the last undocumented chunk of meteorite, the last broken TMRWS, and the only other stash of Shield in any of its forms. Trust me. You need my knowledge and experience."

Mia shook her head. "You can hardly get out of bed. You're so weak that…that something else took over your body. No, Mom, I can't risk it. Please, give me your notes from the spies I know you sent in there over the years, your journals, everything you have. I'm taking Talia and Raph's Shielded squad. Plus, Jorge from Colville is joining us. He's been infused with Shield and is recovering in Rani's lab as we speak. Stay here. Help Jack so we have a place to come home to."

Her mother's entire body stiffened at her words. "How did you find our vials of Shield?"

"Cooper did when he was down here. He grabbed a vial for his daughter. She was injected with some poison that was incurable without it. That's beside the point."

"It isn't." Eva clasped her head in her hands. "We can't just go injecting everybody with the serum, Mia. We don't know if parts of our batch are tainted with residual raw enzyme. And we have such a limited supply."

"Tainted?"

"I'm not the only one who feels the foreign presence of whatever is in that enzyme, and it originates from the raw form."

"Who else?" Mia demanded.

"Your father, for starters, though he is…different. He had two unstable samples of Shield in New Mexico, then a stable one when we were trapped in the MUC. His Other is more wily, less violent." Eva fidgeted with the edge of the blanket.

Mia tried to make sense of her mother's words. Alien presences? Different samples of Shield? *Other?* "Who else?"

"The cannibals in Montana. Your Aunt Sarah. I'm sure everybody who has been injected to some degree or another, depending on the sample of Shield used. Our samples are usually stable thanks to your blood, but Kaspar has been experimenting on human subjects for years, though we've tried repeatedly to stop it."

"Why haven't you or Dad been able to? Go back and finish what you started seventeen years ago? That man sounds like a monster." Mia had heard some of the stories from that trip, though both her parents had kept her sheltered for far too long on some of the details.

Eva lay her head back on the pillow and stared up at the ceiling. "We've tried, but he has these enzyme-injected animals— your father likes to call them Aberrant animals, but whatever— they patrol the tunnel around the BUC now that it's excavated. They have also reinforced the wall around Ft. Belvoir. My biggest regret is that we didn't return right away before he could recover enough to keep us out. By that time, we'd already started working on the other machines on the continent. We've helped Stella and Zeke as best as we could to save as many people as we could over the years, but it's difficult when we're clear across the country with a limited supply of fuel." Her mother closed her eyes. "But now we have to. I hate to admit it, but you're probably the best shot we have due to your blood, Mia. The raw enzyme won't affect you, not like it affects others."

The only thing Mia had ever wanted to be was average—or as average as one could be with Shield. Now it looked like she had never even stood a chance of that happening. "Tell me more about the TMRWS and the plan to aerosolize the stable Shield. How is Kaspar even running the machine?"

"He installed Ft. Belvoir's raw meteorite sample into the conduit box that should hold the organic core. The TMRWS agitates the raw enzymes before aerosolizing them into the air when he uses it to water his crops with his damn vortex clouds, and then they are kept under that dome he somehow installed. All of those people have been exposed to small doses for years, with varying results. It can be fixed with one of your father's Shielded cores, but all of the rest of the TMRWS need to be networked for the weather mechanisms to operate effectively and essentially reboot the weather. It needs to happen now, because we only have control of two satellites at this time." Eva snorted, "I guess the apocalypse has really slowed us down."

"That's not funny," Mia said.

"It is a little. I can't imagine how long it would've taken us without the underground tunnel system." Her eyes drooped. "By the way, I agree with you, I just don't like being bossed around by my daughter. I had already decided not to go. Jack needs me here. Talk to Marie Evans, though. And take Rani. She needs to get out more. Both will be able to teach you what you need to know to get the system operational. It'll be difficult to infiltrate if you don't have the proper knowledge and resources. I hope Kel is with Stella's group when you get there. It'll be good for her to see Talia. One last thing, and then I need to get some sleep. What about Cooper? He's one of us, whether he likes it or not."

Mia pulled her knees to her chest and contemplated the question, as well as all that her mother had said. She'd hardly let herself think what Cooper could be going through, what Sarah was doing to him. There was the bud of some feelings there, but were they hers, or was it due to Shield? What Cooper called the Seeking, the ability to know each other's locations briefly after they touched, told her the connection went beyond mere attraction. She didn't know what to do with that information. But her memories of the brief interaction they had as children only intensified the feeling.

"Why didn't you allow us to be around each other more when we were younger? He escaped the MUC with us. He was technically family," Mia said.

An uncomfortable look crossed her mother's face. "Well, you reacted to each other."

"Come again?"

"As a small boy, he was very protective of you, almost unnaturally so. He could always find you when you hid from the world. We kept you separated so nothing would happen."

"To me, you mean?"

"And to him," Eva said softly.

A part of Mia balked at her mother's words. Nobody and nothing dictated her feelings, regardless of what she'd just witnessed with her mother.

"I think he'll have to contend with Sarah for a while. We'll have to rescue him on our return trip," Mia said. Every marrow and morsel of her wanted to do the very opposite, but this mission on the East Coast was more urgent. Her father didn't have much time. Besides, Cooper knew how to deal with Sarah, he'd been doing it for years.

And I don't want that kind of connection. Denial would get her everywhere.

Eva examined her hands. "I'll get you my notes, but Mia? Don't let Kaspar get his hands on you. He's the worst kind of evil, even worse than Hensley." Her mother shook her head.

A shiver worked its way down Mia's spine. She nodded to her mother. "I won't, Mom. Now, I'd better check on Jorge."

CHAPTER 4

EVA

Each finger of Eva's hands ached. She'd almost killed her daughter. That foreign rage, red and hot, rarely overtook her anymore. What she had been suspecting for days was solidifying in her brain. Her Other was quiet and contained now, but in her weakened mental state, how long would that last?

Grief lined her soul in such a deep purple it was almost black.

She scooted off the bed, slipping into her boots. The effort took her breath away, almost to pre-Shield levels. Rani couldn't explain it. Her bloodwork came back normal—well, normal for her.

She made her way to the lab where Daniel's cryo container was stored. The length of the refrigeration units stretched across the room in a smooth line, opening the narrow door to the secret compartment where she and Daniel kept their most sensitive information and samples. Now that included the man himself.

The coffin-like tube made her claustrophobia bubble up in a vicarious reaction. *Dios*, even in unconsciousness, he looked so serious. She placed her hand over the small rectangle of glass above his face. Something stirred inside, settling her Other, which in turn unsettled her more than she wanted to admit.

"He's one tough sonofabitch, Eva. He'll be fine." Jack's warm hand rested on her shoulder.

She covered it with her own, still gazing at the face inside the cryounit. "I know. He and I have been—I don't know how to explain it, Jack. Each other's everything sounds trite and a bit cliche, but it's probably the closest description I have."

"Trust me, I know. I've been here for most of it," he said wryly.

"If he doesn't pull through…" She drifted off.

"Mia will get the antidote. He'll be fine. Speaking of which, you're going to let Mia go alone?" Incredulity threaded his words.

"Did she tell you what happened?"

"No. But it doesn't matter, she can't do this on her own."

"Her father and I did. We didn't have a choice. I…I don't think I can get too far away from Daniel. The Other's close to the surface. I almost killed my own daughter this time."

Jack's hand fell away from her shoulder, and he turned her around. "You good? You need to be locked in a room some-where, darlin'? I can find one."

His tone was only half teasing.

"I don't think it'll come to that. But she needs to go, and you need to stay here. Keep Sector Nine in line, fix the wall, and get the evacuation orders in place." *Keep an eye on me.* The words choked her throat.

Jack pulled her to him and enfolded her into a warm, familiar hug. "We got this, Eves. Mia's got this. She has a good team, and we can send Rani with her. We can also give her the coordinates to find Stella and that bunch; they'll watch out for all of them."

"Thank you, Jack. And great minds think alike, I already told her Rani was going."

"Anytime. Now, let's go light a fire under Rani's ass so our girl can get out of here before the world ends for good."

Eva huffed out a little half-hearted laugh and slung her arm around Jack's waist. The two walked out of the secret lab, even though her soul remained behind with Daniel. "We also need to get those settlements within the borders of the Territory and fix the wall. We also—"

"Woah, slow down, chickadee. No worries, I have a plan."

Eva snorted halfheartedly. "That's what I'm worried about."

CHAPTER 5
COOPER

Cracked and broken earth filled the horizon for as far as the eye could see. The destroyed remains of Chicago consisted of the hollow eyes of buildings and burnt-out carcasses of high rises, thrust to the sky like broken teeth. Cooper swore he could still smell the death that lingered, even though it had been thirty years since the bombs fell.

The caravan crept around the suburbs, passing abandoned houses, faded red Xs prominent on most front doors. First Wave markings. In the distance, the vast, deep canyon created by the receding waters of Lake Michigan shone in the afternoon light. The broken wreckages of boats from decades past lay exposed and sun-hardened.

The jeeps bumped over the potholed and disintegrating road. What he wouldn't give for a horse right now.

Miles passed with the same scenery, the same devastation. The people they passed scattered like rats as they retreated from Sarah's soldiers. He breathed a sigh of relief as they skirted a half dozen small settlements and didn't stop. Sarah's laser focus was on their Virginia and not on torturing innocents for resources.

The late fall air was dry but crisp this late in the afternoon. A week from their target, he asked a question that had been weighing on him since they'd left Montana. "Why didn't we take the underground rail?"

Sarah wouldn't meet his eyes, keeping them on the road in front of her. "Why would I answer that?"

Cooper quirked an eyebrow and countered, "Is it a secret?"

"It isn't."

"Then why not answer the question?"

She frowned, sneering. "You take orders from me, slave, not the other way around."

"I'm just asking a question about tactics. Don't I need to know your plans if I'm to help? I would think approaching from the surface gives Kaspar a tactical advantage. He can see us coming from miles away."

"So? We're not invading. Yet."

"That still doesn't answer my question. Why not the tracks? You have an engine and several carts. It would have been faster, regardless of whether we were invading."

This time, she shifted, left eye twitching. "Those tunnels get more unstable the further east they go, that's all."

That was a lie. He'd traveled quite a distance from near the Virginia entrance to Track Three less than a year ago. The tracks had been cleared. A lot of debris filled the open spaces, but nothing had been on the tracks themselves.

"Bullshit. What did you find while I was gone?"

She backhanded him with a quick pop from her right hand. Blood welled from his nose and mouth. Cooper cursed.

"Enough questions, boy, or I'll make you ride with the Trolls."

"When we all get taken out because of your lack of communication, don't come crying to me in the afterlife." He licked the blood from his lip and wiped the rest on the sleeve of his threadbare flannel. His nose stopped bleeding almost immediately. At this rate, all of his clothes would be blood-stained from Sarah's tender reminders about her rules.

It wasn't until Hagerstown, Virginia, that they encountered the first real obstacle of their trip.

As he understood from old books, pre-Collapse billboards were once used to advertise businesses. He didn't know what this one was supposed to be advertising, but the four bodies, nailed spread-eagled and in various stages of decomposition, were certainly a message. To whom was up for grabs.

Sarah glared at the remains. "We stop here for the night. Cooper, I have a job for you."

Just what he wanted to hear.

Unlike other parts of the country, where vestiges of old-world cities remained, beaten and broken, with only a whisper of what was, the surface of Virginia had been pounded to powder. Only hills of dirt-encrusted steel remained in most places, mounded around the metallic leftovers from random buildings.

In the years after the Collapse, dust storms plagued the area, swirling and drifting the debris into metal carcasses of a bygone era.

The head covering he wore kept the worst of the powdery soil from his lungs. Déjà vu hit. The last time he'd made this run, he'd also been scouting for Sarah, spying on their ally. Perhaps 'ally' was too strong a term. Sarah liked to say there were no allies, only situationships. And in her opinion, those situations happened day by day, sometimes hour by hour. Especially with General Lee Kaspar. Trust issues, that was Sarah Zapada. But in this case, he agreed with her.

He weaved his way between the little that remained of civilization. Washington DC, and the surrounding suburbs, had been hit hardest, the bombs dropping for months straight in an attempt to destroy the Western Coalition's central leadership. The leaders had burrowed in their secret underground facilities, waiting for the smoke to clear. All the Eastern Bloc had done was kill millions of innocent civilians, some too poor or incapable to make it to safety.

The path of destruction left a very barren barrier around most of Ft. Belvoir. Daniel and Eva had finished off the destruction with the fire they'd set. Both events had also done something else: created a clear line of sight with little cover.

Cooper jogged in a reasonably direct route southeast. About an hour into his trip, he slowed at the chirp of radio chatter. He ducked behind a small mound of twisted metal.

Too late.

A bullet sliced through his left calf, and he choked back a cry of pain. He was getting damned tired of being shot in the leg.

Two people in full body armor, faces included, approached, weapons drawn from opposite sides. Goody. Soldier One and Soldier Two.

Cooper raised his arms, his leg burning. It had felt like a through-and-through, which would be better in the long run. He hated digging out bullets from half-healed wounds.

"How ya'll doing? Nice place you have here, though I would talk to your cleaners. It's a little dusty."

No comment.

Wonderful. He kept talking.

"So, I was just taking a little walk and got turned around. Do y'all know how to get to the nearest McDonald's? I seemed to have lost my map."

Soldier One slammed the butt of his rifle into Cooper's gut, and he fell to the ground.

"I take that as a no," he choked out.

Soldier Two gestured for him to stand up and start walking.

Cooper rolled to his feet, gut and leg burning, though the pain was receding as Shield healed the damage.

"So? Not the chatty types. Roger that."

The two soldiers remained mute behind their masks.

Cooper wasn't known for keeping his mouth shut. "That was a great shot. Well, if you meant to hit my leg. If you didn't mean to hit my leg, it was a crappy shot. But that gut punch. Smooth. Impactful, even. I'm still feeling it."

"Shut up."

Cooper kept his smile to himself. "I'm just not in the mood. Somebody real close to me once told me I'm incapable of keeping my mouth shut. Deep inside, I'm pretty introverted. Put me in a tough spot, and I just keep talking. Must be the nerves."

"Shut up, or I'll shoot you again," Soldier Two said, emotionless.

Up to seven words. Progress.

"Then it *was* you who shot me. Remind me to repay you for that later. So, where we going? I really did get turned around back there and lost my compass some time ago. Ever since, it's been circles, especially out in this gray monotony of nothingness. Shit, if I wrote books, that might need to be spiced up a bit. Maybe, the gray dredges at the ends of the earth? No, that's too much of a mouthful, maybe—"

Whack.

The rifle took him in the back by a kidney. He stumbled but kept his footing. Barely.

"I thought you were going to shoot me," the words grated out between clenched teeth.

"If you hadn't come from that rabble up north by H-town, I would have. Now, shut the hell up before I sew your mouth closed."

So, they did have a spotter up by the billboard of death. He hated it when Sarah was right.

Cooper filed the information away and kept his mouth shut this time.

In the distance, an actual building appeared. Metal girders were constructed into a tent shape, and what looked like tin or metal roofing was thrown up as walls. Guard outpost? Cooper eyed the camp around it—fifteen, no, twenty canvas tents. No occupants milled around. Nobody entered or exited the tents.

He and the soldiers ducked into what Cooper took to be the

makeshift headquarters. Portable plastic tables lined two of the walls, guns and ammo containers along every surface. A two-way radio station sat along another wall, an armored and face-covered soldier operating it.

"Sit there." Soldier Two pointed to a folding camp chair set next to the radio, and then he and his comrade whispered at the back of the building.

Cooper turned his attention to Soldier Three beside him. "Nice radio. It must really reach far. Not a lot of places to put a repeater these days, but people are anything if not resourceful."

Black, black eyes just stared at him through the eyeholes of the polyurethane face mask. Really, until they talked, he wouldn't even be able to tell if the person was male or female. Good body armor was difficult to find these days. Great body armor? Almost impossible. The last time he'd been here with Sarah, nobody wore it. That was what? A year, year and a half ago?

"And really nice armor. I didn't know that stuff was still around. I'm young enough, I've only read about it here and there. Whoever's running your ops sure has resources."

A deep male voice materialized behind him. "You know who's running ops here, Killian Cooper. Stop your digging. I've trained them better than that. Why are you and Sarah here? I haven't called either of you."

Cooper tensed, then turned around as nonchalantly as possible. He hadn't even heard the footsteps of the man's approach. He shuttered his surprise. Quickly. "General Kaspar. How are you, sir?"

"I'd be better if I knew why an ally was caught sneaking into my territory."

Cooper contemplated the man. He'd been graying before he took Shield—or whatever variant he had access to post-Collapse—and the silvery hair was cut short in a high and tight cut. Like Soldier Three, his eyes were darker than usual. Twin lines of what appeared to be a black tattoo bled down the right side of his face. He stood at attention, shoulders loose, arms behind his back, and legs shoulder-width apart. Like his people, he wore the black body armor but no face covering.

Cooper gathered his story and took on the friendly tone he'd been using with the others. "Ah, well, Sarah was a little put off by the dead bodies on your doorstep. Thought maybe something was going on. We just wanted to ensure everything was in order before initiating contact. No spying, sir. That's why she only sent one to scout."

"Hmm. I see. Still doesn't explain why she showed up with an army." The general took a step forward, head tilting like a bird eyeing a tasty bit of prey.

"Yes, the Trolls. She has a few requests and wants to use them for payment." Cooper bared his teeth in his toothiest grin.

Kaspar quirked a brow. "Must be a pretty big ask?"

"Daniel Burgess."

For the first time since appearing behind him, the general blinked those black, hollowed-out eyes, his jaw clenching. "What about him?"

Cooper smiled. For real this time. He always liked surprising the enemy. "Sarah's going on the offensive and needs your help."

CHAPTER 6

COOPER

Razor wire–topped pens lined the single lane into the heart of Kaspar's territory. In one, a woman, the left side of her face twisted and roped with scars held a squalling baby. She peered at him with a predatory gaze, eyes black as the most bottomless pits of hell and skin pale to the point of actual white. Behind her, nameless others roamed, some swaying in place and looking into the nothingness of the sky, clothes hanging in rags on skeletal bodies. The woman hissed at him. Actually hissed, like a cat, while hugging the struggling infant to her emaciated breast.

A chill skittered along Cooper's spine. And disgust.

Pen after pen of feral humans, some with their guts growing out of bulging stomachs, some barely showing signs of change. Except those eyes. Those black, black eyes staring a hole into his soul. In one pen, naked people with stringy hair crouched over a littering of half-chewed bodies.

So many of them.

One little girl, dressed neat with the exception of blood splattered all over the front, grinned a blood-soaked grin at him as he passed, her little hands with sharp nails grasping the wire of the fence. Gorge lurched in his stomach, the memory of the cannibal family he'd killed in his parents' old home before entering the Basin Territory still fresh in his mind. Had it only been a couple of weeks ago? It felt like a lifetime.

The last time Cooper had been in Kaspar's territory, he'd entered from the south, along dirt-encrusted paths through the powdered destruction of the old Richmond Highway. On that end, there had been no pens of half-humans, their eyes so dilated that they were permanently black. Did Sarah know they were here? And, was Kaspar bringing him through here on purpose?

A foreign presence swirled in his blood, restless. The presence had only awoken a few times before this week, all of them with Mia, blood calling to blood. He'd never really acknowledged that feeling, that otherness. It had always been there, in the background, content to stay there in his subconscious. Now it stirred, deep and disturbed, mirroring his own emotions but distinctly coming from somewhere else. This time, he didn't push it away; instead, he welcomed it, letting it surface in comforting silence in his mind.

"Nice little army you have here, Kaspar." Was his voice deeper?

Kaspar's head whipped around, and he stopped, brows drawing together and nostrils flaring like he'd smelled something foul. Maybe he had.

"What are you doing?" Kaspar demanded.

Cooper tilted his head, blinking innocently. "I don't know what you mean."

"Don't try that with me, you little shit. You're in my territory, I own your ass. Put it away."

"Put what away, Kaspar?"

"Your darkness."

Except to Cooper, it didn't feel dark. On the contrary, it felt… good. Powerful. "No."

A flicker of something—was that fear? —flashed through Kaspar's eyes. There and gone, but Cooper had caught it.

A momentary little thrill surged through him.

Kaspar caught the eye of the guard behind Cooper. "Take him to Level One holding and get that bitch down here from Hagerstown. I want answers. If she gives you problems, start tranqing her tellurium monstrosities. That'll get her to cooperate. And remind her she's only as useful as she makes herself, and I have no problem putting her and her little band of misfits out of their misery."

Somebody shoved him from behind, and he caught the masked face and cold, soulless eyes of Soldier One. Cooper had two options: go with the person or fight his way back to Sarah.

He eyed the slave pens behind Soldier One, the hundreds and hundreds of infected people in each one. Infected. Sarah's words from the black rock cavern that she'd used to describe Eva and Daniel. Yet Eva and Daniel hadn't developed psychosis. Despite their flaws—and there were many—they were essentially trying to feed and help people. They allowed the smaller settlements a large amount of autonomy and self-rule. Compared to the other territory leaders on the continent, that was a lot. He didn't realize how much until just this moment.

Cooper allowed the soldier to push him in front of Kaspar toward wherever Level One holding happened to be. The Other inside him railed against the idea, but Cooper quieted it without forcing it back into his subconscious. He had a plan, and something told him he'd need that alien presence sooner rather than later.

So, to a holding cell he went.

The dream hit Cooper hard.

A woman's shadow flickered at the edge of his periphery, long dark hair and stormy gray eyes flitting in and out of focus until she stood in front of him, her white t-shirt and jeans worn but clean.

Her mouth moved.

"What? I can't hear you," he said.

She reached out a hand toward his face, but it missed its mark.

Cooper took a step closer, but she remained at the same distance away. It was like tuning to a radio and only hearing static. "Mia, I can't hear you."

The shadows danced in and out. She raised her other hand. Her mouth formed the same words, over and over.

The alien presence within him, buried in his blood and bones, pressed forward until Cooper could almost make it out as a shape standing beside him. Pressure, so much pressure compressing his sternum.

Mia was screaming the words now, shouting as she faded into the ether.

His Other grabbed his hand with a wisp of smoke, and her words finally solidified, taking form and sound.

"I'm coming."

And she disappeared.

CHAPTER 7

MIA

Mia's eyes flew open, and a sharp pain shot through her head and tingled down her spine. The hum of the train's engines droned on and on, the dim light of the interior casting shadows on the floor. She cradled her head in her hands. The throb pounded a hole into her skull.

Had it been a dream or something else?

Kiva whined beside her, settling her head on Mia's lap. She petted the dog's head in reassurance.

Cooper's eyes had been so dark. And the shadowy figure next to him…Mia shivered. It had to be the stress of the situation playing tricks on her, and the guilt from not rescuing Cooper from Sarah first.

He'll be all right. He's worked for Sarah before.

The self-pep talk only made her feel slightly better.

"You all right?" Rani sat down next to her, scooting Kiva out of the way.

The dog dropped to the floor, settling her head on her front paws, and chuffed out a breath. Mia was glad she'd decided to bring the canine at the last minute—like she'd had a choice.

Mia peeked through her splayed fingers, still covering her face. Genuine concern wrinkled the older woman's forehead. She didn't want to voice her concerns about Cooper. He felt private, as if talking about him made his situation more severe—their connection more real.

"I should be asking you the same question," Mia evaded.

Rani's eyes narrowed in suspicion. "What has your mother been saying?"

Head clearing, Mia dropped her hands and quirked a brow. "She hasn't been saying anything. But Rani, you haven't left the MUC or tunnels for years."

"Pssh. I've gone on many trips with Eva. I guard the train, and she does the adventurous stuff."

Mia blinked in surprise. Had she really been so focused on her own issues over the years that she hadn't noticed when both Rani and her mother were absent? The lightbulb blinked on. All those extra-long training sessions in the desert. It pissed her off that everybody had been hiding so many secrets from her. Like somebody who couldn't be trusted. Like a damn child.

"How many?"

"Trips? I don't know, a half dozen or so. After your parents found the maps labeling all of the TMRWS, she went around repairing or shutting them down. Took years, but she got it done. Your father would go on some, but they didn't like leaving you alone too often, so one would stay."

The trips to the outer settlements. That's what she thought they were doing, and they never contradicted her.

"Why so many secrets? I could've helped."

Rani shrugged. "They were protecting you. I also think it was guilt over how Shield and the TMRWS were used. They didn't want you exposed to anything. And, well, dear, you are a little headstrong."

Mia had already considered all of this. Knowing the inherent risk of a discovery with far-reaching implications was always something scientists had faced. Knowing specifically how much those discoveries contributed to the downfall of society, however, was a different matter entirely.

"My blood is unique. I get it. I'm surprised I wasn't bubble-wrapped and kept in a secret room in the MUC my entire life if what everybody says is true."

Talia came by and scooted in to plop down in the end seat next to Rani. "We're coming up on the hub, boss. We stopping?"

A beanie covered the young woman's short brown hair. At the moment, she didn't have any guns attached to any part of her, but that could change at a moment's notice. A knife hilt poked out of the top of her black boot and was sheathed at her side. A hint of a smile tipped Mia's mouth. Talia was a good person to have in a fight, even if she was inexperienced. Jorge sat sleeping, the only apparent side effect from the dose of Shield he'd taken two days ago.

Mia considered the question. On one hand, everybody needed to stretch their legs after twelve hours on the train. But on the other hand, they were very close to the tunnel that took them on the bypass around Kansas City. She almost looked at Rani for confirmation on what to do, then berated herself. It was her decision.

"We'll stop but for no longer than an hour."

Talia jumped up, a smile breaking out across her face. "Yes, ma'am. I'll let the others know."

Not that the others hadn't already heard. The engine wasn't that big, and all were Shielded. Everybody had heard the plan.

Rani rested her head against the back of the seat, eyes closed, hands in her lap. Relaxed. "I always thought your parents should've been a little less controlling with you, by the way. Let you spread your wings earlier."

"Thank you, Rani. Better late than never, I guess. And thank you for coming."

Rani nodded. "My pleasure, girl."

#

Fewer debris piles littered the hub fifty miles west of Kansas

City. Unlike other switching areas, this one had been opened up to bypass Hensley's domain. If followed to its final destination on the main branch, it would end up by the Great Lakes. At the junction, before doing so, a spur looped around to rejoin Track Three on the other side of the city. Daniel had secured the bypass against Hensley years ago. Mia couldn't blame them, not after what the man had done to their people and had done to Talia's mother, Kel.

She hoped to avoid the same series of events.

Clem, one of the soldiers from the militia who had taken control of the train for Rani, positioned it on the correct track before shutting it down and leaving the large front headlight on to shine brightly against the wall.

"Perimeter barriers, fifteen-minute rotation on sentry duty, so everybody gets a chance to move around. We load up in an hour."

Murmured affirmatives rumbled through the group, and like a well-oiled machine, the others disembarked and took the barriers off the sides and top of the engine like they'd been doing for three days. Mia made her way to the back, where their greatest treasure on this trip was stored.

Mia clicked the case open. The organic core infused with stabilized Shield, its liquid center glowing, nestled in the cushioned depths. *It's all right. It'll be all right.* Mia straightened and closed the lid, her paranoia dampened for the time being. Nothing could happen to that thing, or it would be a slow agonizing death for all of them. Another twenty years at most, her mom had warned, and then there would be no more water to support human life. Everything hinged on this trip.

Mia picked up her gun and walked off the engine.

Nobody saw or heard the creatures until it was too late.

The first large cat, black as death, leaped onto Clem, clamping its powerful jaws on his arm with a snarl. A panther on steroids. Or Shield. Her mother's journals often mentioned the possibility of a facility somewhere testing Shield on animals, though they'd never been able to find it.

More animals of all types flooded into the tunnel. So many that she couldn't count.

Lions, tigers, and bears, my ass. Holy shit.

A small wolf snapped its jaws in front of her, eyes completely black.

Like Cooper's.

Mia didn't have time for a reaction. It lunged, its furry body flying through the air. She slammed a fist into its face. The animal yelped and scrambled back, growling, hackles raised, and teeth bared.

The gun case was open in the bottom compartment of the train. From now on, they'd travel armed.

She inched her way toward it, but the wolf padded closer.

Something furry dropped from the roof of the train onto her head.

Mia held her panic in check with effort. Pain lanced down her back as something dug its back claws into her back through the flannel shirt and its front claws into her scalp.

Blood streaming down the side of her face, she stumbled back against the train and slammed the creature between her body and the side panel.

Thunk. Thunk. Thunk. Growls and hisses accompanied each impact.

She dropped to the ground. The creature on her head—a cat of some kind—disappeared in a flurry of fur. Just as the claws loosened from her back, the wolf hurled itself across the empty space. Hot, lupine breath, rank and rotten, fanned across her face. With one hand, she kept its jaws from her throat, and with the other, she reached for the gun case.

Slobber dripped onto her skin like acid. Mia clawed for a weapon, any weapon. God, the thing was strong.

The arm holding back the wolf weakened and began to shake with the effort. She dug into the ground with the heels of her feet, propelling her closer to the compartment with the gun case. A long pink tongue escaped from a mouth of razor-sharp teeth. It lapped up a drop of her blood.

One moment she was centimeters from having her throat ravaged, the next, the animal started convulsing.

Not one to look a gift horse in the mouth, Mia shoved the wolf off of her and scrambled back to find the first gun she could.

Froth foamed from between lupine lips.

Mia stared at it in horror. Her blood wasn't supposed to work like that.[AR1] She thought it was supposed to be refined somehow. This was new.

Later, contemplate it later.

Now that the immediate danger had passed for her, she took a moment to process the chaos around her.

Two Shielded militia members fought back-to-back against two bear-like creatures. The bears' rigid, muscled bodies bulged, fur so thin as to be non-existent.

Cats of every shape and size clawed and pounced, bounding higher than any feline had a right to. Rani swatted at them mid-air with a rifle, shooting them as they landed on the ground before they could reach the bear fighters.

Talia and Jorge had backed up against a tunnel wall on the far side of the hub and clubbed and shot at feral dogs and wolves. The other half dozen fighters did their best to keep the other animals at bay. Hell, there were even a couple of monkeys. For each shot fired, another animal recovered and rejoined the fray.

A moment of helplessness gripped Mia. *Take off their heads.* The words came from nowhere.

Not questioning the advice, she yelled out into the group, "Knives out! Cut off their heads if you can."

Nobody glanced her way, too involved in not getting eaten by monster animals, but the energy shifted. Mia gripped her

Bowie knife, opened a wound on her arm, and stepped over the now-still body of the wolf she'd killed.

She covered the knife in her blood and joined the fray at Rani's side.

The older woman looked at her with relief. She batted a frizzed-out black cat from the air and shot it once it hit the ground in front of Mia.

She chopped off its furry head. Black blood spurted onto the ground. She and Rani worked their way through the wild, unthinking clowder of mutated cats. Blood and fur flew. Scratches marred every inch of her exposed skin by the time they'd dispatched the last one.

One of the bear fighters whirled and jabbed at the monstrous creature, keeping him away from where his comrade rode the other bear. Muscles burgeoning, the young, Shielded soldier cursed, trying to slam the knife between the bear's neck.

Mia wiped more of her blood onto her dripping blade and yelled at the man. "Malic! Use this one!"

Not skipping a beat, he caught it from the air by its hilt and plunged it into the ursine's vertebrae. It dropped like a sack of rocks to the ground, roaring its displeasure. White foam erupted from its mouth like the wolf.

Mia didn't contemplate it, just repeated the process for the other bear fighter and ran back to the train to retrieve two more knives.

She ran towards Talia and Jorge, both of whom were now cornered by a ring of dogs and wolves. Crap. Whatever lab they came from had to be close for there to be so many of the super-charged creatures.

"Catch!" Mia tossed a bloody knife each to Talia and Jorge. Rani and the bear fighters helped clear the other animals, screeching, clawing, and biting through the other soldiers.

Mia catapulted herself onto the back of a large timber wolf. Its rank fur made her gag, but she clung to its powerful body.

Clutching at with one hand, she knifed it in the side before being flung off. It was enough; it went down like the others.

Encouraged, she twisted and lunged, stabbed and swiped her way through any animal that came her way, reapplying her blood when necessary.

Gasping for air, adrenaline running like a freight train, she paused when another creature didn't present itself.

Something scraped against the wall, and she whirled around.

Friend.

One of the Shielded soldiers had slipped down the wall with her legs splayed in front of her, limp and bloody arm clamped to her stomach.

Piles of dead animals were spread out all around the hub, some piled where they'd charged in groups.

Drip, drip.

A growing puddle grew beneath the tip of her combat knife. Harsh breath sounds and the moans of the wounded mingled in the air.

"Everybody back on the train, help your neighbor," Mia ordered.

Whatever they had just encountered, they would have to either shut it down or face it on the return trip. She closed her eyes for a beat and felt time slipping further and further away for her father. For Cooper. Time to see what the rest of her mother's journals had to say.

CHAPTER 8

EVA

Work on the wall continued. Eva monitored the build while Jack coordinated the stream of settlers coming into the Territory from the east. The people had received the message loud and clear from the scouts, and nobody wanted to be left out in the cold. Despite Sector Nine's protests, Jack had the refugees set up in a tent city out on their land. Let them try treasonous acts with hundreds of extra people in their way.

Eva shoved her canteen back in her backpack and wiped a tired hand over her sweaty brow. Reconstruction was slow going. Jack had found an old semi-truck to disassemble and fill in the largest of the gaps, but they still required a substantial amount of material. For the wall to be fully energized, it had to be mostly metallic objects, large enough to make a difference but small enough to maneuver. Once it was turned on, all other electrical activity would cease due to the amount of volts pumped into the grid buried within. It took electrical fencing to an entirely different level.

All she wanted to do was sleep.

"Ma'am, it's coming on four o'clock. I'm going to get these

folks fed. You need anything else before the night crew comes on?" Tad, one of the foremen, crouched beside her chair.

"Were you able to salvage any of the top planks from the old wall?" *Have I asked this before?*

Tad regarded her with patient brown eyes. If she had asked the question before, he wasn't going to give anything away. "No, ma'am, they were a total loss. We have a line on some replacements west toward Yakima, but as you know, it gets…tricky over there."

She nodded. "Take Bradley's team, they're more seasoned."

"Yes, ma'am."

"Then I'll see you tomorrow." She stood from her chair and stumbled into the younger man in the process. He grabbed her arm and steadied her, genuine concern flashing across his face.

"Can I help you back to your side-by-side, ma'am?"

She shook his arm off weakly, embarrassed. "No, I got it, thank you."

Tad shoved his hands into his pockets and took a step back. "Should I call Mr. Allen?"

"Absolutely not." Irritation threaded her words. "I can drive myself back home, Thaddeus."

The tips of his ears reddened, and his lips compressed from the use of his full name. "Yes, ma'am."

Eva climbed into the ATV and turned over the electric engine. It started with a hum, and she jammed her foot against the gas pedal without looking back at the foreman. Irritation flooded her system, sharp and tangy. Call Mr. Allen? Seriously? She didn't need Jack. Everybody had been treating her like some decrepit beast needing coddling and babying.

Eva sped the machine down the gravel road, dust billowing behind her. The faster she went, the more worked up she became. The black haze that came when her Other was at the surface blurred her vision and gave her a spurt of energy. She turned into a corner, back tires skittering and gravel flying. The side-by-side careened onto the two passenger-side wheels while hot tears fell onto her cheeks. She wiped them away with a trembling hand.

Relief flooded her at the sight of her driveway, the long line of poplar trees, their yellowing leaves fluttering in the breeze, led the way to the two-story farmhouse. Its sandy color reflected the dying light of the day.

Jack's ATV sat parked in front. His sturdy frame leaned against the back, arms crossed, waiting for her.

She skidded to a stop and hopped out, riding the adrenaline still flowing through her veins and keeping her upright. "That traitor called you anyway."

He held his hands in front of him. "He said you almost fell."

"I tripped standing up, it can happen to anybody." She stalked past him to the front door. Her adrenaline was already dissipating and being replaced by the ever-present weakness since Sarah had injected her with the bioagent…since Daniel had gone into cryo.

"You're forgetting conversations, you're weak. Look at you, you're shaking." He followed her up the front stoop, and she opened the door.

"Do not follow me in here." She tried slamming the door into his face, but he shoved a booted foot in between the door and the jamb.

"Will another dose of Shield help? You need more testing, or something. Hell, darlin', you would know more about that than I would." Jack pushed through the door.

"Boundaries, Jack, I don't want you here." Dots and spots sparked in her vision, usually indicating she needed to lie down. Now.

"Normally, I would comply, but not when your safety is at stake."

As if to prove his point, all the strength left her body, and her knees gave out. Jack caught her and carried her to the worn leather sofa.

She gazed up at him through teary pools, her words slurred, "What's happening to me?"

###

Eva awoke to Tamara Foster sitting in a chair, reading a book next to her, her socked feet crossed and resting on the end of the bed. Jack must have moved her here after she'd passed out.

"What time is it?" She croaked.

"Welcome back, my friend. You've been out for fourteen hours, give or take. It's"—Tamara looked at her watch— "just past eight. In the morning."

Eva scrubbed her hands over her face and shoved the panic down. She'd done many, many scary things over the years. Had thought she was going to die on more than one occasion. But this...this was different. This felt like the real thing. The end. *El fin.*

"*Dios mio.*"

Tamara ignored her. "Jack sent me. He thinks we may need to do some work down in the lab to figure out what's going on and that you may need some help."

Eva looked at her old friend. All of them had been through hell and back together. This was just another version. "Yes."

"I got you, girl. We'll get this figured out. What did Rani say before she left?"

"That with the extra dose of Shield and the antidote, I shouldn't still be this weak. That Shield probably just needed a little extra time to work."

Tamara frowned. "She left you even though it wasn't?"

Eva quirked a rueful brow. "I lied and said it was improving so she'd go with Mia."

The other woman shook her head. "Damn, you're stubborn. I'll gather a few of the techs, and we'll see what we find. Do you have a starting place?"

That was the rub, wasn't it?

She looked down and shrugged. Her collarbones were in stark relief above her thin T-shirt. Weight loss was added as another symptom. "Blood and tissue samples again. Maybe now that more time has passed, we'll find something else."

"You need help getting dressed?" Tamara masked it well, but a deep concern was reflected in the tension of her shoulders and the grip on her book.

Yes. "No, I got it."

With an effort born of pure will, she sat up and swung her bare legs over the edge of her bed. Dizziness swept over her, and she closed her eyes. A warm hand settled on her arm, and though she knew it was a cranky move, she shook it off. "I'm fine."

"Obviously," Tamara said wryly.

"Let me do this. Please. If you'd like to do something, could you make me something to eat? I'm starving."

Another lie, but at least it would get the other woman out of the room.

Tamara was silent for a beat but finally said, "Fine, you stubborn ass. Soup or sandwich?"

"Soup, please."

Eva waited until Tamara had left to open her eyes and fall back into the cushy pile of comforter and pillows. The clean scent of line-dried linen was the scent of home, love, and laughter—the scent of better days before the Collapse.

She dropped the wall in her mind that she had erected against the influence of her Other. Warmth flooded into her, along with the energy to get dressed. But there it was, the proof glaring her in the eye. Even through the bouts of strength, her Other was weakening, using its reserves when she needed it, but something was hindering the enzyme. And without it, she was as good as gone.

CHAPTER 9
COOPER

Cooper's prison cell had once been a private office with its own bathroom and couch. Thick cement walls and the absence of windows indicated that he was most likely underground. The fluorescent lights shone without end, and there was no switch. A mental game? Probably. It was something he would do in the same situation.

Packed bookshelves lined one wall, and nobody had thought to take them out. He'd read two books by the time they dumped Sarah, bound and gagged, into the room with him.

Cooper turned on his side from his position on the couch, head resting on one hand. He couldn't resist the need to grin.

"Trussed up like a hog, huh?"

Sarah glared, spouting something through the gag. He didn't even try to interpret her words.

"You'll have to speak up. I can't hear you." Cooper sat up and bookmarked the book he was reading. Some monologue on ethical leadership. Maybe he should give it to his captors and the woman tied up on the floor in front of him.

Sarah bucked and wriggled like a fish on the line, trying to loosen the knots, no doubt. To untie her, or not? Cooper sighed, audibly and long before slapping his hands on his thighs and standing up. "Well, what kind of minion would I be if I didn't untie my boss? Stop moving and hold still."

The knots were tight and well-made. They'd have to be to hold Sarah. It took the better part of twenty minutes to undo them. He took the gag off last.

"You worthless piece of shit—" she started.

He cut her off. "No, no. You don't get to call me that. I followed your directions to the letter. Notice you are also here with me. And you're welcome, by the way, for untying you. I had half a mind to keep you trussed up."

Sarah rubbed her wrists, the red marks already disappearing due to Shield. A constant glare was creasing the space between her brows in semi-permanent wrinkles. "They're tranquing my Trolls and putting them in pens. They're also rounding up the rest of the soldiers. It's a clusterfuck."

"Might as well settle in. I've already tried all routes of possible escape, even trying to bash through the wall. It's enforced with steel, by the way." Cooper stretched back out onto the couch and reopened the book. Let her find a place on the floor. He couldn't care less.

"Scoot over."

"No."

Sarah grabbed his legs and swung them off the couch with a sweep of her arms. He grunted and cursed. She sat at the opposite end and crossed her arms, inspecting every inch of the room they found themselves in like a caged animal. It was probably the most apt comparison he could have made for her. The mighty foe brought to her knees by an even bigger monster. And then imprisoned. Karma at its best.

Cooper slunk down on the couch and resumed reading the book, ignoring her. Or trying to. The energy emanating from her was intense, and when she started tapping her foot, he gave up and snapped the book shut.

They probably didn't give her her own cell because they were observing them somehow. Testing his theory, he said, "So did Kaspar say he'd help you attack Daniel's Territory?"

Sarah shot him a sharp glance, then immediate understanding dawned behind her dark, dark eyes. "No. He thought I was trying to start something."

"Yeah, he didn't seem to believe me either. What's the plan?"

Sarah threw up her hands in frustration. "I don't know, Cooper, storm the walls and bomb the ramparts. It's a little difficult to make plans when I'm in here."

"Not used to losing, huh?"

Sarah clenched her fists, and he did not doubt that if she didn't need him, she would have hit him. Her version of effective leadership. He really should give her the book.

"I'm not losing, it's just a minor setback." She frowned.

"He took your only bargaining chips, Sarah. I would say it's more than a minor setback," Cooper said.

The wheels spun behind her narrowed eyes. Something was definitely brewing in their devious depths.

"We'll see." And she smiled an evil smile.

#

A day passed in monotonous silence. Cooper ended up sleeping with a pillow on the floor for the few hours he required it, leaving Sarah the couch, not by choice. After all the things the woman had done, giving her any amount of comfort was not at the top of his list.

Hopefully, she wouldn't get hungry.

On what Cooper concluded was his third morning in the cell, the door opened, and a massive bear of a man, with blue eyes that were almost white, gestured for him to come—no dark-lined tattoos.

Sarah jumped to her feet. "I demand to speak to Kaspar. Our longstanding agreement is being violated, and I won't stand for it."

Soldier Four—Cooper was surprised the soldier count wasn't higher—stopped her progress with the barrel of his tranq gun. "Only him."

Almost monosyllabic, but not quite. It would be a fun challenge to see how many words he could get the mountain of a man up to. He strolled to the door, Sarah's curses and threats following him.

"Thanks, man. She can get a little vile after a while if you know what I mean."

Sarah hollered an insult, and Soldier Four closed the door in her face. She pounded on it, the frame flexing with each impact of fist against metal. Interesting.

"So, what does ol' Kaspar want to do to me today? Waterboarding? Fingernail pulling? You know, I would almost prefer a good dose of strategic beating to going back into that room with that woman."

"Shut up."

Well, it was a better start than with Soldier Two.

"Now, that's not nice. What did I ever do to you? Are you always this dour?"

The quick snap of a fist against Cooper's back, right in the kidney, doubled him over. He stumbled forward with a gasp.

"I said shut up."

"Roger that." At least he'd gotten four words out of the asshat before his kidney took the consequences. Shield went to work, though, and by the time they reached an elevator, only an ache remained.

Soldier Four pushed a floor, and a down arrow appeared on the readout above the controls. S4, S5, S6. His interest piqued. S for sublevel? Had to be if they were going down. Logic dictated they were in the lab beneath Ft. Belvoir. How many other old government buildings with sublevels could there be in this area?

At S8, they disembarked and followed a narrow, cement-walled hallway, doors to half a dozen offices closed tight. At a T in the hallway, they turned right into what looked to be an infirmary.

"Sit on the table."

Uneasiness heightened his already focused senses. Orders, infirmaries, and hospital beds never mixed well in his experience.

"What if I say no?"

The fist took him in the gut this time, and he tipped over onto the hospital bed, its steel frame twice as thick as a standard bed frame. Chunky manacles soon encircled his wrists and ankles. *So not good.* He'd rather be tortured than be experimented on, and he had a sneaking suspicion this was headed that direction. Soldier Four walked out, and only the distant sound of people in distant rooms doing distant things reached his ears.

Cooper strained against the manacles. No give.

Bucking and fighting against the restraints didn't loosen one chain. After a few minutes, he lay still, panting in frustration and a good dose of fear. He remembered his parents' sick, frail bodies writhing after a failed experiment had ravaged them.

He closed his eyes and reached for that Other that was so close to the surface these days. It flooded his system with calmness, and his heart rate steadied.

Somehow, since he'd been in that blasted cavern back in Montana with the black rock, that Otherness had been so close. It had crossed his mind, especially after his encounters with Mia and the mutual Seeking—and not to forget that dream that felt so real—that maybe it was there more than he suspected, guiding his actions and body in subtle ways. And he just hadn't noticed.

Like it or not, it was a part of him. Whether it was the enzyme in Shield or something else, he didn't know. All of that science was beyond him. His body warmed as if the Other was responding to his thoughts. Hell, it might be due to its presence in his bloodstream and tissues, infused in every part of his body since he was six.

"Mr. Killian Cooper. A pleasure to meet you. I am Dr. Hausman." A short man, black hair matching the black in his eyes and the inky lines of tattoo on his face, walked in. He wore a white doctor's coat and held a tablet. An assistant wheeled a cart full of instruments to the foot of the hospital bed and clicked down the stoppers so it wouldn't roll away.

"Can't say the same. I work with one of General Kaspar's allies. She won't like this very much." Not that he thought Sarah gave two damns about him other than what he could do for her, but it was worth a try.

"The way I understand it, you're one of her slaves. A unique slave, but a slave nonetheless. If we harm you too much, we'll just compensate her. Now, you were injected with the Manhattan Complex's fourth-generation Shield serum when you were a boy, is that correct?"

The man tapped at this screen before gazing at Cooper with a clinical detachment.

"My parents joined the circus when I was young, and I grew up with carnies before the bombs dropped. I ran the pony riding station with a man named Boo. I dreamed of owning my own circus one day." Cooper blinked innocently.

Dr. Evans sighed. "Miss Jones, please prepare the syringe."

Cooper jerked against his restraints. "No, Miss Jones, don't prepare the syringe."

"This will go easier if you cooperate, Mr. Cooper." The doctor tilted his head to the side and hugged the tablet. No emotion, not even a flicker of disgust or hate.

"It won't, and we both know it." Cooper flailed harder, focusing every ounce of his being on that Other warming him and making his vision red-rimmed. Blood ringed his wrists and dripped onto the matte metal surface.

"Darius, come hold his body down." Soldier Four powered into the room and lay across his body to hold his arms against the bed. Cooper went wild. Then the poke of a syringe, and everything faded to gray.

Two soldiers dumped him in the office prison cell right in front of the door. Sarah rushed to him, cursing the two who slammed the door in her face. Again.

Oh, that would piss her off.

Thoughts were fuzzy and his vision even fuzzier, so he tried to get an arm under himself to sit up, but failed.

"What happened to you?" The derisive question came from the glaring woman above him, with her hands on her hips.

"Dr. Mengele, though I think in this iteration of the multiverse he calls himself Dr. Hausman." His Other slumped in the corner of his mind, quiescent. Spent. As was he.

"Get up."

"Pretty sure that's not happening," he slurred. Oops. Vision was going again. The funny purple…

When he came to, he was lying on the couch. Surprise fizzled through him. Sarah had moved him to the sofa? Inconceivable. He giggled.

A purple haze swam around the edges of his sight. So pretty. He waved a hand back and forth through the beams of purple light streaming out from behind his fingers.

Sarah slapped his face. Ooh, that was more like the evil woman he knew. "Get it together, Cooper. I need you."

"Need? I need a lot of things…" Was that a fairy flying over by the bookcase? No, fairies weren't real….

The next time he returned to himself, a headache shot through his brain and scorched his optic nerves along the way. Sarah sat at the end of the couch on the floor, paging through a book.

"Hey, evil queen, whatcha reading?" He squeezed his eyes shut.

"You back for good, or do I need to beat some sense back into you?" She dropped the book next to her legs and rose smoothly.

"No more tender ministrations. Please," he intoned. At least everything wasn't surreal anymore.

"Report."

"Oh, manacles, syringes, and brain surgeries, oh my."

"In plain speech, Cooper." She put her hands on her hips and waited with her normal murderous look firmly in place.

"In short, they drained most of my blood, looked inside my skull, and a lot of other things I prefer not to talk about." He kept an arm over his eyes.

"But, why?"

Her question had to be rhetorical. Why would Kaspar do any of it?

"I don't know. Why do you do what you do?"

"People need a strict structure to function. And power equals freedom," she replied.

Shock shot through him. She had answered him. He looked at her through the pain of the headache, flabbergasted.

"Human flesh–eating cannibals and killing people at random doesn't qualify as structure, Sarah."

She snorted. "You know nothing, Cooper."

Hadn't he read that line somewhere? "Eating people, bad. Killing, wrong. Helping people, good. See, it's that easy."

Sarah frowned at him, but he replaced the arm across his eyes. This time, he forced himself to sleep, and she didn't say another word.

CHAPTER 10

MIA

From the journal of Dr. Eva Zapada:

Nala isn't a normal dog. I knew it right away, but after Kansas City and the tunnels under Virginia, I tested her blood, and my suspicions were confirmed; she has some Shield variant in her blood. All the tests showed the enzyme, but it had mutations I'd never seen, like some borehole straight through the center. I wonder which lab was in charge of such experiments and how many different animals were involved in them. Those things in the tunnel with Stella's crew were definitely not human, and I wish I had gotten a sample of blood or tissue. I'm ninety-nine percent positive I would have seen the same markers. My biggest question is, why is Nala not feral? And why doesn't she have physical mutations along with the cellular ones? Both questions will probably never be answered, not these days with our limited resources and time to explore. Suffice it to say, she has similar attributes to the MUC's Shielded: strength, resilience, rapid healing, limited cellular aging, which will likely lead to limited aging overall, and a lack of erosion in the prefrontal cortex. Not that it's our biggest concern at the moment, but the facility where she was created will eventually need to be found and destroyed. It does lead to my biggest concern: how many more laboratories out there have a version of Shield besides the MUC and Ft. Belvoir? We were supposed to be the only ones.

#

Mia searched her mother's journals, Eva's spidery cursive almost indecipherable, and ran across a passage about Nala. It was only a couple of pages long in the small book.

She read the passage and then reread it. So, her parents knew that a lab testing Shield on animals existed, but hadn't done anything about it.

It must have been why her mother gave her the rest of her journals to read. These little nuggets were probably scattered throughout the area.

Mia dropped her hand to the silky fur of Kiva's head and petted the dog's ears. Kiva groaned in her sleep, stretching her legs, relaxed as her side puffed out on a deep sigh. The dog had been magnificent in the fight. Almost preternatural in movement and speed. It was a miracle Cooper had found her—the same animal who had found her mom. Kiva or Nala? Both names suited, and the dog responded to both with equal enthusiasm. But there was just something about the name Kiva.

Her next step was to find the lab. They couldn't leave such a massive resource at their backs if they were going to take Kaspar out.

"Rani, what have my parents told you about Kansas City?"

The other woman held out a bowl of stew and eased into the seat beside her, avoiding stepping on the canine sprawled on the floor. Somebody had rehydrated a pack of the stuff over a camp stove, and now the sounds of slurping and chewing filled the train engine. Malic, one of the bear fighters, munched while guarding the door, wary eyes scanning the outside through the windows.

"Nothing good. Hensley uses the meteorites to enhance his Shield injection, allowing him to appear godlike to his cult of followers. And the things they did to our people." Rani shivered. "Not many people know this, but Talia is his daughter. She came home with your parents, then Chet and Ana raised her."

"What happened to her mother?" Mia was aghast.

"Kel? She decided she wanted her baby to be as safe as she could. She stayed in Virginia and helped Stella and her lot rescue people from Kaspar's camps. I often thought your parents didn't give her much of a choice about that. I met her once. Kel is… interesting to say the least."

"Is that why my mom sent her with us? To possibly see her mother?"

Rani shrugged. "Maybe. I think the bigger reason was that you needed as many people as you could trust on your side. Now, what are you thinking?"

Mia digested the last comment. "I think we use Kiva to track the animals back to their source. Keep a crew down here to protect the engine and set up mines just in case, but we need to locate this lab if it exists and shut it down. I don't want such a thing at our backs or facing us on the return trip."

Rani nodded, "I agree. Who are we leaving here?"

"Malic and Jorge to lead, and three of the Shielded militia? Split them up and bring you and Talia."

"I'll stay here."

"Rani—"

"No, I already told you. Your mom would do the adventurous stuff, and I would guard the train. I don't see why that needs to change now."

Mia regarded her with a slight frown, but if she'd learned anything over the years, it was that when Rani got something in her head, it stuck, and nobody was going to change her mind.

"Fine. I'll take Malic, but I think Jorge needs to stay here."

Rani nodded. "That will work. And Mia? Be careful. I know firsthand the old government hid a lot of, to use a Christian term, sins in these tunnels. This one will be no different if you find it."

It was Mia's turn to nod. "I know. Thank you, Rani."

\#\#\#

The pungent mix of blood and dirty animal punched Mia in the nose as she exited the train with her team. Kiva picked her way through the piles of furry bodies on dainty feet, sniffing here and there, ears forward. The black part of her coat blended with the shadows until all that could be seen were the bluish lights shining in her eyes.

The dog tracked one way and the other before leaping over dead animal bodies and disappearing into a blocked-off tunnel.

"Didn't most of the animals come from that tunnel?" Talia pointed down the branch.

"Let's see where she takes us. We can always backtrack." Mia's mom trusted the dog. So would she.

A questioning, low woof came from the tunnel. Mia gestured for the rest of the crew to follow her, and she joined Kiva behind the barricade across the small tunnel, almost hidden in the dark. A chunk of track had been removed at some point, easy enough to repair, but enough of a deterrent for anybody with a train or other means of travel by rail. Along with the barricade, most people wouldn't find it worthwhile.

"Is this marked on Eva's maps?" Talia asked.

"No, but the entrance is. It looks too narrow to fit the engine. Perhaps a modified carrier of some kind, like our converted mining carts, could fit? There are many such entrances marked on the maps, but I think Mom and Dad were more concerned about saving the world than exploring every inch of the tunnel system." Mia said it wryly, but the seriousness of the words weren't lost on her. Her mom spending so much time finding and fixing the rest of the TMRWS, and not being at home, said enough about the direness of the mission.

Malic and the two Shielded militia followed at a distance, heads on swivels. Talia walked beside her, and Kiva trotted well ahead of the group, only stopping here and there to sniff out her progress. As the light from the main tunnel faded away, Mia broke a glow stick. The eerie green was enough for all the Shielded to see every inch of the tunnel, but it was diffused enough that it didn't travel for miles.

The tunnel curved to the left. Mia checked her compass. Northeast. She tried to visualize where they were, just outside Lincoln. Northeast would take them right beneath it.

Talia must have come to the same conclusion. "What was in Lincoln, Nebraska?"

"I don't know. I think I remember reading that there was a small lab studying infectious diseases and a National Guard center. None of it really that special." Mia considered the lab. To create what those feral, Shielded animals represented, there needed to be a lab a lot bigger than what showed up in her parents' notes. And Nebraska wasn't suitable for many underground facilities due to the high water table. It was basically a swamp.

"Are you sure?" Talia nodded at the dog trotting along, straight as an arrow into the darkness of the tunnel.

"I guess we'll find out."

CHAPTER 11

MIA

After what seemed like hours but was more like one, the tunnel brightened, and emergency lights glowed a deep, bloody red, casting everything in a macabre glaze. The foreign sound of water dripping in the distance, echoed against concrete. If Mia's calculations were correct, they were now right below Lincoln.

Before the Collapse, Lincoln, Nebraska, was a quiet capital city, rarely mentioned beyond state lines. Its reputation as one of America's safest havens was a beacon of Midwestern calm. But Mia's mother, during a pre-Collapse geography lesson, had warned her of such places. "Sleepy cities can be the best hiding places," she'd said, her voice low, as if the walls might listen. "Governments preyed on their isolation, burying truths where no one looks." She hadn't named Lincoln specifically, but now, creeping through its underbelly, Mia felt the weight of those words.

A sharp, chemical stench stung Mia's nostrils, growing stronger with each step down the tunnel.

Talia's nose wrinkled, too, as she tightened her grip on her rifle. "God, what *is* that? Smells like death and bleach."

Kiva growled, low and guttural. Her hackles bristled, ears

pinned forward. The group froze and snapped up their rifles, barrels trained on the gloom ahead.

As they stepped gingerly around the curve in the tunnel, they saw a crumbling barricade of warped wood and rusted metal slumped against a pitted concrete wall. Shadows danced beyond, stirred by something unseen. Mia's pulse quickened, and the air thickened with the promise of danger.

"No need for that," a woman's voice said from the shadows. "Who is that beautiful baby with you?"

Did she mean Kiva? Goosebumps popped out on Mia's arms, and the short hairs on her neck stood on end.

"My people were attacked. I would say there is a need." Mia peered into the darkness. A faint outline of a door, its seams flush with the tunnel walls, creaked open. "Show yourself or we'll open fire."

"Hmm. That won't do. That won't do at all. I just want a closer look. Yes, just a peek." The door opened all the way, and a slight figure hobbled forward. By her side was something on four paws as big as Kiva.

As the crimson light hit the woman's face, Mia almost flinched. Ropy scars ate into the flesh on the right side of her face. Ragged hair sprang from a scarred scalp, and a dirty, white hospital coat covered a filthy sweat suit coated in animal fur. She held her right arm to her stomach.

The woman laid her left hand on the head of the great beast by her side. Kiva growled, and the other animal tipped its head to the side like it was domineering over something inferior. Neither wolf nor dog, it was a black combination of both.

"Kiva, wait."

"Kiva? What a nice name. This is Bob. He is quite docile unless you threaten me, then, well, he can be very vicious. What does that man want now? He already has so many of my babies, I'm not giving him any more."

Mia blinked in surprise. "Excuse me?"

"That monster in Kansas City. He took my babies. Did he send you to take the rest?" She petted the head of the wolfdog.

"Is that why you attacked us?"

"I want to keep my babies safe. I'm all they have left." The woman stopped the repetitive strokes, and a fierce, determined look scrunched her scarred face. "No more."

"Got it. No more. What's your name?"

The woman frowned in confusion. "My name is Dr. Henderson."

"But, Dr. Henderson, we aren't here for your animals. We don't work with Hensley."

At the name, the woman slammed her hands over her ears and rocked back and forth, head shaking from side to side in agitation. "No, no, no, no."

Bob, in all his glory, growled a deep, thunderous sound and crouched in front of the doctor.

Kiva responded with her own growl in turn.

Mia dropped her rifle and put her hands in the air. "I'm sorry, Dr. Henderson, my apologies. Please calm down before the animals get into a fight. We're not here to harm you."

Almost as suddenly as it had started, the doctor stopped and straightened. "No more animals hurt. No more."

"No more, I promise." Mia spread her hands in front of her placatingly.

Bob plunked his butt on the ground, eyes intent on Kiva.

Kiva glanced up, the gray luminescence swirling in the dark depths created by the red emergency lighting.

"Thank you," Mia told her.

The dog grunted but straightened, still on high alert.

"We're here to make sure no more of your animals die." Mia started slowly, not wanting to trigger the woman again. "How many do you have?"

"The monster took them all with him. I just have Bob and a few others." She gripped Bob's coat.

If she meant the mass of furry bodies lying dead in the tunnel outside of their train, Dr. Henderson would flip.

"Uh, where are they now?"

"I sent them to attack the monster's people. They'll be back soon." *Stroke, stroke, stroke.* Bob stood stock-still, leaning into the doctor.

"I see. What if they don't return?"

Confusion wrinkled the woman's face. "They always come back."

"Okay. Could we wait with you until they do? Have something to drink and discuss if we can help get your, uh, friends back?"

Dr. Henderson pulled out a small but long cylindrical device and blew into it. Both Bob and Kiva stood at attention, their focus entirely on the doctor. "There, that'll bring them back faster. Follow me."

She walked through the door, Bob and Kiva following.

Mia grabbed Malic before he could go through the door. "Get back to the train and have everybody clean up those bodies. We're bringing her with us."

"Are you crazy?" Talia's mouth gaped open. "Kidnapping her?"

"Maybe, but did you see what happened to Kiva and Bob when she blew on that whistle? It might be useful in the future."

"Then just take the whistle from her," Malic said.

"No, she might have information we need. Just go back and get those bodies cleaned up. This shouldn't take too long. And please bring back some refrigeration units while you're at it."

Malic nodded, albeit reluctantly, and turned to jog back down the tunnel toward their train.

"Let's go see what this lab looks like."

"On your six, boss," Talia's gaze intent on Malic's progress into the darkness. "You sure about this?"

Mia considered Talia's concerns. On one hand, having another person on the train—especially one slightly out of touch with reality—would make it tricky. However, on the other hand, if she had been involved in creating these animals, she might know how to control them without necessarily killing them. That would make her a strong ally if it came to them fighting their way out of Virginia through Kaspar's creations.

"Yeah, I'm sure. Now let's catch up to our host."

As the group threaded through the cavernous room, she could've sworn she was back in the MUC, seventeen stories beneath the earth in Track Three's receiving room.

Pitted cement walls, streaked with rust and grime, mirrored her base's brutal simplicity. Warped lockers leaned against tables littered with shattered glass and faded manifests dulled by dust. A long, clouded window overlooked the track's platform, where crates—some splintered, others sealed tight—hinted at supplies once shuttled by trains now long silent. The familiarity unnerved her, as if Lincoln's secrets had been molded from the exact blueprint as her own.

The emergency stairwell door was painted in a chipped red and stenciled with numbers and words—S17, EXIT. If not for the tunnel's chemical reek still clinging to her clothes, Mia might've believed she'd never left.

Dr. Henderson shoved the door open, revealing a spiral of concrete steps twisting upward into flickering light and downward into shadow. She and her beast climbed up without a word, her boots scuffing the worn treads. Mia's gaze lingered on the descending path, a pull in her gut urging her to explore the darkness below. Something waited there—she felt it, sharp and insistent, like a truth she wasn't ready to face.

"What's down there?"

"Lots of water." Dr. Henderson hummed, and Bob placed himself between the doctor and the rest of the rabble. Kiva followed, no longer on edge after that whistle went off. Mia narrowed her eyes on the dog.

"And where are we headed?"

"Topside."

Pulling teeth and herding kittens would be easier to accomplish than informative answers from the doc.

"I see. Will your babies find us there?" Mia turned to raise her brows at Talia. The woman just shook her head.

"Oh no. They have their own place. I can see it on the screen."

Lights flickered in the stairwell. They passed through two floors lit by the residual glow from beneath the doors. Where was she still getting electricity?

On the third landing from the tunnel, Dr. Henderson opened the door into a hall lined with even more doors. Offices, most likely.

At the end of the corridor, she entered a room, late afternoon sun streaming from floor-to-ceiling windows. A couch with a threadbare blanket and portable heater had been dragged right in front of the window. A desk pushed to the side had a screen with a security feed in quadrants flashing across it. Most were filled with fuzzy static, indicating no camera, but a half dozen others had 3D pictures of empty cages in various sizes and unoccupied rooms. One showed an entire room almost filled to the ceiling, and to the camera, with water.

"How long have you been here, Dr. Henderson?"

Confused forehead scrunching and pursed lips met her question. "I don't know. Always? It feels like always."

"And where do you get food and water?"

Dr. Henderson walked to the screen and typed in something on an attached keyboard. A quadrant appeared, revealing a massive greenhouse overgrown with plants. "And Bob gets me meat. Some of the cats will bring me treats, too."

"Is there anybody else here?" Mia had already assumed no, but she wanted to make sure.

"Oh no, the closest settlement is scared of my babies. It's just me taking care of them."

She flipped through the feed and frowned when she came back to the empty cages. "That's not right. They should be back by now."

"Maybe they got held up."

The screen flashed, and the doctor gave a sudden, shrill shriek. "That monster killed my babies!"

Undecipherable figures moved across the screen, picking up and disappearing with furry bodies. Malic must have made his way back to Rani and the train.

"Can we do something?" Mia asked.

Almost hyperventilating now, the doctor stared intently into the screen and tipped her head this way and that to try to find answers.

Mia repeated the question. "Dr. Henderson? Ma'am?"

"That monster needs to die." Tears now streamed down her face, a totally unhinged light shining in her aquamarine eyes.

"If you come with us, we might be able to help you get some of your babies back." Mia now doubted the wisdom of inviting this woman along.

Dr. Henderson brushed away the tears. "I can't leave."

"I don't like the idea of leaving you here by yourself without any protection, animal or otherwise, ma'am." Mia reached out a hand but stopped when Bob dipped his head, sitting between her and the doctor.

"She's completely insane," Talia murmured next to her.

"Shhh." Mia brushed her away.

Dr. Henderson took another look at the security feed, then met Mia's eyes. "Only to save some of my friends. You bring me right back?"

"Yes, ma'am. But we have to make a stop somewhere else first. Okay?"

The doctor nodded, tears still leaking out of her eyes. "Okay."

"Now, you mind if I look around?"

#

The third lab they explored contained what Mia had been looking for: a large, Level Two refrigerator, half full of samples. At first glance, they looked to be Shield but with some variant in coding.

"Dr. Henderson? What is this?"

The doctor glanced at the vials with disinterest and went back to stroking Bob's fur, an action she repeated since seeing the security feed. "Medicine for the animals. It makes them stronger."

"I see. Do you mind if we secure these before you leave? Since you and Bob won't be here to protect it?" It was astounding to Mia that the samples had not been stolen before now. Then again, who in their right mind would want to go up against Dr. Henderson and her creations of their own volition?

At this, Dr. Henderson paused her petting of the giant wolf-dog. "I'm not stupid, you know. I had it secured before the water flooded the lower levels. I had to bring it upstairs in case my babies needed more injections. The flood took out half of my supply."

"I see. I don't think you're stupid, Dr. Henderson." Mia searched the rest of the floor. She found handwritten journals and ejected a hard drive. Dr. Henderson just looked on without putting up any resistance, or siccing Bob on them—a win-win all around.

After she was sure they hadn't left anything that could be used against them in the future, Malic returned with the refrigeration units. Mia gathered all of the modified Shield serum—time to leave Lincoln, Nebraska, behind.

CHAPTER 12

EVA

At one time, the MUC's lab had held all of Eva's hopes and dreams. Its gleaming steel counters and pristine white walls had been a testament to precision and purpose. She'd poured her dreams into its sterile order, believing her research could save a nation crumbling under a losing war. Mindlessly, she followed the government's decrees—until the night the lab locked down and Daniel told her they were starting human trials against all research.

Where would they be now if she had discovered the truth earlier? Would it have even mattered? The old government would have just stolen her research and had somebody else perform the experiments, somebody less skilled. So many ancient questions, buried in the dust of a broken world, and in all honesty, totally irrelevant now. The past could never be undone, only mitigated.

Eva stared, transfixed by the images from both the light microscope and electron microscope.

"Is that what I think it is?" Tamara stood above her, arms crossed, and a lab coat covering her jeans and sweatshirt.

"Mia said they got hold of her blood when they kidnapped her. What I don't understand is how they synthesized an antigen so quickly. Sarah injected me mere hours after." Eva shuffled through the images on the computer. One after the other, showing holes bored into the very cells of not only the Shield enzymes, but of her white blood cells, too.

Unless.

Crap.

"Pull up this file." She wrote the number on a piece of paper. Dread settled its cloying, sharp fingers over her.

Tamara squinted at the computer screen, shuffling through files, until a satisfied tap of fingers against the touch screen produced a log of blood tests for Mia and Cooper over the years. She sent the log to Eva's screen with a flick of her wrist.

"Rani should come up with a different filing system," she mumbled.

The old log glared at her. Obvious. Incriminating.

Sarah had somehow mixed Cooper and Mia's blood with the bioagent poison before injecting it into Eva. If she could do that to her, she could've done it to Daniel as well.

Mia's blood. Both stabilizer and, in the right conditions, an enzyme neutralizer. Cooper's enzyme counts had always been high, but they had never affected him like others: no aggression or lack of empathy. But, under certain conditions, he could tune into Shield injected like he was finding them on a radio.

Each of them were unique in their own way, like all Shielded.

"What is it?" Genuine concern infused Tamara's voice.

"She aggregated their blood. What if she re-injected the mixture into Mia? God, just a bit of her blood would be toxic to most Shielded if injected until her system flushed it out."

Tamara's eyes widened at Eva's words. "What did you and Daniel do this time?"

"Not me. Not at first anyway. But I did help him in the end. When they were children, we noticed that the enzymes in Mia and Cooper's blood interacted in unusual ways. It was too trau-matizing for Cooper, so we didn't do any further experiments at that time. We did when we returned from Virginia." Eva slumped in her chair.

"What did you find? With Cooper and Mia's blood?" Tamara's eyes were saucers.

"When they mixed, the cells divided and then reformed into something new. It weakened some Shielded cells, destroyed others, and strengthened those with enzymes from the same meteorite. Sarah has mixed their combined blood with the poison. To simplify it, she's created an entirely different compound. A different poison."

"So, you're saying the combination of their blood is like red kryptonite and supercharges enzymes?" She took a bite from a fruit roll.

"Are you comparing this to Superman? Seriously?" Eva was aghast.

"Have to wrap my mind around it somehow. I'm an engineer, not a lab geek. This," she waved her fingers at the microscope, "has always been more difficult for me to process, even if I've been around it most of my life. Could the combination of their blood be used in conjunction with Shield to cure you?"

"It depends on whether Sarah has injected Mia with it, and if she has, how long it takes her system to flush it out. I would need a fresh sample of both of their blood, anyway, so it's a future problem." Eva frowned, contemplating Tamara's words. "But, yes, in theory, it could work. Daniel and I never pursued the research further. Mostly because fixing the TMRWS network was our highest priority, but also because..."

"You didn't want to possibly break the world further with more super-secret, possible 'human experimentation,' enzyme research," Tamara murmured. "I get it. All of the survivors from the MUC have felt that at one time or another over the years, Eva. You and Daniel like to shoulder it all, but every one of us was down there with you during that year."

Eva choked on a sob, all her emotions hovering just beneath the surface these days. "This is a tired conversation, Tamara. The government didn't use your research to destroy civilization, they used mine. If we get the TMRWS networked, maybe, just maybe, some of that guilt will...be resolved."

"Ach. So arrogant." Tamara rolled her eyes. "Let's move on. We can't test your theory about the blood until Mia and Cooper return, anyway, so I'd like to run something else by you. Something I've thought a lot about."

"What are you cooking up, now?" Exhaustion washed over Eva in a wave, but she forced her eyes to stay open. Tamara's theories usually panned out, so she didn't want to miss it and fall asleep now.

"Okay, so, these bigger chunks of meteorite, I have a theory." The rest of the roll disappeared into Tamara's mouth. "What if they're like a version of an Ark? You know? To seed other planets?"

A chill ran down Eva's spine. "Let's not even go there."

Tamara ignored her. "Like, how did they get below the Earth? Into mines? Somebody had to put them there."

Her voice sharpened. "I said enough, Tamara."

Tamara put her hands up, as if surrendering. "Wow. I got it. No theorizing about the scary black rocks."

"It's just...we messed with stuff we didn't completely understand in the first place, and I should have questioned their origins from the start. It's too late now, and theorizing about it isn't going to solve the current problem."

Tamara squeezed her arm. "I understand. Have faith, Mia will find the antidote for Daniel, find Cooper, and get back here in time, I know it. You and Daniel raised her right."

Visions of everything that could go wrong flashed in Eva's mind's eye. "I just hope you're right.

CHAPTER 13

COOPER

hack.

Thud.

Punches rained over Cooper's body. An electrified prod was soon added to the mix for flavor. He dangled between two manacles set in metal posts. The sun blasted his already shredded skin and blood pooled below him and splattered over the rusty stains of tortures past staining the ground.

The only positive out of any of it was Sarah beside him in the same position.

"What do you know about Daniel Burgess's operations? How many people can he mobilize? Armament? How many injected soldiers?" Soldier One didn't give him time to respond. He snapped another punch to Cooper's screaming torso. At this rate, he would be one big bruise for days. Sometime ago, a blessed numbness had spread through him, the Other inside of him doing its best to control the nerve endings. Even its strength was waning, though.

The questions fired at Sarah were of a different tune. "What are your plans to attack the general? What are the keywords to control the pseudo-humans under your command? Why are you here?"

And on and on. Cooper's lips puffed out, so mangled and bruised he couldn't answer with any type of coherent sentence, even if he wanted to.

A howling crescendo filled the air as Kaspar's monsters—and probably Sarah's—caught the scent of blood. If the electrified fences around the pens didn't hold, they were all done for.

Rows and columns of hundreds of soldiers, in the dark blue and black fatigues of an urban police officer, watched the beatings with indifferent, black eyes and guns at the ready. Their tattooed faces were so uniform in design and placement that Cooper wanted to know who the artist was.

Without warning, the questions and hits ceased, and the only sounds were the pseudo-human animals in their pens and the drip of blood. Cooper opened the swollen slits of his eyelids.

A giant bear of a man, his black fatigues spotless, wove his way through the soldiers. He had one of Sarah's Trolls in a collar attached to a long stick with buttons on one end. Electrified. It growled and hissed, its vaguely human form so deformed, it was more beast than *homo sapiens*. Dr. Mengele indeed.

The soldiers bowed. In unison. Horror engulfed Cooper in its enormous maw. This wasn't a man to these people; he was a god. Hensley had nothing on General Kaspar.

The red haze on the edges of his vision that meant his Other was in the forefront darkened, then shrunk to the background. That, right there, more than anything else that had happened in the past five days, scared him beyond measure. If these people could somehow make it to the Basin Territory—where hopefully his daughter now resided—they wouldn't be able to hold them off for long. Maybe the rail guns out by the east wall for a while, but what else did they have? A wall of junk wasn't good enough to stand against these organized and single-minded people.

Sarah stirred beside him. "Asshole."

"Me or him." Cooper murmured through his puffy lips.

"Both. He's a bigger one." She conserved her words, her lips just as swollen.

"His will, our law. His will, our law." The soldiers roared the words, repeating them over and over as General Kaspar climbed the stairs to the platform.

No, that didn't add to the horror at all.

"Idiot." Sarah's words were barely audible over the roars of the crowd. "Never make them think you're God."

Cooper's thoughts exactly. Which left an uncomfortable taste in his mouth. He'd agreed with the evil queen. Bleck.

General Kaspar stopped in front of them, his back to their beaten and battered bodies. The Troll on the pole—he snorted, Dr. Seuss eat your heart out—dropped to all fours to lap at the blood pooled on the ground below Cooper. Cooper made a half-hearted attempt to move, his arms almost out of their sockets from hanging like a side of meat, before the monster started gnawing on his leg.

Sarah spat a glob of blood at the general's feet. The general punched Sarah in the side of the head. Her head whipped back, and her neck cracked with the force. Eyes so dark worlds would get lost in their depths, stared at her.

"I hear all. You'd be good to remember that."

The words fell on deaf ears. Sarah was unconscious, dangling by her arms. The filthy black t-shirt and cargo pants she wore were so densely saturated with blood, sweat, and piss they were stiff as a board. The Troll on the ground whined, jerking at the smell of fresh blood. General Kaspar yanked on his end of the pole to bring the creature to heel.

He brought his arm up and the crowd fell silent. "When an enemy dares to come knocking at our doors, we must show them we won't back down. They seek to challenge not just our walls, but the very essence of our existence. Let me tell you, my soldiers, what befalls those who dare to cross us: First, they will see our Dogs, fierce and formidable. They will see our fortifications, rebuilt from the wreckage of the past. When they approach, they will find no forgiveness, for we are the storm that does not pass. We take from the enemy not just their lives but their technology, their knowledge, and their fear. And when the smoke clears, they'll have a reminder at what awaits those who awaken our wrath. Let this be a warning to all: We are not mere survivors; we are the rulers of this new era. We are the ones who turned survival into strength. Let them come. We will crush them and make them bow before us."

If Cooper could have slow-clapped, he would have. Damn the man was a scary bastard and hyped up on whatever version of Shield was coursing through his veins. The crowd stamped their feet; he guessed it was their idea of beating the war drums.

The general began to speak again and Cooper tuned it out. Warmonger drivel. Besides, something was happening to his body.

His Other's presence changed, became more frantic. It zipped from his mind to his body. Some of the strength returned to his limbs, and his vision cleared.

Not questioning it, he made an effort to appear still out of it, barely responsive, but Cooper could now open both eyes if he wanted.

Kaspar swung around on him with eyes narrowed to tiny beads of ebony. "Stop it. Now."

The presence inside him froze. As did Cooper. A frisson of fear slid into him and pulsed against his gut. The man had just talked to his Other. Like he could see it.

A smart-ass remark probably wouldn't go over well, even if Cooper defaulted to sarcasm when he was uncomfortable. Now didn't seem to be the time to test it.

A ragged female voice croaked beside him. "You're still a bully, Kas. Leave the kid alone. You think I'd tell one of my slaves anything about my plans? You are an idiot."

The general slammed a fist into Cooper's abdomen, right where his Other had paused its rapid healing efforts. Cooper grunted at the impact and warmth flooded his stomach. Though there still wasn't a lot of pain, something had definitely ruptured.

"He knows about Danny's plans. I can almost taste it. I don't care about your little schemes, Sarah. I always knew how to rein you in. Control can take many forms." Kaspar jerked at the pole and the creature attached to it whined. Its mouth was inches from Cooper's bare, left foot. It resumed licking up any remaining blood on the ground.

"You still think Daniel just leaves his secrets lying around? Pathetic. I breached their walls and found nothing of value. Weak and idealistic as usual. You could take them within a week." Sarah rasped, her head resting on her outstretched arm.

What was she up to?

Whatever it was, it was distracting Kaspar.

The man walked to stand in front of Sarah, almost nose to nose. "You're lying. You forget, *I* trained that man. *I* taught him everything he knows. If he didn't show you his hand it was because he didn't feel it was necessary. I thought you were smarter than that."

Damn, there were a lot of *I*'s in those sentences. The words almost slipped out of his mouth, but he caught them. Slowly, his Other moved, warming his stomach, and he didn't want Kaspar's focus back on him.

A macabre, bloody grin split Sarah's mouth. "Smarter than you think."

And she slammed her forehead against the man's nose with a crunch.

General Kaspar bellowed. The soldiers that had been standing behind Cooper and Sarah swarmed the woman, battering her to unconsciousness again.

Kaspar turned to him with that laser focus. No hint of a busted nose, not even one drop of blood showed on his face. Whatever was inside him had healed him that quickly. Did all those soldiers have the same thing running in their veins? Cooper didn't think they had enough explosives to combat that.

"What is Daniel planning?"

"What will you do if I don't tell you? Hit me? Been there,

done that." Cooper knew he shouldn't egg the man on, but he couldn't fight his nature. Okay, maybe sometimes, but apparently now wasn't one of those.

"No. I will find everything you care about in this world and destroy it. While you watch."

God, the man was a walking cliche. "If you think you can take him on, go do it. Hell, isn't that why you've been grooming the demon-witch over there? To have a muster point close to Basin?"

"Daniel was developing something more powerful than your puny brain can imagine, boy. I want to know where it is and how much of a threat it poses. It's why Sarah sent you into the lion's den. So, tell me now. Where is it? Where is Daniel hiding it?"

Cooper's puffy lips hung open in surprise, or as much open as they could go. "I really have no idea what you're talking about."

"Mia, Cooper. He wants to know about Mia." The manacles above Sarah clanked together.

His Other shifted once again as the blows resumed and he was left to watch General Kaspar's voracious face enjoy every hit.

And to top it all off, the Troll on a pole now waited, luminescent eyes eager to finish what it had gotten a taste of.

CHAPTER 14
MIA

The rest of the trip passed in dull monotony. Mia half expected resistance as the bypass track intersected with Track Three once again, but not even a blip or a bump. It was almost too quiet.

Every member of the Basin team was on edge with Dr. Henderson and Bob on board. The woman's crazy claims and frequent mumblings to herself spoke of too much time spent alone. And the smell. Bathing wasn't the top of her priority list— even with all that water available. All of it had done something to the doc's mental state.

The only member of the party not on edge was Kiva. She bounced around Bob like a puppy, nipping and prancing, wanting him to play with her. Bob would respond in kind until Mia had to lock Kiva in the bathroom after they'd knocked over supplies and rammed into chairs and people with their antics.

When the dogs had busted down the door, they decided the train would take more frequent breaks to let the animals expend a little energy.

Just fifty miles from their final destination, the tension finally filled to bursting.

"Stop that damn talking! I can't even hear myself think!"

Malic stood over a cowering Dr. Henderson, Bob next to her, growling at Malic. "And you, mutt, shut your pie hole. You're just as annoying."

Not that Bob could talk back, though Mia was pretty sure he could understand just about every English word Kiva could.

"That's enough, Malic," Mia said mildly. This close to Ft. Belvoir, these spats didn't need to escalate.

Sofia, one of the other Shielded militia members, interjected, "He's not wrong, ma'am. I can hardly rest as she mumbles equations and food counts and on and on about the monster and what she's going to do to him. She could whisper, and we'd still hear it like her voice was on a megaphone."

Talia and Jorge grunted their agreement.

Mia sighed. They were all in on it, then—almost a mutiny. The team wasn't wrong, but until they could find her a space of her own, they were all stuck together.

"Hey, Rani," Mia called to her longtime mentor, who was currently operating the engine, "I think we need a break."

"Are you sure? We're almost there." Rani responded.

"Yeah, I'm sure."

Malic threw his hands in the air and stalked to the door to stand with his arms crossed. "A break? We need this nut job off our train. I told you it was going to be a problem."

"Well, it wasn't your decision, and I wasn't going to leave her there undefended." *With all those vials of Shield,* she didn't add. And they weren't murderers. Like her mother often said, if they didn't have their honor, they would be worse than their enemies.

Bob growled a retort and stared at her with his eerie wolf eyes as if taking offense to her argument that Dr. Henderson would have been left undefended.

"You're tough, but not tough enough to fight an army from Kansas City on your own," Mia said to the wolfdog. Kiva eased next to her furry friend and sat, ears perked, and whined a little.

He chuffed indignantly but put his hackles and teeth away now that Malic was across the train and Kiva was next to him.

Dr. Henderson clung to his fur, her pale, pale face a mess of confusion and fear. Her agitation had increased with each mile from Lincoln. Lord knew if she'd even be able to control any altered animals they came across in her current frame of mind. Kiva and Bob were tame compared to what was out there.

The train screeched to a stop in the middle of the track. Rani opened the door with a swish, and everybody but Mia, Dr. Henderson—she needed to find out the woman's first name— and the two animals disembarked.

"Are you all right, Doc?" Mia said.

"That kid is angry. There is so much in my head…so much." She mumbled something else, indecipherable, and curled into her seat like a child.

Right, then.

"Look after her." She ordered Kiva and Bob. The two lay on the floor by the doc, and Mia heaved herself out of the chair to exit the train.

The Shielded militia members were running sprints back and forth on the side of the track, the gravel crunching beneath their boots. Malic led the pack. Good.

The others had disappeared into the dark somewhere.

Truth be told, she had needed a break as well. Something about nearing Ft Belvoir left her on edge. She'd been able to suppress the feeling by dealing with other things, but what waited for her in that place frightened her to the core.

Mia didn't understand why her parents had avoided it since their first trip. Yes, her mom was busy fixing the rest of the TMRWS, but why allow General Kaspar to build his forces? At least they could've sent small groups in to destroy supplies and keep him from making any huge gains. Her dad was usually more proactive.

"Mia!" Rani shouted from the shadows in front of the train. They'd kept the leading light off while they were stopped, and the only source came from the cab of the engine. Just enough for their Shielded eyes to see in the dark.

"Coming," she called back. There was urgency in Rani's voice, but not panic.

Mia made her way down the tall concrete tunnel. This part of the tunnel didn't sport any walkways, which usually indicated no maintenance rooms or hubs, so she was surprised when she caught up to Rani and Talia talking to a thin young man in front of a metal door. It was flush with the side of the tunnel wall. He had a rifle slung on one shoulder and a pistol in a holster and nodded to Mia. Not exactly relaxed, but not on high alert either.

"Mia Zapada?" His deep voice negated his otherwise smallish appearance. She had learned a long time ago that looks could be deceiving. Talia was a prime example.

"Yes. And you are?" Mia shook the proffered hand.

"Evan, Stella, and Zeke's son. We were told to be on the lookout for you and the train. Welcome to Virginia."

Sometimes God did the darndest things. Like made you stop right by where you would find an ally.

Mia shook her head and followed Evan into the depths of the room built into the side of the tunnel.

###

"That will never work! Have you seen the wall they have around the fort on the surface? I didn't think so. It was built to withstand Eastern Bloc M-758 Class MIRV weaponry. The entire dome is a titanium composite designed to distribute energy evenly across its surface, utilizing advanced electromagnetic distribution as per pre-Collapse technology. They used to double their sports stadiums as bomb shelters back then. There is one main way in and out on the surface that doesn't require entering the control center, shutting down the wall, and retracting the dome and main gate. It's the service door beside the main gate. This tunnel is the only plausible way to enter the BUC. Evans's hands flew in the air as he talked with his hands, clearly agitated. "They got their shit together after your parents' infiltration."

Stella placed a hand on her son's arm. "Excuse him, he's been working on a solution to this problem for quite a while. After they reestablished wall and dome operations, we were left with one option for access: underground. They keep imploding the track, and we keep finding a different way around. At this point, it's a game to them."

Mia slumped in her chair—a metal-framed camp chair that had seen better days and had been fixed way too many times.

"What do you suggest?" she asked.

The older woman sat beside her, arms resting on her knees. Her black fatigues were mended but neat, and the small camp where they found themselves was compact and organized in such a way that it could be moved quickly. Efficient was the word that came to Mia's mind. These people had been in this area for years without being caught or killed, constantly on the move, constantly burrowing holes like ninja gophers. She had to remember that.

Mia clasped the warm metal of her dad's compass in her pocket. Was she out of her depth? Maybe. She should never have let Rani and Talia stay with the train. But if she hadn't, she may not have had a train to come back to, with everybody so on edge. Kiva lay at her feet, head on her front paws, disgruntled at being parted from Bob. She gave another doggie sigh, and Mia ran her fingers over her silky ears.

"It's not so much that you wouldn't be able to get into the first floor of Belvoir's central facility. We have many of their uniforms and face paint. I even have eyedrops to match their eye color for a short time. They add to their ranks so often that a new face isn't that interesting as long as it looks like theirs. No, the problem is clearance once you're in the elevator."

"What about the emergency ladder my parents used?" Mia asked.

Stella tilted her head and regarded Mia curiously. "Moved. First thing Kaspar did after Daniel and Eva escaped."

Damn it. She'd do anything to have either one of them here with her right now. This type of situation had been their life, she'd always just been on the sidelines at home. Sheltered. Safe.

She still couldn't put a finger on why her mother hadn't made more of an argument against her coming on this trip.

Your blood.

The words whispered through her brain, and Mia shivered.

"Then that leaves only one option." Mia met Kiva's luminous eyes as the dog's head came up, ears swiveling forward on her head.

Stella froze at Mia's tone, horror filling her voice. "No, your mother would kill me."

"Well, a lot of people will die if I don't try."

"It's suicide."

"What are you two talking about?" Evans's eyes flew from Stella to Mia and back.

Mia shrugged. "I just need to get captured. Then tell them who I am. That should present enough of a distraction."

CHAPTER 15

MIA

The plan was simple: get captured, get Kaspar alone, stab him with a knife coated in her blood, then get down to sublevel three to open up the doors to Track Three and let her people in.

Simple didn't always equate to easy.

The retractable dome shone in the late afternoon sunlight, blinding in its intensity. Apparently, at one time, it had covered some sport stadium. How Kaspar had transported here and installed spoke of just how much influence he had over the East Coast. How the man thought any attack would come from above these days was a mystery. Or maybe he just didn't want anybody climbing over a wall.

Mia straightened the foreign clothes and tried not to itch her painted face.

If Stella was correct, the supply team would enter through the service gate. If Mia timed it just right, she could tail the crew through the gate dressed as one of them. They'd filter their own people inside, and wait for her signal.

If there was one thing Mia knew after reading Eva's journals, it was that General Kaspar would want to study her. Study her and interrogate her but definitely the former. She'd have to make it look authentic, this infiltration, if she wanted to keep his suspicions directed on other things.

Antidote. Then TMRWS. Everything else is secondary. Focusing on the objective was key, and not the myriad other horrors trapped within the walls of Ft. Belvoir.

Anxiety and adrenaline coursed through her veins as she slid into line behind some soldiers in a supply convoy, their black tattooed faces and eyes scanning for threats.

Nobody eyed her twice.

Strange. Even stranger than their appearance. Programmed and brainwashed to look only for differences. Arrogance at its finest. Kaspar thought so little of any minor infiltration that he wasn't as vigilant as she'd thought.

The tattoos on one of the women's faces shifted.

That hadn't been in Stella's debrief. She stared ahead, keeping her outer appearance from reflecting her inner turmoil. Every cell in her body was on fire, and her heart pounded against her ribcage. Too late to turn back now.

The group walked through the gate, super-iridescent LED lights shining like daylight from the dome. Pens and pens of people stared out of dead eyes as the soldiers walked by. These soon bled into cages of pseudo-humans, staked to the ground like animals, wailing and yanking against their chains. Half-eaten human corpses littered the ground around them.

Various types of animals in razor wire–topped enclosures hooted and hollered, growled and roared as they passed. Dr. Henderson's babies in all their glory.

One lone child, her eyes so black it covered any white, stared out of a gaunt, expressionless face as they passed.

Horror after horror lined the path to a gray government building, one side patched with newer brick. In front of it was a platform where steel beams shot up from the ground, and manacles dangled from a support beam above. Rusty patches of blood stained the ground.

The supply wagon skirted the platform and rumbled along

toward another red brick building that had a steeple and bell tower. Government housing stretched beyond it, out of place with the powdery streets and pens of reeking, writhing biology in front of the main gate.

As soon as she entered the storage facility—the fort's chapel from the looks of the remains of stained glass—she veered off down a hall and into a bathroom. She closed the door with a click.

And listened.

The distant noise of boxes being stacked and orders being shouted to subordinates made its way to her. Nobody came down the hall to look for her. Nobody shouted an alarm. Stella had been right. They really hadn't noticed her.

Soon, the noise from the nearby room stopped, and footsteps shuffled away.

Easing out of the bathroom, Mia went further into the building, looking for a back door.

Bingo.

Through the old church kitchen stood a door to the outside. She opened it until a slit of light showed itself. Outside, stacks of shipping crates, large shipping containers, and old houses lined what once was a street. Nobody moved around the houses. Her mom had shown her pictures from old magazines. Mia could imagine the lawn, trees, and cars parked in the driveways pre-Collapse. The swing sets and trampolines. Eva had longed for such a place where survival wasn't the top priority. Where life wasn't so tenuous.

She slipped out onto the back stoop and glided between two shipping containers. No alarm was raised, so she made her way along the containers, keeping them between her and the road. As soon as she made it to the back of the main building with the patched walls, she walked across the road. Any quick movement would be picked up by the predators who surrounded her, so she needed to keep things smooth and even. Act like them, move like them.

All the doors on the back had been covered with large sheets of metal fastened to the door frames. Even the loading dock was blocked off. She walked clear to the other end of the building and paused again before making her way to the front.

Something brushed against the barriers in her mind. Something familiar. Mia froze and closed her eyes. What was that? Crouching now so she wouldn't be outlined against the wall, Mia focused all of her attention inward.

A faint pulse of light beat behind her eyelids. There was only one sensation that had ever done that. The Seeking.

Cooper was nearby. Shock and a frisson of alarm ran up and down Mia's spine. She could sense him without an initial physical touch.

And then a second thought hit: if Cooper was here, so was Sarah.

This could ruin the entire plan, as feeble as it was. Her aunt could ruin everything.

First off, could Cooper sense her? He had to. If she had only started sensing him when she neared this part of the building, then he was inside somewhere, possibly in the underground sublevels if her sense of direction was correct.

This complicated matters. She wasn't going to leave him here. Dammit.

She straightened and walked out into the light shining down from the dome.

General Kaspar really must have been secure in his absolute control of the region, especially within the dome. No security met her at the door, no guards even meandered in the halls. The entry hall was completely empty. Two winding staircases looped on either side of a long, curved front desk guarding a bank of elevators. Cooper's signal—for lack of a better word—strengthened, though it was well below her feet. Why couldn't he be in one of the upper rooms?

Upstairs first. Because maybe Stella was wrong, maybe she could find security codes to the elevator hidden away somewhere, like one of those old James Bond movies her parents talked about.

A girl could only hope.

Mia padded up one of the winding stairs. Two hallways took off from a balcony overlooking the front entrance. She started down the left-hand side. Doorways opened to stale rooms long empty of any office equipment. Hope faded as she worked her way down the right-hand hallway, with the same results. Okay. No secret codes.

If she was being honest with herself, she was stalling. Once she walked into that elevator, there really was no turning back.

Nothing like ripping off the bandage.

She walked to the elevators. Only one set of doors was lit up, the arrow pointing down. She pushed the button and the doors hummed open.

Taking a breath, Mia stepped into the elevator and faced the numbers on the side. Above her in a corner, her image was reflected on a screen back at her.

The doors slid closed. She instinctively made to reach her hand to stop them, but it was too late.

"Welcome, Miss Burgess." A disjointed male voice said over a speaker. Mia backed up until she felt the wall of the elevator press against her back. She watched as the numbers above the elevator changed: S4, S5, and so on until the elevator bumped to a stop on S8. Sublevel 8. She clenched her shaking hands at her side.

The door opened. An older gentleman stood on the other side, smiling. His eyes were like the soldiers around him, but the lines of tattoos on his face were wider and longer. Nausea knotted her stomach.

The man didn't just look evil, he exuded a malevolence she's only ever read about. This wasn't what her parents' Shield serum was supposed to do. They'd created it to help people survive the planet's warming cycle and the drought. They made it to cure cancer and disease. They made it to help all of humanity. Kaspar was the result of the power chamber of the TMRWS, her parents had broken so many years ago. Their worst fears made real.

A soldier, his eyes so clear and pale they stood in direct contrast to everyone else in this crazy place, held a gun on her from behind the man she'd only seen in pictures, though his appearance had drastically changed since it had been taken.

General Kaspar.

"Miss Burgess, come with me."

"What if I say no?" Mia crossed her arms over her chest to quiet her nerves. This man was everything her mother's journals said he was.

"Let's not play games. We both know you won't get very far. Though it might be fun to see you try. We haven't had a good hunt here in a few weeks."

A hungry look lit the guard's face, though his rifle didn't twitch. Cooper's signal was stronger than ever, somewhere down the hallway and to the right behind General Kaspar and White Eyes.

Then, something foreign brushed against her mind, so insidious that she put up her mental defenses. She could still sense Cooper, but it had faded.

The general smiled. "Beautiful. I don't believe in any deities, but I certainly wonder how else it could be explained that I required your presence and now you're here. Kismet."

Mia hid her unease. "Definitely isn't karma."

He chuckled. "Come. I really would rather not have Olin here drag you by your hair."

The hungry look on the soldier's face intensified tenfold. Suffocating tentacles of doubt screamed their way through her system. Stupid. This was stupid. She thought she had some idea about what Kaspar would be like, that she could trade with him or persuade him somehow. But this? Time for Plan B.

The lines shifted on his face, turning her stomach. Just like the female guard. Like some kind of parasite had invaded his mind. This wasn't in any of her mother's journals. Stella had tried to warn her, but like an idiot, she thought her capabilities could get her through anything.

Mia's back itched as she walked between the general and Olin. Waves of malice emanated from the man, almost palpable in their intensity.

A zing of warning shot to her from Cooper. No words, but definitely feelings. He knew she was there.

Somehow, this bolstered her, which was probably the opposite of what Cooper had intended. But she came here for a reason, and she needed to remember that.

Kaspar led her into an office lined with books of every shape and size. An enormous cherrywood desk filled one entire side of the room, and a rug, worn in patches, covered the concrete floor. Two wooden chairs were placed in front of the desk.

Olin stopped at the door and Kaspar waved for her to take a seat. Nothing would be accomplished by non-compliance at this point, so she sat.

"So, tell me, girlie, how's the old man?" A low, evil-sounding chuckle followed the question.

And Mia knew to the depths of her soul she had made a huge mistake.

CHAPTER 16

EVA

Refugees streamed through the new North Gate from the outlying settlements. The ragged columns, along with their horses, carts, and other farm animals, were hustled to their assigned Sectors to set up camp. Any able-bodied fighters would be cut from the pack and given extra rations. Harsh but necessary if they stood a chance against Sarah's people. Without Mia or Cooper's blood, fighting the pseudo-humans would be difficult at best.

Sarah. Her sister rose like a fever dream in her mind. Memories of their childhood overlaid the images of what she had become—a violent, homicidal psychopath. Yet, Daniel had the same type of Shield running in his veins. Eva puzzled over the difference in outcomes. Maybe the mixture of enzymes from different samples…

Jack's ex-wife, Peta, interrupted Eva's train of thought and rolled to a stop in front of her with her horse and cart, their teenage kids on the seat beside her. "Seen Jack?"

Having refused the Shield injection, Peta looked like a normal sixty-year-old, with graying hair and fine lines fanning out around her eyes. Still beautiful, but still aging twice as fast as the Shielded—including Jack.

"He's at the South Gate letting the Craigmont settlement through." Eva didn't attempt to rise from her seat beneath the canopy. The lethargy was deafening.

Peta's eyebrows shot up in surprise. "Craigmont? Seriously? They came off the mountain?"

"Everybody's taking the threat seriously. The last scout reported that Sarah's forces are emptying out of Montana. Another, smaller force went back east last week. We're trying to determine why."

"Are you all right?" Concern etched her face.

The very thought of explaining all that had passed exhausted Eva. She waved her hand. "Fine. A little tired. I'll have one of the guards radio Jack."

"Tired? That's absurd—"

"Peta, please. I'm all right." Eva struggled to her feet, the dizziness causing black spots to dot her vision. With a stubbornness born of pure will, she remained standing. She refused to use her Other's reserves more than she had to.

A long moment passed as Peta examined her over from head to foot. "You're full of shit, and I'm going to talk to Jack about this."

"He knows. I'm sure he'll tell you the entire story." Eva gave up and sat back in her chair. She closed her eyes, willing the spinning to stop.

"Eva?" The cart creaked as Peta stood up.

Eva opened her eyes and pleaded with the other woman. "Peta, please, just go find Jack. There is nothing you can do."

Peta glared at her. Eva expected nothing less. Jack's ex-wife had to be hard-headed and fiery to put up with him over the years.

"I'm going to go drop off the kids with Jack and then come back and take you home. You don't need to be out here like... like that." She waved a hand up and down to encompass all that was Eva.

A hint of rebelliousness reared its head. "I'm not an invalid. Not yet. Please go talk to Jack."

For crying out loud, how many times did she have to say it?

Ire gleamed from Peta's eyes. "Fine. We'll see about you staying here."

She snapped the leads against the rumps of the horses, and the cart lurched forward once again.

Just in time for a side-by-side to approach, dust billows behind it. The late afternoon sun gleamed off the dirty windshield—one of the scouts.

The little run-in with Peta had left her weak—well, weaker—and she could only scoot to the end of her camp chair and lean forward, arms braced against her thighs.

A young man, a soldier from the Shielded militia, screeched the ATV to a stop and jumped out. He stopped in front of her. "Ma'am, they're on the move. I estimate four days, maybe five?"

Eva's stomach lurched. Sarah wouldn't go on the offensive unless she felt like she had a good chance of winning.

"How many?"

"Two hundred fighters, twenty pseudo-humans. I couldn't get an idea of weaponry; they have it all covered on wagons, and I couldn't get close enough." He stood at attention, hands behind his back.

"No, you did the right thing. Go find Mr. Allen and tell him to meet me at the Council House in two hours."

"Yes, ma'am." He nodded and turned to go.

"And, Adam? Good job."

###

Built out of an old community center, the Council House housed the trade center and Anne, the administrative assistant who crunched all of the numbers for all of the Basin's resources. Ruling with an iron fist, she didn't take crap from anybody, including Daniel.

The ride here had taken whatever energy Eva had left and stomped on it. She sat in one of the rolling chairs and dozed, waiting for Jack and the rest of the council to arrive.

A firm hand touched her shoulder, and Eva jerked awake to peer up at Jack.

"Morning, sleepyhead." Brows drawn together in concern, he kneeled next to her chair without removing his hand. She didn't mind. The small amount of human contact was comforting.

Peta walked in and made a beeline for them. Good, they would need as many allies as possible in the room.

Since Mia had made her pronouncement calling martial law, a few of the different Sectors had made life difficult in the Territory, especially Sector Nine. This meeting needed to focus everybody. The last thing they needed was internal strife when they had enemies showing up on their doorstep in less than a week.

Carmen, the remaining leader from Sector Nine, sat with a pinched-looking man, hair carefully combed to one side. Earl.

One of the original residents of the Basin before the Collapse, the older man was set in his ways. He used to hold Gustav's seat on the Council. With Gustav out of commission after his failed attempt to breach the MUC, Earl must have thought he'd get his old position back.

Eva clenched her hands in her lap. Just what she needed.

Jack squeezed her shoulder and stood, meeting Peta's eyes and nodding toward Earl. Peta course corrected, heading straight toward the seat next to the older man.

Good, that would keep Sector Nine occupied for a while.

Carmen narrowed her eyes at Peta and glared at Eva. Eva just smiled. So much said without a word uttered. This sure would be a fun meeting.

The other representatives trickled in, murmuring softly.

At least there wasn't shouting. Yet. Eva glanced at Jack's holster just in case. Yep. He was armed. She smiled a half smile. The meeting in which Mia had taken control couldn't have gone better. Before the meeting, Jack had let the Sector representatives off their leashes and had not reeled them back in. But Mia was stubborn and hard-headed. It had taken longer than either of them had thought—Jorge and Claire's appearance partially to blame for that—but when Mia'd let loose, she had caught everyone's attention in the room. Eva glanced at the bullet hole in the ceiling. Not the most diplomatic, but that would have to come later when they all weren't on the verge of being overrun by lunatics.

As the last Council member filed in, Jack called the meeting to order.

He didn't beat around the bush, either. "Montana is on its way; they're not just preparing their resources anymore. The scout believes they'll be here within five days. All Sectors need to be ready with their section of the wall. Sectors outside the wall need to secure your resources and make sure all your people are in their assigned areas no later than three days from now."

Disgruntled chatter filled the silence.

"Quiet! We need—"

"...enough rations..."

"Those damn settlement people..."

"What about the tunnels, I can't..."

Jack rubbed the bridge of his nose. For some reason, the Sector leaders rarely talked over Daniel. Whether his very presence commanded attention or something else, they usually listened better than this. Acted like grown-ups.

Jack took out his pistol and added another hole to the ceiling.

Blessed silence fell over the room. They really needed to invest in a gavel.

"If we can't come to some kind of order, Eva and I will just make the decisions for everybody and the council be damned."

"Aren't we in martial law, anyway?" said a disgruntled Sector Five rep.

Jack continued, "That's only for rations, curfews, and fighters. You still have a say in how your people are deployed, but it's all hands on deck. Children and those watching them, including the older people too unfit to fight, need to head to the shelters. After we energize the outside section of the wall, nobody's going to want to be outside of it."

Earl stirred in his chair. "What about the settlement folks? Some of them are stirring up trouble."

A stern impatience entered Jack's voice, and he leaned forward, hands planted on the table in front of him. "Anybody, and I mean no matter where they're from, who causes issues will be put out at the dam. The folks from the settlement have just as much right to our protection as Sector people. You got it? I mean it, Earl."

The sour, pinched expression screwed even tighter. At this rate, the man's face would never be normal again.

"Are we still being put below the railguns to defend the dam?" Carmen asked.

Jack didn't hesitate. "Yes, ma'am. Moving on. Rations need to be distributed…"

And on it went. Discussion of supplies, militia deployment, strategy, and where the settlement fighters could assist, as well as lines of communication, all of which increased the tension in the room. It wouldn't be enough, not with those pseudo-humans. They needed a way to disperse a stabilizer quicker than by bullet.

The core. A rush of adrenaline shot through her, and she straightened. Dammit, this constant fatigue had dulled her mind. She should have thought of it sooner. They could do the same thing she'd sent Mia to do in Belvoir right here in the Territory.

She needed to talk to Tamara.

"Why aren't you saying anything? What's wrong with you?" Carmen interrupted a conversation between Jack and Sector One and looked right at Eva. "You haven't said a word this entire time. What do you think of all of this? It's your sister attacking us after all."

Leave it to Carmen to point out the obvious.

"What would you feel if your sister were attacking, Carmen?" She threw the question back at the unhappy woman.

"We all know it's your and Daniel's fault that all of this is happening. And Jack. If he hadn't partnered himself with you all from that godforsaken hole in the ground, we wouldn't be here. Injecting himself with your poison. Infecting himself. Why should we follow any of you?" The woman's voice became more vicious with each word.

"Easy, Carmen, that's my husband and friends you're talking about." Peta looked past Earl to glare at the other woman.

"It's all right, Peta," Eva said and turned back to Carmen. "Is that why Sector Nine betrayed the Territory? Were you a part of the plot to destroy the MUC after all?" Long monologues were beyond Eva at this point. Better to just cut to the chase.

"No, but I did agree with their reasoning. We've been controlled and demeaned by you all for years. It's time we had better leadership. We all know you hoard resources."

Eva choked back a hard laugh. Her Other stirred for the first time in days, and she sat forward, hands folded on the table. "Do we now? Should I tell everybody what we found underneath *your* Sector, Carmen?"

"Go ahead. I don't care. What else were we supposed to do? Every winter, we're on the brink of starvation, while you and the other Infected lord it over us."

And there it was in a nutshell.

"Is that what you want? To be injected with Shield? I'm telling you, it's not all sunshine and roses, Carmen, as you're going to see when Sarah's soldiers show up. Controlled and demeaned," Eva snorted. "You don't know the true meaning of those words. I admit, some of my and Daniel's research was used for very bad things, but our intent was never to harm, just to heal."

Carmen frowned but was either unwilling or just smart enough to realize she needed to stop before escalating the point. "Is that what's wrong with you?"

"Don't we have bigger things to worry about than our own internal conflict? Can we table all these other topics for now until the crisis has passed? We have a war to prepare for," Eva deflected.

At the word war, fear replaced the anger on many faces around the table. Except Carmen and Earl.

"Oh, we'll talk about it. It's not over yet," Carmen spat.

Eva's Other faded back into the corners of her mind, and all the strength left her limbs. She slumped back in the chair, her entire body once again too heavy to support her.

"Easy does it, darlin'," Jack murmured next to her. Discussions started up in corners of the room as he leaned her way.

"Watch out for them," Eva whispered. "They're not done with all of this, and I can see them sabotaging the fight."

Jack shifted in his chair. "If they try anything while we're defending ourselves, if they side with Sarah's troops, if they even so much as look at anybody else in the Territory the wrong way, I'll wipe their leadership off the map."

So would she, if she could even move. "Hopefully it won't come to that."

CHAPTER 17
COOPER

ooper's entire body burned along every nerve ending. His Other had stopped blocking the pain receptors. He'd concluded that even it needed rest.

He sprawled on the threadbare carpet of his and Sarah's office cell, the chill leeching from the cement a balm to his bruised and broken skin. Sarah sprawled next to him.

They'd been given one glass of water and a bowl of some kind of vegetable soup. Definitely not enough to repair all the damage inflicted on their bodies. He didn't even have the energy to move away from the vile woman.

To top it all off, Mia was somewhere in the building. At first, he thought it was some reaction to the beatings and crap being injected into his veins by Dr. Hausman, but as soon as he could think clearly, he realized it was real. The fact that the Seeking worked after all this time without touching her was the least disturbing thing that had happened recently and would require more thought in the future—if there was a future. Right now, he tried to figure out exactly how close she was.

The door to the hallway opened, and he rolled his head to try to determine what fresh hell Kaspar and his ilk were bringing to bear now.

They dumped a body just inside the doorway and closed it with a clang.

Well, that answered that question. With a groan, he pushed himself to his hands and knees and crawled over to Mia. She lay curled and unconscious on the floor, her heartbeat barely a thump. Ol' Hausman administering his plethora of poisons again. Wonderful.

Cooper dragged her and himself the short distance to the wall and sat with it at his back and her head on his lap. Smears of paint smudged off on his hands from her face.

"What's she doing here?" Was that a tremor of fear in Sarah's voice? The world must be ending.

"You know as much as I do," he said.

"I would hope my niece isn't stupid enough to travel across the country to rescue you."

"Thanks, Sarah, you make me feel all warm and cozy, but I doubt it. She didn't even know I was here."

A flicker of panic colored her next question. "How long has it been since that little tussle at Jack's house? Ten days? Two weeks?"

"Something like that, maybe a little longer. We're not exactly in a position to determine the time down here, boss."

Sarah grunted and stood up. She started pacing in slow, limping steps across the short distance of the office, mumbling under her breath. It was so low, Cooper couldn't even make out the words. The woman was crazy.

He felt Mia's eyes on him and looked down. Specks of dye still dotted the irises. "Hey, slugger," he said. "We gotta quit meeting like this."

"Cooper?"

At her niece's voice, Sarah stopped pacing and stood over the top of them. In any other circumstance, the move would have worried Cooper, but he just didn't have the energy.

"Did they take any of your blood?"

In contrast, at the sound of her aunt's voice, Mia tensed. "What are you doing here? Cooper, what is this?"

"Welcome to jail. There's a bucket in the corner, and we get some semblance of a meal about once a day."

"Prison?"

Sarah's voice was impatient. "Enough chatter, did Kaspar or his vile little minion get any of your blood, niece? This is important."

Mia blinked, her brow scrunching as she tried to process Sarah's words. "I...yes, he drew blood, and then the doctor gave me something, he said it was to make me talk, but it just made my entire body spasm. He gave me something else to stop that, and the next thing I know, I'm in here. What do you think Kaspar will do with my blood?"

Cooper watched Mia watch her aunt. And she watched her carefully.

Sarah's hands landed on her hips, and she looked at the ceiling, ignoring Mia's questions. "This changes everything. Up, both of you. You need to work out the kinks, the more you move the better. It gets Shield circulating."

"I've never heard that before," Mia scoffed.

Sarah snorted. "Your parents don't know everything, girl. Now, up."

"Sarah?" he inquired.

"What Cooper?"

"You're planning something? Mind telling the other adults in the room what that is?" An ugly thought blossomed. She wouldn't.

Sarah narrowed her eyes. "Not yet, no. It's Plan B. Should've been Plan A because I knew you would fail. I'm not telling you a word because who's to say if either of you is going to get questioned again in the next ten minutes? I got this."

Trust her? Cooper snorted. "You're out of your mind, lady."

"Enough talk. Move."

Every fiber in his body ached. Shield was unable to keep up with this level of damage without adequate calories and water.

"Cooper?" Mia's stormy gray eyes met his. Her presence inside his head, that bright light that indicated her location, was now so close it blazed like a star in his mind.

"Mia."

"What is going on?"

"Kaspar didn't believe Sarah when she said she brought her Trolls in trade. He thought it was a preemptive strike."

"Was it?"

Cooper shrugged. "Maybe. Your aunt doesn't tell me much. I don't think she trusts me."

Mia blinked in confusion. "Trolls?"

"Your parents and every other sane person call them pseudo-humans or monsters. Well, your father calls them Aberrants, but he's too sentimental. Any one of those is more accurate in my opinion."

This time, alarm crossed Mia's face, and she struggled to sit. "Kaspar has her pseudo-humans? What the hell is she thinking?"

"Why don't you just ask my niece. After you get your ass up and moving." Sarah bent as if to grab Mia's arm. Mia slapped it away and used the wall to stand. Cooper followed suit, but a little slower.

"Fine. What the hell were you thinking, bringing those canni-balistic freaks here? Even giving allies such things is beyond idiotic. It's like giving them nukes with no oversight."

Cooper wanted to slow-clap. There'd been a lot of that on this trip.

"I'm still not telling you." Back and forth, Sarah walked across the office, looking up at the ceiling, the walls, the floor, even the lights.

The sneaking suspicion took root and blossomed. She was looking for listening devices. He'd swept the room days ago, but not today. It would only make sense to do it again. It was probably why they dumped Mia in with him and Sarah. Not for any reason of comfort.

Cooper stood and searched the walls next to them. He met Mia's eyes, trying to communicate what they were doing. The light dawned in her eyes, and she took the far wall. The three of them plodded and limped around the small space.

"Well, I don't like it. Did you see what was in those cages? He doesn't need any more monsters." Mia stopped and tilted her head at one of the corners. Cooper joined her and smiled. He reached up, pinched the bug from the wall, and crunched it under his boot.

Between the three of them, they found two more, all suffering the same fate as the others. After crushing the last one, the trio dropped to the rug in a huddle, as distasteful as it was with Sarah.

Sarah dropped her voice to below a whisper.

"The Trolls are preprogrammed to bust through their cages and make for the tunnels on my mark. I've had to wait for their tranqs to wear off. They'll breach the lower tunnel entrance and find me. After that, you two will be coming with me to Montana. If you don't, I'll kill everything you love." So, matter of fact. So, Sarah.

"I don't think you can," Cooper said. "Or you would have done it already. I think something else is going on, and you need us."

Sarah glared at him. "If you didn't believe the veracity of my intentions, then why have you remained with me for so long after your daughter was safe?"

Cooper shrugged. "I wanted to see where this carnival ride ended. You were definitely up to something. And Kaspar needs to meet his maker."

"And that turned out so well for you."

"Which brings up the next question. Why haven't we blown this joint yet?" Cooper indicated the dried blood on their shirts and the bruises and flayed skin. "Why go through this?"

An evil grin lit Sarah's mouth. "He needed to believe that I was completely brought to heel. The only way the Trolls can get down here is if I'm already here. They can track me, we can communicate. It's a fascinating side effect of that slop my sister produced."

Like a messed-up version of the Seeking. He'd never thought that other Shielded—in any of its forms—could have the same effect. He should have.

As if she were having similar thoughts, Mia said, "But this place is just as secure as the MUC—more so, even. How can you be sure they'll make it?"

"Because, my dear, there is only one way they can die efficiently, and I have her here in the room with me." The evil grin on Sarah's face remained firmly in place.

Except now Kaspar had Mia's blood as well. That's why Sarah said it changed everything. She must have something else up her sleeve.

"What about being beheaded?" Mia asked.

"Have you ever fought one of my Trolls? It would take a lot to do that, niece. Only your father has succeeded, and I don't see him anywhere near."

"What about—"

"Enough questions. We'll rest up and then I'll call them." Sarah scooted to the corner of the room, curled up, and was asleep before Cooper and Mia could do much more than gape at the woman.

"You trust her?" Mia whispered.

"No, but I don't see any other way out. Pick your evil, my friend, and at this point, she's the lesser one here."

Mia leaned in, her mouth at the curve of his ear, the words little more than a soft breath. "I have a plan, too."

Goosebumps popped out on his neck and down his arms.

And here he was without one.

"I'm glad somebody sane does."

Mia grabbed his hand in hers and lay her head on his shoulder. "She does have one thing right."

"What's that?"

"We'd better rest so we're not left behind."

Cooper rested the side of his head against her hair, suppressing a sigh. Tough guys didn't do that.

Before he knew it, he'd drifted to sleep, the warm, bright star of the woman next to him implanted into his mind.

CHAPTER 18

MIA

Mia's aunt was definitely going to double-cross them. A leopard didn't change its spots, a tiger its stripes, and all the other sayings that indicate some people never really changed. She and Cooper were a means to an end, and if Sarah thought she could force them into her service after all of this, she had another think coming.

"She almost looks normal," Cooper murmured, so close to Mia's ear she could feel his breath against the side of her face. They stood shoulder to shoulder against the far wall of the office prison.

"Almost being the operative word." Mia examined the smooth lines of her aunt's face, the black hair slicked back into a greasy braid, the sturdy boots, and the filthy clothes. She sat in the middle of the room, legs crisscrossed, and eyes closed in concentration. Calling the Trolls. Crazy bitch.

"Shut your mouths, idiots, I need to concentrate." The furrow between Sarah's eyes deepened, but they didn't open. At one point, she froze, and her entire body tensed while a grimace of pain replaced her concentration.

Mia could hear Sarah's heart racing and her breath shallow and quick.

Damn, if her aunt weren't such an evil psychopath, she'd be impressed.

Ten minutes, then fifteen passed without a sound except Sarah's labored breathing and Cooper pacing back and forth along the far wall. The movement flickered across her mind's eye like a ping-pong ball. She grabbed his arm on the next pass, and tingling traveled through her fingertips. Right. Magnetic super-blood—or whatever her mother called it. The other, more disturbing aspects of the enzymes and their effects would have to be contemplated later. Or never. Either or.

Cooper met her eyes, and she quirked an eyebrow. His lips thinned, but he stopped moving, heaved a sigh, and leaned against the wall beside her once again, shoulder to shoulder.

Pop.

Pop, pop, pop.

The chatter of more gunfire intensified as did the screams, followed by the gurgles and death throes of people on this sublevel. The Trolls had arrived.

Perhaps Olin and Dr. Hausman were among the dead. One could only hope. She shivered, shoving what the doctor had done to her further to the back of her mind.

Mia shivered and leaned closer to Cooper, his presence comforting. Whether that was just his aura or because of their shared super-soldier Shield blood, it didn't matter in that moment.

"Get ready," Sarah rasped almost inaudibly.

Grunts, a shot. Then the deafening squeal of metal being twisted and wrenched from the frame.

Two enormous, androgynous pseudo-humans lumbered just inside the door and stopped, their bulging eyes intent on Sarah.

Slow and easy, she unfolded from her position on the floor and stood. "Go, you idiots. I shouldn't have to tell you what to do."

The utter derision in her aunt's voice spurred Mia and Cooper forward in unison, and they skirted the behemoths blocking the doorway. She didn't even want to contemplate how they would fight such things.

Your blood. The words drifted into her mind from nowhere and everywhere, there and gone in a split second.

Right. Her blood. Just not right now, while they were trying to escape.

Without a word, she and Cooper swept into the hall, pilfering guns from what was left of the guards in the hallway, and ran in lockstep toward the elevator.

From what little remained, none of the bodies was Olin.

Disappointment joined the rest of her heightened senses. She would see that monster die if it was the last thing she did.

Cooper's presence beside her and inside her mind combined even more until she could anticipate his every move and matched it without any extra thought. Coordinated. Efficient. Unsettling.

Mia attempted to ignore the creatures and her aunt stalking her down the hall. Close enough she wouldn't get left behind when they reached the elevator, but far enough to allow her and Cooper to do the dirty work when they came upon soldiers. Mia had to develop a new plan to ditch Sarah and her monsters—Trolls, whatever.

The doors to the elevator were propped open. If Kaspar and his minions weren't on this level, they could be anywhere.

"We need to get to sublevel three. That's where Track Three, the labs, and bio storage are located." Cooper crossed the threshold and removed the dead body, holding the elevator open.

"How long until Kaspar's soldiers get here?" Mia chanced a glance back at Sarah.

The older woman had paused between the Trolls. "Ten minutes. Maybe more once we make it to the third sublevel, where Cooper will perform feats of precision in breathing to open up the door blocking the track."

Mia held the elevator doors open warily for the monsters—all of them, including her aunt. Cooper waited for her to get in.

"Come again?" Mia asked.

"She means I get to run a quarter mile while holding my breath so I can reach the controls to the titanium and steel–plated doors blocking us from the track."

The track where the core she needed to insert into TMRWS would be with her people on the other side of Kaspar's barrier.

Stella and her crew would be up top. "There's something I need to do after we get what we need from the lab."

"Not happening—" "No." Both Sarah and Cooper spoke over each other.

Mia lifted her chin. Neither of you is my parent. I'm going."

"Do it, and my Trolls will restrain you. We can't risk it." Sarah's battered face glared at her.

The doors to the elevator closed, and Mia punched in the number for the third sublevel.

If she could only get Cooper alone, off to the side, to explain.

The doors swished open, and Cooper and Mia parted, guns up and aimed in front of them. They each took a wall while the Trolls and Sarah shot straight down the middle.

Startled faces appeared at some of the doors. Nobody stood a chance against the Trolls.

Screams and cries as unarmed people were torn limb from limb echoed along the corridor.

Disgust and faint nausea washed over Mia. A look of contempt took up residence on Cooper's face, but there was nothing either of them could do.

They followed Sarah halfway down the hall and into one of the labs. Rows of glass-fronted storage refrigerators showed vials and jars of every shape and size. Her heart fell. How would she find anything to help her father in all of that?

She whispered the code into Cooper's ear. "That's the antidote we need to help my dad."

"Got it." Without another word, he began at one end, and she started at the other. Of course, it would help if Sarah just told them where to get it. Not that she knew what they were looking for. And not that the woman would help fix what she broke.

Sarah went to a blank wall on either end of the long, narrow lab and touched a section of it. The entire fence clicked, and she rolled it on a seam along the floor, not unlike the one at the MUC—a hidden room.

Mia peered in at the secret refrigerators.

As if reading her mind, Cooper said, "Go. I'll check these."

She nodded, grateful, and followed her aunt into the lab. Sarah was scanning the rows and rows of higher-level storage refrigerators. Mia started at one end. Her aunt ignored her.

Solutions in neatly labeled vials filled the shelves. Some were variants on the Shield coding, others were unfamiliar. If they weren't running low on time, she would have taken samples to bring home for her mother.

Fridge after fridge failed to yield what she wanted.

Sarah opened a door and took out a tray, stuffing some of the vials into her bra and dropping the rest to crush them beneath her boot.

Mia's heart fell. Surely they weren't the antidote? She wouldn't put it past Sarah.

Sarah moved on, quicker as she searched the rest of the fridges. Mia prayed that Sarah would continue with her original goal—whatever that was.

Sarah froze, going rigid. "Hurry, niece, we need to leave."

Heart accelerating, she sped up.

"Got it." Cooper's voice reached her ears from the other lab.

She looked into the last fridge, saw the code she was looking for, and her brow furrowed in confusion. How could he have it if it was right here? She grabbed a couple of the vials and stuffed them into the top of her boot—the bra was a stupid place to put anything breakable—and walked out to see what Cooper was on about.

He was stuffing two vials of something into his pants pocket and didn't meet her eyes. A strong feeling to keep her mouth shut washed over her, and she closed her mouth. He was up to something.

One of Sarah's behemoths grabbed Cooper from behind. He made a show of struggling, and Mia understood. Sarah didn't want her to succeed in helping her father.

Sarah smacked him on both cheeks with her hands. "Not happening, dear. Thanks for finding this for me, though. I've been trying to find it for years, but I didn't have the classification number."

Sarah took the vial from Cooper's pocket. "Now come. Niece, stop lurking and get going. We're almost out of time."

"I'll kill you for that." Mia didn't have to try too hard to make the statement sincere.

"Get going or I'll have one of my Trolls carry you."

Mia stalked out of the lab. The elevator down the hall was still propped open. No real resistance had met them. It left her uneasy.

Kaspar wouldn't let this pass. Not by a long shot.

On the third floor, déjà vu hit. Again.

A viewing window looked out onto a loading dock that looked out over a track. Like at the MUC, this one had been blocked off, though Kaspar had acquired enough steel and titanium to make it next to impossible to blast through.

"Your turn, kid." Sarah had one of her pseudo-humans punch through the wall next to the edge of the viewing window. A passage with another steel door appeared behind the stone. A keypad next to it. "Just like you trained."

Cooper didn't pretend to hide his disgust. "You do anything to her, and I won't stop hunting you."

"Yeah, yeah. Now go, they're almost here. I think they expected us to come to the surface. Idiots."

Cooper gripped Mia's hand and squeezed it once. "Giv'er hell."

Mia's heart dropped. "See you on the other side."

Shouting and bootsteps filled the room beyond the viewing window.

"No more time, boy. In you go." Sarah typed a code on the keypad, and the door clicked open, then closed behind Cooper.

Mia turned to face Kaspar and thirty of his best soldiers streaming through the door.

CHAPTER 19

COOPER

The bright green glow of exit signs filled the narrow, rocky passage—at least to Cooper's Shielded eyes. He didn't hesitate, he didn't look back. Lungs screaming for air, Cooper sprinted down the corridor. A noxious gas settled along his route from vented tubes drilled into the side of the rock wall and swirled around him as he barely kept from ping-ponging against the walls.

A hundred more yards.

Mia's location in his head fluttered. She was terrified. His Other responded in kind, wanting him to return to the tunnel.

No, we need to open the doors and vent the passage.

And now he was talking to it as if it were alive. He'd gone mad.

Black dots spotted his vision, and tears streamed down his bruised and swollen face.

Fifty yards to go.

If he breathed, they were all done for.

He practiced the sequence of numbers in his head and palmed the small pebble of black rock that had hung out in his back pocket for days. Too tiny to do much more than make his fingers tingle, he'd need to place it beneath the scanner by the door, at least according to Sarah. He trusted she wanted to save herself, so hopefully, he hadn't just gotten himself recaptured based on her word.

Twenty yards.

The bright green glow intensified.

His steps faltered on the rough floor, and sparks of light replaced the dots in his vision.

Damn it, he had to make it.

He opened the barrier between him and his Other and allowed the presence to flood his senses. It helped.

Cooper stumbled the last few yards to the scanner. His meaty fingers fumbled over the keys. He shook his hand and tried the numbers again—one green light. The pebble clicked against the metal dish beneath the scanner. He rocked from foot to foot, bracing against the wall and urging his brain and Other to hold on a few more seconds.

Twin lines of a laser swished over the tiny rock.

Cooper fell to his knees beside the door, his lungs on the verge of exploding. Right before he was sure he was done for, the heavy metal door clicked open and cool air hit his face. He hauled himself over the barrier and forced himself to stand up before gasping and gulping for the fresh air above the gas billowing from the passageway.

"Fancy meeting you here." The barrel of a gun pressed against his forehead. At the moment, though, breathing seemed more important than talking, so he closed his eyes and allowed his lungs to expand in his chest. In and out. In and out.

When he could finally form a coherent thought, he opened his eyes and stared into the headlamp of a short woman. He blinked, and she scooted the headlamp up. Talia. Of course, Mia would bring the feisty nineteen-year-old.

"Lower your gun. He's one of the good guys." Jorge's voice said from the shadows. More people materialized behind him. The rebel group that Sarah was always on about.

I'll be damned.

"Have you seen Mia?" Talia demanded, though she did lower the gun.

"Yeah. Give me a sec. And find cover. There's a small army behind that wall. No time to explain." Cooper stumbled back into the now-vented passageway. He punched another code into the keypad, and a panel beneath the scanner opened, exposing the handle of a hydraulic lever.

Harried footsteps moved behind him. He couldn't be sure if the rebel fighters followed his advice or not. At least no one shot him. Mia's heart rate was rapid, her presence in his head erratic. She was fighting for her life.

Hurry. His Other was frantic.

Cooper ripped the panel door from its hinges and yanked the lever down.

The floor rumbled in response. He took out the two pistols he'd stolen from the guards and used the door to the passage as cover.

The enormous door retracted up into the ceiling of the tunnel. Cooper squatted, trying to catch movement from the other side of the barrier and make himself blend in with the background. If anybody came down the narrow passage, he was screwed.

A shadow moved along the wall on the far side of the tracks, too small to be human. Cooper ignored it, it wasn't heading toward him.

Bright light shone beneath the slow-moving door, and Cooper squinted against the abrasive glow, trying to see a target, any target.

Chaos materialized on the other side. Sarah's Trolls wreaked havoc on Kaspar's forces. Limbs flew, and gun chatter and ricochets filled the air.

And Kaspar held Mia with a Bowie knife against her throat.

"Enough!" Kaspar roared.

A Troll dropped the torso of a man it had just pulled apart. All motion in the room ceased.

Not in the tunnel. So focused on his quarry, Kaspar failed to hear the movement on the other side of the massive blockade door.

Sarah glared at Kaspar and Mia. "Pathetic, niece."

"Give me what you took from the labs, Sarah, or I will drain her dry here and now."

An evil grin split Sarah's face. "You know your problem? Besides letting that black rock consume your world? You've always been self-centered, Kas. There's a bigger picture out there. One that needs control and order."

Now, that was the scariest thing he'd heard all day.

Then, a black and brown German Shepherd leaped from the base of the wall near the track onto the back of General Kaspar.

CHAPTER 20

MIA

If Mia had swerved left instead of right, or grabbed something sharp on their way to the third sublevel, she wouldn't be in this position. She didn't have much time to think about what Kaspar had just proclaimed to her aunt before something knocked into them from behind, snarling and ripping with teeth and claws.

Kaspar grunted in shock, his hand loosened on the knife, and it clattered to the floor.

Mia didn't stop to contemplate her next move. She dropped to her knees and retrieved the knife, cutting her arm to get the blood flowing. Covering the knife blade, she spun to see Kiva and the general rolling on the ground.

A shout of voices from the shadowed tunnel charged toward the soldiers, and soon grunts, groans, and more gunfire filled the air.

Cooper materialized beside her, pistol at the ready. No words needed to be spoken. They took flanking positions on either side of the rolling mass of fur and almost humanity.

Mia circled around to try for a better angle, she didn't want to hurt Kiva. Cooper mirrored her in the other direction. His eyes were all for his dog, now holding the general by the carotid.

Good girl.

Kaspar got a hold of the dog's fur, and she growled around her mouthful of flesh, then shook her head like he was a rag doll. He whacked her in the side, pummeling and punching. Again, and again.

But Kiva clamped on like a tick on a deer.

Kaspar bellowed in pain and got a few fingers into the corner of Kiva's maw. She yelped, clawing for purchase against the sides of the large man. Large furrows ripped through his uniform shirt, bloodless as they regenerated instantly. Her eyes glowed with an ethereal luminescence, and Shielded dog fought tooth and claw against pseudo-human male.

The tattoos on Kaspar's face swirled and coalesced into wavelengths pulsing across his skin.

Horror beat its tattoo in Mia's mind.

Sarah and her Trolls had joined the fray with Stella's rebels and Talia and Jorge. The rebels' guns and knives were making quick work of Kaspar's monsters. Knives with her blood smeared on them. She hadn't known if it would work dry, but it seemed to still be effective.

"Kiva, we got it." Cooper rasped. He saw what she'd done. Kaspar had gone still, and the lids of his eyes drooped to half-mast. The pulsing lines on his face sped up, swirling and twisting like an enormous heartbeat.

The connection between her and Cooper snapped full circle, and his Other was frantic.

Their eyes met.

"Kiva, now!" he shouted.

But it was too late. Kaspar got his hands around her neck and snapped it with a twist. Her yelp was cut off, and the giant bear of a man threw the canine across the receiving platform.

She hit the wall and didn't move.

"No!" Mia screamed.

Anger swept her up in its jaws. In unison, she and Cooper attacked the monster in front of them.

Their blows landed on cold, hard steel wrapped in skin.

Cooper stumbled back, drawing the pistol at his waistband.

She did the same.

A roar of rage from one of Sarah's Trolls echoed throughout the chamber and tunnel. She couldn't take the time to look. The man in front of her was transforming further, his eyes blacker than death, the pulsing lines of tattoo strumming now. Whatever darkness had settled in his bones was on full display.

They shot Kaspar in unison. Mia didn't even know if she could get close enough with a knife.

The creature howled, but the bullets fell out of the wounds in his head and healed in seconds.

"Shit." Cooper unloaded the clip, and Mia followed suit. The man-thing punched out, and only Cooper's quick, Shielded reflexes saved him.

Keep him occupied, I have an idea. Mia forced the words along the connection with Cooper, testing a theory. Not that it didn't freak her out that Shield could make it possible, just that now wasn't the time to contemplate such things. Her mother had a lot to explain when it came to the Shield serum—if they survived this.

For a brief second, Cooper's startled eyes met hers before he had to dodge another blow from the creature stalking him. Soon, his back would be up against the wall of the loading dock.

She would only have one chance.

Mia backed up to get out of Kaspar's peripheral. He was now totally consumed by Cooper, who ducked and weaved just out of the thing's reach.

Now would be just dandy.

So, he'd figured out how to push his thoughts, too, along the wavelength of energy.

Not wanting to grab Kaspar's attention, she eased herself closer, smooth and easy, no jerky movements. That's what predators focused on.

Cooper avoided the next swipe of a hand, but the left hook

caught him on the chin, and he slammed into the wall behind him.

Kaspar zipped closed the space between them and caught him around the neck, holding him against the cold cement. He bared his teeth and growled.

Mia leaped onto his back, not unlike what Kiva had done, and plunged the blood-coated knife into his neck.

Cooper crumpled to the ground. He gagged, his hands at his neck.

Kaspar yanked the knife out with both hands. His face cleared of darkness for a split second. His shocked eyes met Mia's from where she had stumbled to the ground. "Thank you."

Like a giant tree being felled in the woods, the man landed on the loading dock in a heap. His black tattoos flaked away like dust. He stared into the nothingness of the void with sightless eyes.

Cooper crawled to his knees and made his way to where Kiva had fallen. "She's alive!"

"Thank God." Mia struggled to sit.

The dog lifted her head and whined. Cooper puffed out a raspy breath. "Good girl, shhh. Brave dog. I think you'll be just fine."

He ran his hands over the soft fur of her head and ears, and the canine heaved out a painful sigh.

"Sarah." Mia's breath came in quick puffs in time with her racing heart. It was wonderful to see Kiva alive, but they had more pressing matters at the moment.

"Copy that." He rose to his feet and hauled Mia to hers in a swift movement. "She can't be allowed to leave with whatever serum she has in her bra. You got one more in ya?"

"Let's go find out. But first..." She walked over and started hacking at Kaspar's head until it separated from his body.

Cooper whistled, "Well, that should do it."

She wiped Kaspar's blood on her already filthy cargo pants and opened the same half-healed wound on her arm, smearing the blade in it. If those black tattooed freaks of nature came after her or her people, she'd be ready, and so would Cooper. She handed him the knife.

"We have one more thing we need to do before we leave." She dropped to the tracks.

The fight had trickled further down the tunnel. Limbs and bodies littered the ground, some of Kaspar's soldiers still twitching. Without hesitation, she plunged her knife into the still-intact bodies.

They ceased all movement after that.

Some of the bodies were from Stella's crew, the hardened fighters who weren't Shielded but gave it their all. Parts of one of Sarah's Trolls also lay strewn on the floor. With a bit of maniacal glee, she plunged the blade into the creature's heart. It convulsed, then almost seemed to deflate.

Talia had dropped the core's box against the wall of the tunnel, hidden in the shadows, out of the way where it wouldn't draw attention.

Mia dropped to her knees and opened the box. The core sparked, the liquid inside swirling with an iridescent blue. She pocketed it.

Cooper's eyes widened. "Is that what I think it is?"

"Yeah. We need to get it to the control vault on the second level and to the TMRWS before Stella's rebels blow the surface and the tunnel. Then we'll find Sarah. This is more important." She cradled the core. "By the way, what serum did my aunt take from you?"

"Not the one she thought she did." A smile tipped the corner of Cooper's mouth. He leaned over and drew out a vial. "I switched them. It says *Reanimate 159-20*. What would your aunt want to reanimate?"

She wouldn't? Would she? Was it even possible? Daniel had shot Sarah's lover over thirty years ago in Seattle.

Mia dropped the vial into the refrigerated case, where the core had been, and closed and locked it. Jorge and Talia jogged toward her, bloody but whole, grim, satisfied smiles on both of their faces.

Mia waved them over. "What's the status?"

"Everything's about secure. The pseudo's took off with your aunt about ten minutes ago." Talia eyed her and Cooper standing shoulder to shoulder. "You both look like hell."

"Take this back to the train and get everybody ready to leave. Move it to the location I told you about." She handed her the box with the antidote from her boot and the reanimate serum. Sarah leaving without a word had been too easy. "And make sure to secure it fully. Sarah's still out there somewhere." Mia cut her arm and recoated their knives.

Jorge gulped in air and nodded, hefting the box. The remaining rebels helped the injured stumble back down the tunnel, along with Talia, Jorge, and some of the Shielded militia from the train.

Cooper joined her at the elevators. "You good?"

"Let's get this done."

CHAPTER 21

COOPER

Cooper's boots skidded on blood-slicked concrete as he picked his way through the aftermath of the chaos in Ft. Belvoir's tunnel. A slaughterhouse would have been cleaner. Kiva limped at their heels, her left flank oozing red from a claw swipe, her teeth bared in defiance. She had refused to join the others who would guard the train. Shield had healed her broken neck, but only time would tell if there was permanent damage.

Bodies—some human, some not—littered the floor, and the air reeked of gunpowder and that acrid, chemical tang he associated with prolific levels of the tellurium enzyme. Cooper picked up a rifle and shouldered it with one hand, Mia trailing him.

"After you," he drawled, dodging another body and letting her pass on their way up the platform.

Mia brushed past him, the case with the TMRWS core cradled in her arms. "According to my mom, the control vault for the TMRWS is on the second sublevel."

That undefinable something strummed between them. Now they could communicate through the super-soldier bond, it was even stronger. He didn't know what to make of it, and truth be told, it unnerved him. Why wasn't she as freaked out? "Lead the way."

Kiva's limp improved as they wove through the fray.

"We need to get this installed before the rebels blow the dome," Mia said, side-stepping a dead pseudo-human soldier in the receiving room. "If my father's right, initializing this TMRWS will bring all of the weather control units online in the other machines and counteract any freerange raw enzyme in the air by aerosolizing the stabilized Shield serum from the cores. If we can't get the dome down—no clouds."

"And then what? All will be rainbows and sunshine?"

She puffed out a frustrated breath. "It'll heal who can be healed—though my mom thinks some are too far gone."

Cooper snorted, holding the elevator door for her and Kiva. "Saving the world and watering the lawn. Multitasking at its best, huh? Your parents know how to maximize damage, you know that?"

"They did their best with the resources they had available to them at the time," Mia shot back, her tone clipped but not defensive. "The meteorite's raw enzyme was too much, and they couldn't replace it the last time they were here without doing more damage to themselves and the others on the surface. They thought they had halted Kaspar's progress more than they had and haven't been able to come back and fix their mistake. Trust me, they've tried."

"Yeah, well, good intentions pave the road to hell," Cooper muttered, pushing the elevator call button. The doors groaned closed.

As the car lurched upward, Cooper leaned against the wall, his sarcasm a thin shield against the ache in his chest. The Shield serum had saved him, sure, but it also damaged him, made him do stupid things to get away from it. But letting it define him had gotten his daughter captured, him trapped in servitude to an evil psychopath, and on the wrong side of things with the only family he'd ever known. He had to stop being stubborn and face the facts. Shield was who he was.

"So," he said, eyeing her, "wanna explain why I heard your voice in my head back there, telling me to distract Kaspar? What's next, we start finishing each other's sentences?"

Mia's brow furrowed, all scientist now. "It's a side effect, probably the tellurium enzymes in Shield syncing our neural pathways. We're…connected, Cooper. We both developed the Seeking, maybe that has something to do with it. My mom will have a heyday studying it, I'm sure."

"Connected," he echoed. "I don't know what to feel about that."

Well, besides the desire to kiss her. But was it attraction or the weird enzyme bond? Did it matter?

She quirked a brow, unfazed. "Me either, but it worked to kill Kaspar, didn't it?. We'll deal with the why after. We've got bigger problems."

"No shit," he quipped.

The elevator dinged, and the doors slid open to a small room off of a larger office space, empty except for a rusted desk and a couple of chairs. A door with a broken exit sign was in front of them, hanging at an angle. Mia said her mother's notes and map indicated it led to the antechamber and then through to the TMRWS control vault.

"It'll be through that door. You ready?" she said, eyes never leaving it.

"Yeah. One question, why no guards?"

Kaspar should've had this entire area packed with the worst of his creatures, but there was nothing.

"I don't know." She opened the door.

The antechamber held a long observation window and a closed, glass pneumatic door.

Beyond the window was an enormous machine he'd only seen in drawings, the control vault and chamber enclosed in the same thick glass as the observation window and door looking out over the massive turbine spinning in its shaft. It loomed above him, the metallic cylinder kept stabilized by an electromagnetic coil.

And the entire control vault chamber was swarming with enzyme residue, encasing the core and daring them to breach it.

Cooper's eyes widened in shock, his Other zipping around wildly. Well, that answered the question about the guards. Not much was getting through. Kiva's hackles rose. Her growl was weak but fierce, her gaze peering through the door.

"Looks like a sci-fi snow globe from hell," Cooper said, squinting. "How do we even get in there?"

Mia's jaw tightened, scanning the turbine through the window and clutching the hard-shelled container. "My mom doesn't think it'll affect me, at least not for a few minutes. I need to get in there, clear the conduit box, and install the core. Shut down the entire system, then reboot. Easy peasy." She met his gaze, fear kept in firm check behind her eyes. "Stay here. I don't know what it will do to you."

"Love your optimism," he muttered, "but Kiva and I are coming with you. Better together, right?"

Indecision flickered across her face. "Fine, but at the first sign of distress, you need to get out of there. The raw enzyme particles can burrow beneath your skin and enter your bloodstream."

"Peachy." He braced himself and then hit the button that opened the door.

The air grew heavy, the dust's metallic tang stinging his lungs. The exit sealed in a swish behind them.

Instantly, the tellurium dust attacked, a living cloud clawing at his skin, his mind. Pain lanced through Cooper like knives carving his nerves. He hit the floor, writhing. Mia fell beside him, her gasps mirroring his—helluva time for Eva to be wrong. Kiva howled in pain and curled up on the floor. The box with the core fell to the floor between them.

"Son of a—" Cooper choked, clawing at the floor. "It's alive!"

Mia fumbled for his hand. He grasped and caught her

fingers. Energy coursed between them. His Other surged along the connection. Inch by inch, his fingers laced with hers, and something snapped into place.

A gesture that was initially just a search for strength and support became, unintentionally, something entirely new. His Other, that alien fragment from the serum, surged within him and combined with the force that was Mia. He suddenly felt it. She didn't have individual fragments blending into a whole; her entire being *was* the whole. She was an Other all by herself and was finally waking up.

Cooper locked eyes with Mia. Their minds brushed against each other again, like tuning forks syncing their rhythms, not with words but with shared strength and instincts. Together, they pushed back the dust. It recoiled from their combined strength that roared in tandem like a psychic shield flaring bright.

Gasping, they crawled toward the container with the core. Every inch was agony. Cooper's muscles screamed, but Mia's grip kept him grounded. "You're not quitting on me, Killian Cooper."

"Wouldn't...dream of it," he rasped. Somehow, they made it to their feet.

Slow, torturous steps brought them to the conduit box that housed the core. Inky pieces of black meteorite, sparks of silver shining in its depths, filled it like a virus. It pulsed with a heartbeat, ebbing and flowing along streams of accumulated enzyme.

She pried the door open with the tip of her knife, and the dust shrieked as if alive.

"Put down the box, grab the knife, and cut my arm. I think if I stab the meteorite with my blood to clear the box, it'll neutralize the enzyme." She pushed the words through the neural bond. Every pulse ignited pain along his nerve endings. Kiva had quieted. Not good.

He set the box down and did as she asked.

Mia stabbed at the cluster of churning particles in the box. They swarmed the blood on her knife.

And nothing happened.

Mia's eyes widened, beautiful storms to contrast the black dust swirling and scattering around them, trying to consume their defenses.

"It's not working." She tried again, thudding at the meteorite in the center.

Still nothing, like whatever had supercharged her blood was now expended.

Time for Plan B.

"Be ready," he told her through the link. Then he dropped her hand and shoved both of his into the box, grasping the original football-sized chunk of the meteorite from the docking port and yanking it free.

Agony, unlike anything he'd ever experienced, shot through him as thousands of particles burrowed into his skin. A scream ripped from his lungs, and he stumbled back, blood dripping until he almost lost his grip on the thing.

"Hurry!" The link disappeared after that as his Other and Shield flooded his system, trying to keep them alive.

The stone wailed, louder until blood also dripped from his eardrums. Particles from the conduit box streamed around his hands, knifing into his wrists and trying to get him to release the stone. He clung to it as if his life depended on it, because it did.

Mia's face contorted in agony. Sweat beaded on her forehead, each breath a ragged gasp against the overwhelming pain she must be feeling. She dropped to her knees by the box, opening the lid, each movement like she swam through a vat of molasses.

The organic core's Shielded chamber shone into the room, like a beacon, scattering the particles in its wake.

She's a hateful thing and needs to die. Something whispered inside him. An overpowering urge to kill the object of his wrath stabbed at him and took his breath away. He sat up.

No. Killing bad. Helping good.

His Other surged through him, offering respite, and all the reserves it still held.

"Throw it across the room, now." Mia rasped. She cleared the connections of dust with the knife and inserted the new core, twisting it until it clicked into place. She cleared the remains of the meteorite around the glass door and shut it.

Cooper panted, eyes locked on the object in his hands. It needed him.

Mia ripped it from him and slung it across the room. It clattered to the grating, and particles of raw enzyme swarmed toward it.

He blinked, the enormous pressure eating his brain, easing. "Th…thanks," he sputtered.

Mia clasped his hand tightly, her face and arms streaked with blood from the dust's assault, and a surge of warmth flooded through him.

God, he hadn't realized how frozen he had been.

"We don't have much time. I need to reboot the system. You with me?"

Words escaped him, and he nodded, the contact of her hand and their link like a salve to his soul.

Now he was getting sentimental.

They walked the three steps to the control vault, the particles in the air more worried about the mother ship lying on the grating across the room.

Mia opened the panel door below, and her brow furrowed. "Help me? I can't do this with one hand."

Cooper shook out his free hand, the circulation returning to the scorched palm. Sonofabitch, that damn rock had burned him. He blinked at it, then dropped to his knees beside Mia. "What do I do?" He asked it through their link, his vocal cords still too raw and painful to use.

"Marie showed me the sequence and drilled it into my brain. I'll take out control server one, you do the same with twelve, then we switch them. I'll initiate override on the computer terminal and restart the system. It all has to be done quickly before the turbine slows too much, or it'll take too long to reboot." She glanced at the particles swarming the black rock like bees.

He nodded. They proceeded with the process.

The turbine slowed. Mia tapped with one hand against the keyboard, face scrunched in concentration. She gave a satisfied grunt, tapped the touchscreen, and the Shielded core glowed a quiet blue. The turbine resumed its normal speed.

The dust collapsed like inert sand littering the floor.

"We did it," Mia breathed, collapsing to the floor, sweat and blood streaking her face. Exhaustion lined every inch of her body.

Cooper wiped blood from his face. "What are we going to do with that thing?" he asked through their link. He gestured toward the tellurium meteorite lying on the ground, looking innocuous.

Mia heaved a sigh. "Put it in the box and bring it back home. Drop it down the hole with the other one and bury it."

"Pardon?" Talking aloud was still a problem, but her words had gotten his attention.

"Yeah, found that out in my mother's journals. After this, my parents and I are going to have a huge conversation about open honesty with those you trust."

"Good luck. It's going to take some major rewiring of their brains to make that happen, sweetheart."

Mia huffed out a laugh. "Ain't that the truth. Come on, we gotta get topside, and help Stella and her crew blow that dome, or this is all for nothing. I synced it with the East Coast satellite, and the other TMRWS should be able to network, or however it works. I just punched the buttons. Somebody from home will have to come check it at a later date."

Cooper drew in a weary breath and climbed to his feet. Reluctantly, he dropped Mia's hand. "Yep. Help people, good."

"I always thought you were a little bit of a caveman," she joked, flexing her fingers.

"Ha."

They turned as one, each movement coordinated to complement the other. He shivered. Damn, it felt nice. Too nice. Then, he saw Kiva lying near the meteorite, guarding it, with large chunks of fur beside her, shivering but alive.

"Good girl." He drew a palm over her fur, feeling for any other injuries.

Kiva whined, her soulful eyes meeting his.

"Is she okay?" Mia asked, dropping the box next to the rock.

"I think so, just a little beat up like the rest of us." He reached out a hand. "Better hold hands while you secure that thing."

She nodded and gingerly picked up the rock, then secured the lid. It barely fit. They untangled their fingers yet again and headed toward the door.

Cooper bent and picked up Kiva in his arms. One more stop and they'd be headed home. The thought of seeing his daughter again flooded him with a hope he hadn't felt in years.

CHAPTER 22

MIA

The elevator's scratched panel blinked as the elevator descended back to the third sublevel and the armory. Mia's mind churned like a flipbook. Images of her mother's gaunt face dissolved into her dad lying in cold storage, lifeless and hanging on by a thread. Cooper held Kiva's injured bulk pressed in his arms, the dog panting in pain.

All the blood and gore, monsters and cannibals were catching up to her. Possibly sensing her unease, Cooper bumped her shoulder with his.

"You good?" he asked.

"Yeah." But the BUC's shadows whispered of death, and the dome still loomed above it all, a steel trap caging all their efforts at a cleansing rain. Failure wasn't an option—not with the rebels' lives, her parents, and maybe the world's survival on the line.

At the third sublevel, the elevator jolted to a stop, cables groaning like a dying beast. Mia's gut twisted, her Shield serum senses flaring in sync with Cooper's subtle shift beside her. Their bond was a double-edged blade—amazing, yet unnerving.

Some dead scientist is gloating in their grave at these results, she thought bitterly. *Thirty years too late.* She could only imagine what an entire platoon of soldiers like her and Cooper could do to an enemy. Not for military application, her ass. The talk with her parents would be a long one.

"Kiva, guard and hold the elevator," Cooper said, setting the German Shepherd back on her wobbly limbs. Kiva, limping but alert, dropped to the threshold, her ears pricked forward. Cooper patted her head and joined Mia.

She turned in the opposite direction from Track Three as they exited the elevator.

"You sure there's an armory on this floor?" Cooper asked, his voice a harsh rasp.

"So far, it's been a similar setup to the MUC, and I got some inside information before I left. If there's nothing there, we'll improvise."

Cooper grinned. "Now, you're speaking my language."

She rolled her eyes, Cooper's bad habits wearing off on her, and continued along the corridor.

Four doors and a right turn later, a dented sign—"ARMORY" —loomed over a steel door with a dark and useless retinal scanner.

"Son of a—" Cooper banged his fist on the metal, frustration flaring.

Mia twisted the handle. It clicked open.

She shot him a sidelong glance, one eyebrow quirked. "Really?"

He shrugged, a lopsided grin breaking through. "What? I'm used to the universe screwing us at the worst possible minute."

"Uh-huh," she said, dryly.

Inside, the armory was a gutted shell—caged gun safes stripped bare, ammo drawers yanked empty. But if Marie Evan's notes were right, the C4 was hidden in a secret compartment. Mia strode to the back wall, yanked open a drawer, and found the release pin. The panel swung down, revealing a black wooden crate and a smaller box. Several handguns with clips were next to it. Cooper pried open the crate, exposing M112 demolition blocks nestled in static-free foam, their olive Mylar wrappers etched with faded warnings: "DANGER: EXPLOSIVE. POISON—DO NOT EAT."

"Are there enough?" she asked.

"To demo the main building and topside entrances? Should be if we're smart about placement." Cooper hefted the crate, and Mia grabbed the smaller box with the detonation cord and timers. It would have to be enough.

Cooper strategically rigged C4 on the walls outside the elevator on the first sublevel and rigged a timer. "You think ten minutes will do it?"

"Better go with fifteen," Mia said.

"We have the main floor left, and we're home free."

She scrunched her face. "We still have to make it through hordes of pseudo-humans and amped up animals to get to the gate, Cooper. It's not like it'll be easy."

"You said these rebels, Stella and Zeke, will have their people in place. And a squad of Basin's Shielded militia?"

She nodded. "Yeah, and somebody with a dog whistle."

Cooper arched an eyebrow. Mia waved him off. "Long story."

The elevator doors opened to the main foyer, and Cooper led the way, his newly obtained pistol ready to shoot anybody who stopped them. Kiva limped along, and Mia carried the two boxes with the meteorite and the C4, bereft without a gun in her hand.

Somebody whistled from across the room.

Cooper swung around and pointed his weapon.

A short woman, with greasy brown hair braided away from her face and dark eyes squinched like she couldn't see much, stood up from behind a fake, potted plant. One pant leg was saturated in blood, and filth coated her skin. Her hands raised beside her head. "Miss Eva?"

Mia startled, peering closer. The woman could be an older version of Talia. "No, my name's Mia, Eva is my mother."

The woman gave a sly, crooked grin. "Ah. Close enough. Where's your mother?"

"Back home. We don't have time for this. Who are you?"

"A shame. Your ma's a decent person. The name's Kel. I was told to wait for you. We found somebody to retract the dome, but we have to get there first." Kel glanced at the dog. "Hi, Nala."

The dog chuffed out a breath, neither happy nor growling, just watching. Maybe she liked the name Kiva better, too. Or perhaps she didn't care too much for Kel.

"What about Dr. Henderson? She ready?" Mia asked.

Kel grimaced. "I still can't believe you brought that woman here. She's crazier than a box of frogs."

Mia tilted her head warily. "She can control the Shielded animals."

Kel shook her head. Disgust laced her words. "Kaspar kept her in Nebraska for a reason. He called her useful but too dangerous for Ft. Belvoir. Sent her supplies, animals, and DNA to breed those…things. She's unhinged."

Mia sighed. "But she's our crazy for now…as long as we return her babies."

Kel snorted. "Henderson's 'babies' are seven-foot monstrosities with finger-sized teeth and can kill with one swipe. I've always said they all need to be put down, but she keeps hoarding animals and making more. The result will be on you."

Cooper's hand steadied Mia's shoulder. "You haven't seen crazy till you've seen us in action."

"Both of you are out of your minds." Kel's eyes flashed.

Mia's heart ached to bolt, to race down the tracks on the second sublevel before the elevator shaft blew and not look back. But her father's voice echoed in her head: *Finish what you start.* Her father may have been a control freak and unyielding on many, many levels, but his drive to help people redeemed him in her eyes. He would be disappointed in her if she didn't finish this.

Outside the building, the distant clamor of rebel gunfire chattered around the skeletal husks of concrete and shattered glass. Shouts and the screech of pseudo-humans pierced the air, dust rising like a shroud. Shadows peeled from the building's edges, and Cooper's pistol snapped up, Kel doing the same as she limped in front of them. She had to find a safe place to store the meteorite box, but a part of her didn't want somebody else to stumble across it.

Several people emerged from the shadows.

Two other rebels, plus Talia and Jorge.

Cooper lowered his barrel. "Status?"

One of the rebels answered. "The temperature inside the dome increased about fifteen minutes ago, and that building behind the one you were in started rumbling. I take you all were successful?"

Talia eyed Kel with narrowed eyes. "Your, Kel"

"And you're the child I grew." Kel's face showed not one trace of emotion at seeing her errant daughter. "Didn't think Eva would ever let you come out this way."

"I never wanted to," Talia retorted.

"You gotta a bit of your 'ol ma in ya after all. Let's go get that dome down, shall we?"

Talia's hands clenched around her rifle, but she didn't say anything else, just resumed her position beside Jorge, who bumped his shoulder against hers in commiseration.

Mia looked at the rebel who'd talked—was it Tommy? Tobin? No, Terrin. "Thank you, Terrin. Get Dr. Henderson up here, tell her her babies are alive and well, and if she helps, we'll find a way to get them home. Got it?"

"Yes, ma'am." He gave her a wary look and something else. "If somebody can get her to listen."

"What happened?"

"That big wolf of hers got shot. He's fine, but she's been batshit crazy for hours. Your person, Rani? Yeah, she had to restrain her until she calmed down, now she won't talk to anybody, just pets that friggin' thing like it's her dying child or something."

Gunfire peppered the air in the distance. Yelling and shouting met their ears, and dust rose in the air from the southeast. The chaos was creeping closer, and the rebels would only be able to hold them off for so long.

"Listen, Terrin. Tell Rani to do whatever she needs to get through to the doc. If all else fails, tranq the woman and steal her whistle."

"It won't work," Kel murmured. "And I told you she'd lose it."

Mia ignored the last remark. "What won't work?"

"That whistle is coded to Dr. Henderson's DNA, and the machine used to change handlers was destroyed in the flood back at her lab. Trust me. If General Kaspar could have gotten his hands on it, he would have."

Mia closed her eyes. She couldn't deal with this right now. New plan. "Fine. I'll head down and see what I can do. Cooper, can you help them hold the line, or whatever it's called?"

"Just clear the way," he said. "And take Kiva with you, maybe it'll help."

"Give me twenty minutes," Mia's mind already on the tunnel below. "Make it count."

He grinned. "Consider it done."

His voice slid into her mind, warm and solid. "Need anything, just yell."

She clung to the feeling. *See you on the other side.*

###

Gunfire erupted, a relentless staccato that clawed at Mia's nerves as she, Terrin, and six other rebels—clad in the tattered rags and filth of Ft. Belvoir's lost souls with makeup mimicking the lines of enzyme on their faces—neared the service entrance in the fort's outer wall. More rebels had maintained tenuous control of their only exit until they could open the gates and the dome.

The shots in the distance seemed to come from everywhere and nowhere. Outmatched, the rebels clung to higher ground among the rooftops, their guerrilla tactics—swift, harrying strikes from shadows and sniper perches—chipping away at Kaspar's remaining forces. Dust, thick with the acrid tang of gunpowder, choked Mia's throat.

Terrin led the way across the kill zone around the fort. Kiva sniffed here and there, her limp less pronounced as she moved.

Kasper had hidden mines among the dirt, and some enterprising soul had flagged a route through with piles of rocks. They had been busy while she and Cooper had been fixing the TMRWS and fighting Kaspar beneath the BUC.

"If we pull this off," Terrin puffed, "maybe we'll all find a little peace."

Mia didn't respond. Peace was a ghost in this world since the Collapse. If they pulled this off, it would mean more than just peace. It would mean survival.

At the hidden entrance to the tunnel, Mia waited for Terrin to yank the camouflaged rug of dirt, pine needles, and forest debris plastered over chicken wire away from the hatch. It included larger logs, hollowed out to reduce weight, that she helped move.

"Kaspar never found this entrance?" Mia asked.

"Years ago, Stella and Zeke created a decoy tunnel and 'accidentally' led him to it. He blew it to hell. This one's for special occasions, like today." He gestured for her to proceed.

Mia descended metallic rungs into the dusty, dry shaft. At the bottom, she brushed her hands together and picked up the box with the meteorite once again. Not that it did any good; they were already so encrusted with dry blood and gore she doubted it would ever come off.

The two took off at a run. The MUC's engine was parked less than a mile away.

They neared the portable barrier, its silhouette stark against the faint glow of the engine. No guards. No Rani. No, Dr. Henderson. None of them came to welcome her and Kiva. She eased the box to the ground and scooted it into the shadows.

The dog growled low in her throat and hunkered low. Mia's blood surged, adrenaline spiking like a blade.

She glanced back. Terrin stood frozen several feet behind her.

"I'm sorry," he whispered. "She'd have killed my family." And he turned to run back the way he'd come.

Mia spun, pistol raised, and froze. Framed in the engine's flickering light stood her Aunt Sarah, her face a mask of cold resolve. Dread lanced Mia's chest, sharper than any pseudo-human's blow.

"Come with me, Mia," Sarah said, voice low, almost sorrowful. Before Mia could respond, Sarah lunged as swiftly as a specter, slamming into her with bone-crushing force. Mia's pistol skittered across the dirt as she hit the ground, breathless.

Kiva barked in a high, staccato pitch, trying to find an opening.

Chaos erupted behind Sarah. One of her remaining Trolls lunged toward the door of the engine. Maybe it wasn't as unoccupied as she'd thought. They must have been hiding.

Bob and Dr. Henderson stumbled through the door of the engine, Bob clamping his giant maw onto the arm of the Troll. Dr. Henderson screamed—a raw, unhinged sound—as Sarah barreled toward her and pounded the doctor's face with her fist.

Rani launched herself at Sarah, but was no match for her. Sarah's fist connected with the shorter scientist's jaw, sending her sprawling. The Trolls clambered up the stairs into the engine, the locomotive swaying due to its bulk. Henderson's equipment and Mia's refrigerated box, camp chairs, coolers, and other paraphernalia crashed to the ground. She heard glass shatter. *Please don't be my father's antidote*, she prayed.

The wolf snarled and lunged, but Sarah sidestepped with eerily precise timing and delivered a kick that sent the beast yelping into the shadows. Kiva zipped in for the kill but suffered the same result.

Mia scrambled to her feet and sprinted to the door. "Sarah, stop! It doesn't have to be like this!"

Sarah didn't answer. Her eyes glinted with a mix of feverish purpose. She vaulted up the stairs and kicked Mia in the chest. "Your father took him away. I'm going to get him back. I'll be seeing you, niece. This isn't over. Oh, and tell Cooper I'll find his daughter." And she slammed the door closed with superhuman strength. The engine roared to life, and Mia pounded on the door to no avail.

Rani groaned and crawled toward Henderson, who curled protectively over her wolf with incoherent mutters and sobs.

As if she were a bug on the windshield, the engine lurched forward, grinding over debris. Mia staggered back to stare at the fading glow. Helplessness plummeted into the very depths of her soul, and she crumpled to the ground. They'd never make it home in time now. Her father was doomed.

Rani limped over. "Is it done?"

Mia blinked, momentarily stunned. "What?"

"The TMRWS? Is it fixed?"

"Yes. But we still need to either retract the dome."

"Then nothing else matters, Mia. Your father would gladly give his life so you and your mother could live. It was his last wish to have his life's work functional and safe."

Mia laughed bitterly. "Yeah, those machines were his family."

"No, I mean you. The TMRWS will make you and your children safe. Well, at least give you a chance. He loves you, Mia. You and your mother are everything to him."

The tunnel was filled with the sounds of a wolf howling, and Dr. Henderson shuffled over. Mia climbed to her feet. Cooper's presence was distant and weak in her mind. *Be okay.*

"My baby boy says we have to help you now." She laid a

hand on the massive wolf's head. "If I do, I get my other babies back." Her swollen face shifted and shuffled as broken bones mended at a rapid rate. Damn, Mia didn't even think Shield worked that quickly on her.

"We'd appreciate it." She ran to the refrigerated case and lifted the false bottom. The antidote was intact and still frozen. It was the testing supplies that had broken. She quickly closed it, relief flooding through her.

Henderson cocked her head to the side. "Let's get these sons-abitches." And she shook the whistle out from beneath her shirt.

CHAPTER 23
COOPER

The streets beneath Ft. Belvoir's wall were a slaughterhouse, the air thick with the guttural roars and unearthly shrieks of Dr. Henderson's monster animals—grotesque hybrids that made his spine crawl. It was like he was trapped in some carnival's house of horrors, except they were real.

Cooper darted through the rubble. He'd picked up a rifle and some ammunition from one of the rebels. He fired it in precise bursts against the chaos. It was like shooting a BB gun into a pond full of fish.

Talia and Jorge flanked him. Their movements were swift and eerily synchronized. Not as seamless as his neural dance with Mia, but damn close—efficient, lethal, like wolves hunting in a pack. Kel stumbled behind with her hurt leg, popping off a round here and there. Their group wove its way around the carnage, making its way to the gate.

"Keep it tight!" Cooper shouted, ducking a well-aimed punch that shredded the air where his head had been.

Talia spun and sank her blade into the creature's black-veined neck. Jorge blasted another into a twitching heap and then plunged his own blood-coated knife into its back, and both monstrosities stopped twitching.

Cooper took off another head, then moved to the next, whacking his way toward the corner of a building that would take them further along toward the edges of the town square and the gate controls.

Mia's presence in his mind, usually a bright pulse, was a faint flicker, dulled by the tunnel's depths. She'd better kick it into gear or there wouldn't be much left to save.

Kaspar's hulking soldiers formed a blockade of the square before the main gate and the control booth. Dr. Henderson's wild beasts—under Kaspar's residual control—and their handlers writhed in the middle of the square in all their grotesque glory.

Cooper's heart sank—end of the road. At least now they knew why the rest of the streets were fairly empty: most of the remaining soldiers were guarding the control booth. There was no way the four of them and a handful of rebels could plow their way through to the other side without getting torn apart. They couldn't even skirt it without a miracle. They'd have to wait and pray Mia talked that lunatic doctor into using her dog whistle.

Minutes trickled by. Their shadowed space against the building wouldn't keep their group hidden for long. Damn it, he should've gone with her. His instincts had told him something was off, and the longer she was gone, the more he knew it was true. Cooper tried sending a message along their neural link, but it failed. Proximity was important, then—unless they were in a dream. Maybe brainwaves traveled better at night?

This time, he really didn't know if he was going to make it.

What would Eva tell Claire? He'd left her a note in case he didn't get back, but that didn't mean his little girl would under-stand. For days, he'd kept her memory locked behind a wall, buried. Now, the thought of Sarah getting her hands on her again was something he couldn't bear. *Focus, Coop.* That was precisely the point of all of this, he chided himself, to protect his daughter from the monsters.

A bearlike beast—a hulking thing with too many eyes—sniffed the air, its head swiveling toward them. Cooper tensed, rifle up. The beast made a whistling call, and several others, handlers in tow, took up the same godawful noise. Then it looked directly at him, all eyes swiveling in their sockets.

"Oh God," Jorge croaked beside him.

Then, the pack charged, claws gouging the earth. Talia and Jorge braced their weapons at the ready. The monsters ate up the ground, gathering followers as they charged their position.

"It was an honor, Jorge. Sorry you couldn't deliver the death blow to Sarah for your grandfather. And Talia, your performance has never been piss poor." Cooper lifted his gun. He'd make every shot count.

"Thank you for trusting me," Jorge murmured.

"I should have brought more weapons." Talia clenched the bloodied knife.

Kel just snorted and braced her legs.

When the creatures were but a hairsbreadth away, they froze in unison, ears twitching as if hearing a silent command. They whirled as one, snarled, and tore into Kaspar's soldiers, shredding armor and flesh. The pseudo-human handlers howled, attacking the animals. Confusion and chaos churned the square.

Cooper's jaw dropped. *What the…?* Then Mia's light shone in his mind, bright as a flare, and her voice echoed through their neural link.

"Got Henderson talking," she said, triumphant. "Her whistle's working."

Relief flooded through him.

"Thought I'd have to save the day, solo." Cooper shot back.

"Couldn't let you have all the fun." The warmth of their connection grounded him, and adrenaline coursed through his veins.

"Move!" Cooper skirted the perimeter, Talia, Jorge, and Kel in tow. A few pseudo-humans lunged with their twisted, tattooed faces, but Henderson's beasts intercepted, tearing them apart in a spray of black blood.

The control house loomed—a squat bunker by the main gate with its door ajar. A ragged group of rebels led by Stella joined them, skirting the meat grinder in the center of the square. In the middle of their group, they had sandwiched an older man, his bald pate slick with sweat.

"This is Frank. Frank can open the dome," stated Stella. "And you are?"

Cooper nodded. "Name's Cooper, and man, are we glad to see you."

Stella shoved Frank toward the controls. He caught himself on the panel and shot her a glare, but went to work.

The enormous touchscreen flared to life, a half-eaten apple appearing in the middle.

"Hurry," said Stella.

"It has to boot up," he ground out. "Be a sec."

The screen displayed a picture with mountains in the background and several colored squares at the bottom. Frank touched one, and a picture of a switchboard appeared. He tapped some of the symbols with his finger, then pushed a button beside the screen.

"There. Now about those food and water rations…"

The dome shuddered, its massive panels retracting with a screech that drowned the gunfire. All movement in the square ceased for a heartbeat as a reversed tornado of mist shot to the sky from somewhere near the center of the fort.

After a few minutes, heavy storm clouds formed and rain poured, warm and heavy, washing over the compound, the slave pens, the cages where the pseudo-humans were kept, and Kaspar's dwindling soldiers. As it hit, most of the tattoo-like lines on the remaining soldiers' faces began to flake away like ash.

Cooper stepped into the deluge. The warmth of the rain slicking his face was startling. It had been a long damn time since he'd felt rain on his face. Mia burst from a side street; her silhouette was sharp against the storm. She reached him, wide-eyed and breathless. "It's working," she said, surprised. "I didn't expect it to hit this fast."

"Yeah, well, miracles happen sometimes," Cooper quipped, but his grin faded as he saw something else on her face. "What's wrong?"

"Sarah," Mia's voice cracked. "She stole the engine, smashed Henderson's gear, and knocked Rani out. I couldn't stop her. She dumped the refrigerated case too, but I don't think she knew what was hidden in the false bottom. I hid the case with the meteorite, too."

Cooper's gut twisted. Sarah had to be put down. She'd done too much damage. He held out his hand, and she grabbed it without a thought. "We're not done yet. I have an idea."

Mia arched a brow. "Mind sharing?"

He smiled. "Nope. You'll see, though I don't think Stella and Zeke will be very pleased because I think it's theirs."

Now to deliver. They may have won this battle, but the real war was back in the Territory with Mia's family, and he bet dollars to donuts that was where Sarah was headed.

"Let's go find us a train."

CHAPTER 24

EVA

Sieges equaled a never-ending vigilance that, after three days, frayed everybody's nerves. Except for the first day, when Sarah's forces lobbed a few explosives toward the wall, they had been hunkering down far enough outside the wall's offensive perimeter that even the Basin's best snipers couldn't get a decent shot off. Not that it prevented them from trying.

The electromagnetic current running through the wall prevented most explosions from making any kind of impact. Unless they somehow planted one on the inside of the wall, it would hold. Eva slumped in her ever-present camp chair in the tower above the north gate. At this point, she should just have the thing glued to her butt; it would make moving it easier. She gazed at the rumbling mass of humanity in the wide-open spaces beyond.

A group of the tunnel engineers—all trained by Tamara over the years—had gone around and set charges in just the right places, and as many of the tunnels to the inner territory had been closed off as possible. It would take months to clear, even with Sarah's pseudo-humans, and thus it would keep the worst of the rabble from getting access—for a while anyway.

The enemy digging trenches in the newly harvested fields, the constant sound of the pseudo-humans howling their anger, and the eerie presence of the watcher just outside the Basin's reach kept their forces on edge. Fights had broken out, which Jack had promptly taken care of, but Eva had a feeling it would only get worse if the stalemate didn't end soon. It was like they were all waiting. Waiting for what, was the question. To make matters worse, Sarah had yet to make her appearance at the gate—just her lieutenants and their blustering arrogance asking for their surrender on a daily basis. Their surrender. The nerve.

Everybody had been cleared from the wall. And now they just waited. Endlessly.

Footsteps thumped up to her perch. A place she'd designated as hers for the duration. Few people ventured up here—something about her being too grumpy. There was only one person brave enough to attempt it.

Jack crouched beside her chair and rested a concerned hand on her shoulder. "How you doin', darlin'?"

She patted the hand, more dismissal than anything. "Fine."

"You know what they say when somebody says their fine. They're not fine." He stood and looked out at the monsters and beasts, humans and animals. "Didn't think this would happen again so soon."

"It's been over fifteen years," Eva murmured.

"Well, time moves differently now. It's like dog years, I suppose."

Eva snorted. "Dog years? *Dios mio*, Jack, I would hope you're not comparing the Shielded to dogs."

"Maybe just the small, yappy ones." A grin split his mouth. "See, things have been on full steam for weeks, isn't it good to smile?"

Eva waved her hand out toward the army. "That's nothing to smile about."

"We can hold this siege longer than they can stay out there without supplies. Let's hope they start eating each other. It would solve all sorts of problems." He unfolded a metal chair and sat down, kicking his booted feet on the edge of the railing and crossing his arms—the picture of laid back and relaxed.

Eva leaned forward. "What if Sarah was with that group that went east? What if they're just waiting for her to get back before trying their next move?"

"Could be. Could be they weren't planning on a siege, and she's just biding her time until they find a way in."

"They could be digging under the wall as we speak. Maybe out by Sector Nine."

Jack just raised an eyebrow. "It would have to be pretty far out for us not to have eyes on an operation like that. We'll get it figured out. Now, Peta's told me you've been up here since dawn. Why don't you go down to the MUC and get some sleep? I'll send somebody to get you when the fun starts."

She didn't tell him, but that was the only thing she wanted to do lately. Sleep. Sometimes she was disappointed when she woke up. Not because she wanted to be dead, but because her dreams were so vivid. Full of a life with Daniel that never existed. A life of happiness and no wars to fight. Of peace and love and grandchildren. Laughter and tears of happiness instead of devastation.

He was so close when she was asleep.

"Fine. But come get me if anything happens, Jack. I mean it."

He just saluted, planted his feet on the wooden planks of the tower floor, and helped her to her feet. "We'll be fine, Eva. And that's coming from a man, so it must be true."

She just snorted and let him help her to her side-by-side.

Fine had fled the scene of the crime a long time ago.

Eva awoke with a start. She reached under her pillow for her pistol and rolled to her feet, the lethargy weighing her down. What had woken her up?

Her Stranger stirred, a flood of warmth energizing her and giving her more energy than she'd felt in weeks.

It sensed something.

She padded out of office she'd turned into a bedroom and into the dim halls. They were lit only by secondary lighting, which meant the main power had gone out. Like a moth to a flame, she headed toward Lab Twenty. Toward Shield and all her life's work buried in the MUC like a nesting doll. Thank God she and Tamara had moved Daniel's cryo container to hook it up to back-up power.

The grip of the pistol was harsh against her palm. There. A low whir like something mechanical running on tracks.

She sped up. The line of refrigerators in the lab made that sound they did when they retracted to reveal the hidden lab where Shield was stored. Eva prayed it was Tamara, but a part of her knew, deep in her soul and bones, it was not. Otherwise, her stranger would preserve its energy.

Eva paused. She could never take on her sister—if that's who it was—in her current condition. How could she level the playing field?

Making a detour to Rani's office, she moved one of the cots to reveal a floor safe. She punched in the code and the door opened. Inside, nestled in a glass container, was her shiny, black objective. Only hesitating for a split second, she grabbed the container and shoved it into her pocket. Last resort.

Daniel wasn't the only one who would do anything to protect those that he cared for.

She slipped into the lab. Like she'd suspected, the refrigerators were pulled away from the wall. Somebody clinked around in the hidden room.

The smell of bleach and cleanser punched her in the nose. Light shone into the dimness of the room, fanning out in bright fingers.

Now or never.

She whipped around the doorway.

Sarah stood on the other side of the room and had opened one of the morgue refrigerators with the extra working cryo bed. What was the crazy bitch doing?

"Hello, sister. It took you long enough." Sarah pushed a button, and the storage container descended slowly to the floor. "Still not recovered?"

"Stop, or I'll shoot." Eva fingered the small vial open in her pocket. The dark tendrils inside hummed against her leg, licked against her palm, energizing her Other far more than anything had in weeks.

Sarah whipped her startled eyes to Eva's hand. "What do we have here? You should put that back. Or even better, hand it over. It's quite dangerous in the wrong hands."

"Why, Sarah? Why all of this? You were an asset to the program. We're family, and you're threatening to destroy everything Daniel and I have built here. For what? Vengeance?"

Sarah's eyes didn't leave Eva's hand, but something flicked beneath the depths. "You and that man are so blind. Put it away."

"What? This?" Eva held up the warm pebble of black rock. Her Other pushed against her mind, a madness of motion she clamped down with effort.

Sarah backed up, never taking her eyes from the gleaming object that was really no bigger than a quarter. A malicious glee flooded her. There was something her sister was frightened of.

"You don't know what that thing is capable of."

"Don't I? You know I swallowed it one time, in Kansas City. There's that old saying, 'With great power comes great responsibility.' Yeah, I couldn't even acknowledge that. It must be what your pseudo-humans feel, and I hate you even more for putting other people through that."

Horror cut across Sarah's face. "You swallowed it? My God, Eva, you are more stupid than I thought. What? You planning on doing it again?"

"If it gets you out of my Territory, yes. Now, answer the question. Why, Sarah? Why go through all of this? The armies and the wars. The death and destruction. We could have worked together. Or at the very least, left each other alone."

"Each rock has a different personality, you know. I've counted five different species, and each one reacts differently to us. I don't know what other countries have hidden in their super-secret dungeons, but all the wars, the Collapse, the rapid evolution of humanity, all of it was because of those rocks. Because humanity wanted to use their strength for their own purposes, and you and Daniel are two of the biggest perpetrators of all." Sarah spat the words like bullets straight at Eva.

"What are you talking about?"

"The meteorites, or what you call meteorites. They're actually incubators. You weaponized their young with the TMRWS, forced them to do your bidding with Shield. They want payback. I was sent to seek retribution and will do so. In return, they'll give me back the only person I've ever loved in this godforsaken world. I found Kaspar's activating agent for all these little nuggets of bioweapons Daniel's been sitting on all these years. What did he call them? Insurance?"

Eva's mouth hung open, her Other frantic. Her sister wasn't just psychotpathic, she was a damn conspiracy theorist.

Not true. Not all. Now. Swallow it now.

Eva popped the black rock into her mouth and swallowed. The energy twined around her limbs and boosted her Other. Unlike so many years ago when she'd saved Daniel and their group in Kansas City, she still felt in control, like she and her Other worked in unison to keep the raw enzyme in check rather than at odds. Powerful. Strong.

I know your ways, now. Do it.

Sarah charged, a macabre mask of rage transforming her face. She raised a vial in her hand and threw it at Eva's feet. It shattered, and a liquid puddled on the floor. The fumes were noxious.

Eva shot Sarah point-blank in the head. All nine rounds, rapid fire.

It slowed her down for a split second, but the holes in her skull sealed, and her sister started toward her again.

No time. Eva leapt over the spreading puddle and slammed the emergency button by the wall. The door closed, and an alarm klaxon blared throughout the facility. No one was getting in. Nobody was getting out. Complete lockdown.

A muscled arm yanked Eva around, and a fist slammed into her nose. Blood streamed down Eva's face. Together, she and her Other slammed their forehead into Sarah's. The other woman rocked back, her eyes now black as night.

Legs were kicked out, arms were pummeled, everything in rapid-fire succession. Eva slammed Sarah against a wall. Sarah slammed Eva into one of the morgue refrigerators, cracking the thick glass. That's when Eva saw what had been hidden amongst them, possibly for years. The face of Sarah's old lover was framed in the glass. This is what she'd wanted all along. Who she'd wanted.

The rock in her gut heated to an almost unbearable temperature, and her Other soaked up the energy it released until the edges of Eva's sight reddened. All pain, all thought fled, and she was pure instinct.

Eva reached over and shut off the cryo tube.

Sarah roared. Everything that had ever been Eva's sister was lost to the wrath of the enzyme flowing in her body.

They crashed together, neither completely human. Something from outside Eva's consciousness called to her, a voice familiar and urgent. She ignored it.

She clawed Sarah's face, the lines of shredded skin reforming in an instant.

Keep going. It's in her right thigh. A different voice, hollower, colder. That wasn't her Other speaking but so similar....

With little effort, she threw her sister across the room.

Opening one of the drawers next to the lab table, she took out a scalpel.

Eva! The voice coming from outside her consciousness was stronger this time. At this rate, she'd develop multiple personalities just from the many voices clambering around inside her head.

She swatted it away. The only important thing was ending her sister.

Leaping over the puddle of bioagent, she kneed Sarah in the gut. It almost raised her to her feet from where she'd fallen.

Eva slashed at Sarah's right pant leg with the scalpel, and her sister bellowed, lurching to stand. She swung a right hook into Eva's face. More blood flowed.

Open the door. Panicked now.

The words flowed over and through her.

No time. She told the voice.

She got her sister into a jujitsu throw and held on tight from behind as Sarah flailed.

Stabbing down with the scalpel, she flayed Sarah's right leg wide open.

A large chunk of black rock, bloody and hot, tumbled to the ground.

Sarah quit struggling, her entire body going limp.

Eva let her go, and awareness crept around the bulging lump in her stomach.

EVA, OPEN THE DOOR!

Daniel. It was Daniel. He was awake!

A wet, cold sensation soaked into her jeans and chilled her skin. A sharp pain knifed through her chest, radiating up to her brain.

Whatever had been in the vial was affecting her.

She pushed the body of her sister away from her and rolled to her knees, heart racing.

I can't. Sarah released something. I don't feel so good.

Daniel cursed on the other end of their connection. *We're getting in biohazard suits. Hang on and open it when we tell you.*

I missed you. The pain spread, shooting down her arm and around to her back. Heart attack.

Hold on.

If I don't make it, I love you. And Mia, tell her…tell her I'm sorry for keeping stuff from her. And Daniel, you won't believe who's in here with me. She crawled to the door, collapsing before reaching the keypad that would open it. Her Other zipped around in a panic. It had encapsulated the colder, darker presence of the black rock in her stomach, but now released it to try to repair the damage from the bioweapon.

You are not dying. You hear me?

She did. But it was too late. The world faded, then went dark.

CHAPTER 25
COOPER

he train ride home had been uneventful. A fact Cooper would be eternally grateful for. They'd gotten Stella and Zeke's old steam engine rolling. It was slow and laborious, and they'd had to stop to fill up every hundred miles or so, sometimes sooner, since water was scarce, but they'd made it.

He and Mia had left Ft. Belvoir in good hands. Stella and her rebels had set up stations to care for any stragglers making their way out. They were planning on keeping everybody from digging into the rubble. Marie had stayed behind to help manage the TMRWS, the only way in now was on Track Three. As long as nobody accessed the lower sublevels, things would be fine.

He snorted. That was never their luck, and he hadn't told Mia, but he planned on making another trip back soon to sort things out with the BUC.

It had rained three more times before they left, the clouds spreading farther and farther afield each time.

Doc Henderson had remained with the rebels, all her babies firmly under her control. Nobody seemed to know what to do with the woman, but sending her back to Nebraska was out of the question. Hensley and his rabble were still out there. At least they could utilize her wards for hunting and protection, as long as they stayed on her good side.

Three miles from home, they ran into a cave-in on Track Three and had to travel topside until they reached the dam, only to get shot at by Sarah's people.

"Sieges suck." Cooper sighed.

"That they do," Mia agreed.

"How the hell are we going to get past that?" Talia's appearance was a little rough around the edges, but both she and Jorge had recovered their energy from the fight during their four-day trek across the underbelly of the country.

The rest of their group waited at the base of the hill, eating rations and drinking water from the outpost well where, once upon a time, he'd hidden his cache on that long night with Jorge.

Rani had been petrified to come to the surface from the train, but after Mia had threatened to hogtie her and bring her anyway, she'd pulled herself together and joined them. Now, she soaked up the sun like some rare flower.

"Shoot our way through and ask nicely not to be taken out by the rail guns once we get to the wall?" Cooper lowered his binoculars. They were on the exact hill he'd been captured on only a month prior. It's funny how things always come full circle.

"The wall will be charged. Nobody's getting through that way," said Mia.

Well, hell. At least Claire was safe. Or somewhat. He'd tried to push his daughter to the back of his mind, not wanting to contemplate the consequences if they failed.

"All right. Then the top entrance to the MUC, where one misstep adds an arm or an extra eye?" he asked.

Mia rolled onto her back and gazed up at the sky. "You know, I was looking forward to a nice long bath."

"Now you're just messing with the natural order of things." He started army crawling backwards off the crest of the hill so they wouldn't be highlighted by the late afternoon sun.

Mia sighed and copied his moves, Talia doing the same. "It's probably the only entrance still intact outside of the wall. Let's go. It'll take us the better part of a day to get there from here on foot. At least we'll be traveling in the dark."

And so it was that they arrived to alarm klaxons ringing throughout the MUC and the secret room off Lab Twenty in complete lockdown. They'd left Talia and Jorge in charge in the guard room at the top and only brought Rani down, not only to open the titanium, high-security door on the twentieth sublevel, but to inject the antidote into her father.

"Where is everybody?" Cooper and Mia swept the corridors, similar to what they'd done the last time Sarah had breached the MUC. "If this is your aunt, we really need to find out how she's sneaking in."

"Daniel and Eva have combed the place and never could figure it out. I have, too." Rani whispered.

"Then why wasn't the place guarded?" Cooper asked incredulously.

Rani shrugged. "It usually is."

"We need to find Daniel's cryo, right away." Rani jogged down the hall, checking rooms. In one, they found Tamara gagged and tied to a chair.

"Well, we know what happened to the guard." Cooper released her.

"Who did this?" Mia asked.

"Sarah," Tamara choked. "Do you have the antidote?"

Mia held up a tube of cloudy liquid.

"Cooper and Mia, cut your fingers. I'll need some of your blood too, no time to explain." Tamara's face was battered, several fingers broken, but she grabbed the cloudy tube and opened the stopper.

"What are you doing?" Mia reached for the liquid.

"Now. Your mother's locked in the lab with Sarah."

Rani handed him a scalpel. Maybe she knew something he

didn't. Who was he kidding? She knew a truckload more than he did.

"Wow, on the first date." He sliced a finger open, and Tamara held the vial underneath, collecting several drops.

He handed the scalpel to Mia. She regarded it in irritation but did the same.

Tamara stopped the vial and shook, jogging down the hallway and turning into the mess hall.

The kitchen's long counter was empty except for a large generator hooked to the cryo storage and a thick cord plugged into the opposite wall like dual types of life support. Which, he supposed, it was.

Rani regarded Mia with serious eyes and grabbed the antidote from Tamara, filling a syringe. "It might not work, girl. Prepare yourself. We might not have gotten it into the cooler fast enough."

"It's his only shot, Rani. Do it."

Cooper rested both hands on Mia's shoulders from behind, and she didn't pull away but backed up until there was no space between them, and her back rested against his chest. He wrapped his arms closer, her hands resting on his arm.

Rani punched in some buttons on the side while Tamara monitored Daniel's vitals. At the moment, all was flatlined.

The top whooshed open in a cloud of super-frozen vapor, and Mia's body tensed.

With gloved hands, the two older women lifted the lid from the coffin-like container and unplugged many of the wires lining the inside. They set it on the ground, and Rani punched in a few more buttons. The panel beeped. "It'll reheat his blood."

She injected the cloudy liquid into the IV.

"With Shield, it shouldn't take very long. If he makes it," Tamara warned.

Seconds seemed like hours.

Blip.

Tamara and Rani's fingers whipped over the controls, making adjustments, their faces animated.

"It's working," Tamara breathed.

Blip. Bleep. Daniel's heart rate strengthened.

Mia's hand came up to clasp Cooper's. Hard. At least it wouldn't bruise.

Color returned to Daniel's face in increments. First, his hands, then his eyes, started twitching as if he were dreaming. Or having a seizure. Either or.

Mia pulled away to grab her father's flailing hand. "Dad, I'm here. Wake up, we need you."

The man jerked to a sitting position, his eyes popping open. "Eva!"

Not seeming to see any of them, Daniel ripped the IV out of his arm and the sensors from his skin.

"Easy, Daniel. If you tell us how to open—" Rani was cut off as the very naked, icy male rolled, then climbed out of the container and stumbled to the ground.

Cooper grabbed Daniel's arm, and the man whacked him. Yep. That would bruise.

Daniel stumbled to his feet and ran down the hall toward Lab Twenty, dragging cords and cables along behind him.

Well, the antidote had worked. And the cryo hadn't killed him. There were always positives.

Cooper and Mia flew down the hall after Daniel. Mia's distraught features were raw, and he could feel her mind racing.

Daniel stopped by the control panel and cursed. The alarm was loud, but not as much as the self-destruct klaxon had been. He massaged the bridge of his nose, his forehead crinkling in concentration.

"Daddy?" Mia attempted to help him again, and Daniel pushed her away.

When he did speak, it was rough and raspy, "Your mother's in there, and she needs help. Get me a hazmat suit, now. Everybody else out and lock down the lab. Nobody in until you sterilize every bug in here."

"I'm staying with you." Mia rushed to the decon room where the suits were held.

"Me, too, sir." Cooper got hold of Daniel's arm before he toppled over. The man flailed, but Cooper had a firm grip.

A weak Daniel wasn't disturbing. No, not at all.

Suddenly, Daniel stiffened his entire body, shaking like a leaf. He grasped his head with both hands, and if Cooper hadn't had a hold of him, he would've been on the ground.

Rani rushed over. "Seizure."

Cooper regarded the man in horror. "I don't think so."

Whispers of voices flooded his head. Not his and not Mia's.

Daniel and Eva's. They could talk to each other, too.

It explained so much.

The voices ceased, and Daniel went limp, unconscious.

Mia rushed in, her eyes wide as she met Cooper's.

"Is she dead?" she choked.

"I don't know. Get suited up, Mia. Tamara, can you drag him out of here?" Cooper grabbed the larger of the hazmat suits out of Mia's arms, tears streaming down her face.

"Yeah." Tamara lifted Daniel under his arms and dragged him backwards out of the room.

Rani punched in buttons before slamming her hands against the controls. "She has it locked from the other side."

The alarms shut off. They all froze.

"What did you push?" Mia asked.

"I didn't do anything." Rani examined the panel, but it was still lit with red.

A whir of machinery had everybody backing up. Cooper shoved Rani behind him toward the door.

It opened, and Sarah stood on the other side, leg shredded and dripping blood. "Save her."

And she collapsed in a heap on the floor.

Time moved funny. Sometimes it seemed to go by at the speed of light. Other times, it was the pace of molasses in January. Northern Hemisphere, not Southern. It was funnier how the universe worked—them arriving right when Eva needed them. Or maybe it was just a coincidence. They weren't that far behind Sarah from the East Coast after all.

He eyed the woman who had tortured him, made him do unspeakable things in the name of her justice, and poisoned his daughter. The incongruency of the shivering, hunched-over woman in front of him created a cognitive dissonance he hadn't felt in quite some time.

Sarah's eyes were clear, her hands cuffed in front of her.

Rani had rushed Eva and Daniel to a separate room. Tamara helped hook up IVs and administer antidotes to all of them. The *necrotizing putreflorum* killed the Shielded sixty-four percent of the time if left to its own devices.

Cooper hovered over Sarah. No hissing, no nasty conversations. It was as if she were a completely different person. After the chunk of meteorite that Eva had ripped from her body, he could almost believe it. Almost.

Mia stopped beside him. "They're stabilized. Dad won't leave her side. It's a little unsettling. I've never seen him act like that before."

"Almost dying will do that," Sarah shivered. Yep, it weirded him out to see her acting vulnerable. It had to be an act.

"They'll make it." Mia grabbed Cooper's hand and turned to Sarah. "So, you had a chunk of black rock in your leg. Did you put it there, or did somebody else?"

"Kaspar did, a long time ago." Sarah looked her niece in the eye—gosh, not even a glare.

Mia cocked her head to the side, confused. "Let's say I believe you. Are you telling me you're normal now?"

"About as normal as our family gets." Sarah shifted uncomfortably.

Cooper didn't feel sorry for her. At. All.

"Then call off your army."

Sarah blinked, then her eyes narrowed. There it was. The black rock couldn't have influenced her to that extent; there had to be a part of her that was naturally vicious. "I will. For ten vials of Shield. The good stuff, not the unstable crap."

Jack strode in, worry etched all over his face. He zeroed in on the woman sitting on the chair. "Sonofabitch."

And he swung one mighty fist in her direction. Cooper intercepted. "Easy. We're negotiating. Why don't you go check on your buddies, then come back to haul her ass to whatever version of prison you have here."

"It's all right, Jack, we got this," Mia added.

Jack eyed them both. "We shouldn't negotiate with terrorists."

"We're not. We're trying to stop a war. Please, trust me for now. Go, see Mom and Dad. They can probably explain better than I could, anyway." Mia shoved the angry man out the door and closed it. Quiet settled in the room.

"Think she'll do it?" he asked Mia through the link.

"I hope so. It would save us another war."

Sarah smirked like she could tell they were talking to each other by other means. Who knew? She most likely could.

"I'll give you five vials, and you euthanize your remaining Trolls. No more enslaved people, Sarah." Mia crossed her arms.

Sarah sat back in the chair, cuffed hands clasped together on her stomach. "What about Hensley? I might need those Trolls."

"Kill the Trolls, and I'll give you the full ten vials, but the Basin Territory has input on who you give them to," Mia countered.

"And the ability to negotiate for food with the Basin on an annual basis. And I want help trying to revive William with

Shield and the reanimation serum. If you do all that, we have a deal." Sarah would kill it at the bargaining table.

Cooper's lips thinned to a line. "Are we seriously making a deal with her? You don't know what she's capable of. Reanimation has never been attempted in this manner. I really don't want the full zombie apocalypse the next time around. She deserves to rot in prison." He sighed. "And what are we going to tell Jorge?"

"Let's stop the war, and then figure out all the details," Mia said back down the link, hands now on her hips."She double-crosses us, we chop off her head, no hesitation."

He peered closer at Sarah.

Her eyes were bloodshot, her shoulders still slumped. She flicked her eyes between him and Mia with a savage interest. Her shredded jeans showed the half-healed wound on her leg. "You gonna let me in on that little side conversation you two are having?"

"You only get one chance at a truce, Sarah, and only because you didn't kill your sister when you could have. If you step out of line even one inch, I'll hunt you to the ends of the earth and chop off your head." Cooper leaned in, all the menace of him and his Other in full force. "Understood?"

Rani wheeled Eva in and parked the wheelchair next to Mia.

"I second that," Eva said.

"My people are a rough crew. It'll take some persuasion without the black rock to…get them to comply. You might also want to get the meteorite in Montana. It's a little antsy now that its friend is depleted. I'm the only one who can get you down there." Sarah hunched her shoulders.

Cooper and Mia glanced at each other. Depleted? She must have meant the meteorite from Ft. Belvoir.

"Next stop, Montana to collect super creepy, possibly alien, meteorite?" Mia said through their connection.

"Absolutely."

A deep voice from the doorway caught their attention.

"I'll give you food negotiation ability on one condition,"

Daniel leaned against the doorjamb, arms crossed. Who knew how long he'd been there? The man could be a shadow when he wanted. He wore sweats, and his skin was still tinged a light blue, but he was up and about.

Sarah quirked an eyebrow but waited.

"You let us inject you with the stabilizing agent and another dose of our Shield to neutralize the free agent raw enzymes that are still running around your blood. If not, no deal." Daniel waited. How the man was standing was another mystery—no wheelchair for him.

Sarah's lips thinned. "Fine."

"I thought you'd say that." He waved Tamara in, and the woman brought in two syringes.

Sarah's eyes opened in shock. "You mean now?"

"I didn't want you to have time to wriggle out of your deal. Yes, now."

"What will it hurt, sister?" Eva asked from her place in the chair.

Sarah leaned forward. "Your experiments kill people, sister."

"Not anymore. And don't talk to me about killing people, you psychotic bitch." Eva pushed out of the wheelchair and took the syringes. "You always had a choice."

"No. I did't. Just get it over with."

Eva didn't even hesitate. "Everything would have been different if this had happened years ago."

And she injected the serum into Sarah's arm.

EPILOGUE

MIA

Sunsets were miracles. Especially ones where the brilliant purples and pinks shone through clouds.

So was the man standing behind Mia, his arms around her. Claire stood beside them on the wall, her hands buried in Kiva's fur. Weeks had passed since Sarah's retreat back to Montana.

A trip, Cooper and Mia had accompanied her on to retrieve the meteorite hidden beneath the mountain near her base. They'd left people there to manage the transition and put Jorge in charge, his settlement being the nearest to Butte. Maybe Sarah would slip up and Jorge could finally get his revenge. It was always a possibility. Talia had remained with him, guarding his backside in more ways than one.

Work on clearing the tunnels had started almost right away. Most of the workers were from Sector Nine under Jack's supervision. He watched them with an eagle eye and a smirk.

"Your parents are right. I think it's going to rain." Cooper breathed in deep. The smell of moisture filled the air, rare and lovely.

"I think it just might." Mia tilted her head up, and Cooper's lips met hers.

"Ooohh." Claire's face scrunched up in disgust.

Cooper chuckled. "Better get used to it pipsqueak."

"Just don't do it in front of me."

Mia smiled. The girl had gotten increasingly comfortable around her but was still hesitant around Eva. Couldn't blame her—Sarah and Eva did resemble each other.

"Got it. Anything else we can do for you?" Cooper's hand landed on top of the girl's head.

"Can we go see if Rani has more cookies? Please?" She gave her best toothy grin

ABOUT THE AUTHOR

About the Author: D.L. Bunch

D.L. Bunch is an author and educator based in Southeastern Washington, where her passion for storytelling intertwines with her love for the great outdoors. With a heart for adventure, D.L. draws inspiration from camping trips, her time with the United States Forest Service in wildland fire, and her many family escapades, weaving these experiences into her gripping narratives. Her debut work, *The Territory Series,* is a thrilling post-apocalyptic saga that explores survival, sacrifice, and the enduring power of hope in a fractured world. When she's not crafting tales of resilience, D.L. shares her expertise through survival tips and exclusive deals on her website, inviting readers to embrace their own adventures. Join her on this journey through the wilds of fiction and the wilderness alike at www. dlbunch.com.

SNEAK PEAK:

A NEW SERIES BY DENISE SPAIN

A New Urban Fantasy Series by Denise Spain:

Prologue:

The New York Globe: America's Best AI, Reporting Today's News Now

June 14, 2030

Cataclysm Unleashes Hell on Earth

Yesterday, at 3:47 p.m., Yellowstone's supervolcano unexpectedly erupted with a force unmatched in human history. The explosion sent pyroclastic flows racing across Idaho, Montana, and Wyoming, incinerating forests and burying communities under ash drifts up to 20 feet deep. A 500-mile-wide circle of destruction from Billings, Montana, to Pocatello, Idaho, and east to Casper, Wyoming, now being called the Inner Sector, is ground zero. Early satellite images—barely piercing the sulfurous haze —reveal a wasteland of scorched earth and shattered rock, with entire towns like West Yellowstone and Cody reduced to smoldering ruins.

The death toll is catastrophic, though numbers remain uncertain. Federal officials estimate 500,000 perished in the initial blast, with ashfall and fires claiming most lives. Tens of thousands more are missing, trapped in collapsed buildings or lost in the chaos of evacuation. Rescue teams—hampered by toxic air and blocked roads—report grim scenes: bodies burned beyond recognition, families suffocated under ash, and survivors wandering in shock. But the strangest reports come from the few images retrieved near ground zero, where the eruption's epicenter has revealed something far worse than lava…

———

L.A. Watch Gazette: Your AI Newsource for the Ages

June 15, 2030

Horrific Tragedy in the Rockies

At the heart of Yellowstone National Park—where hot springs and geysers once drew millions—lies a mile-long gash in the earth, dubbed "the Rift" by shaken geologists. Its depth is unknown as probes fail, and drones crash within its vicinity. Above its midnight-black depths, a shimmering curtain of light pulses, so bright it burns retinas without specialized lenses. Scientists are at a loss. Dr. Marcus Teller of MIT, reached by phone, called it "a geological impossibility," suggesting the eruption may have tapped unknown subterranean energies. Others whisper of something unnatural, a tear in reality itself.

Survivors near the Rift report horrors beyond the ashfall. A park ranger—pulled from the wreckage near Mammoth Hot Springs—described "shadowy figures" moving through the haze, untouched by the choking air. In Pocatello, a group of evacuees found a dozen bodies, drained of blood but unmarked by burns. On the outskirts of Caspar, a farmer swore he saw glowing orbs hovering over his fields, followed by screams that "came from the ground itself." At least 50 deaths—scattered around the outer edges of the Inner Sector—defy explanation: victims frozen in 90-degree heat or torn apart as if by claws, far from any volcanic debris. Military units deployed to the area report equipment failures and sightings of "things with wings" vanishing into the Rift's light…

———

Ft. Worth Sun Times: Writing Real News by Real People!

June 22, 2030

The Unknown Continues after Yellowstone Eruption
By Dr. Gunnar Hendricks

The Rift's anomalies have sparked panic among survivors and responders alike.

As many examples flood out of what is now being termed the Outer Sector by refugees, strange occurrences are flooding the news. In Boise, a firefighter claimed he saw a man wield light and air with his bare hands to clear a path through debris, only to collapse, his skin marked with glowing scars. In Billings, a nurse reported a patient who heard voices from miles away and ended up predicting a landslide before it happened. These incidents, dismissed as hysteria by some, suggest a deeper shift. Studying early data, Dr. Priya Anand of Caltech, warns of "anomalous energy" from the Rift, possibly altering those exposed. "We're seeing things science can't explain," she said. "People are changing."

Military efforts to contain the crisis are failing. Conventional weapons such as tanks and airstrikes have proven useless against the Rift's light, which seems to absorb or deflect them. A nuclear option was reportedly considered and abandoned after a test detonation near the chasm had no effect. Yesterday, a group of twelve civilians calling themselves "wizards" approached a National Guard outpost, claiming they could "feel" the Rift and offering to help "put a ward around it." Desperate officials are now listening to what just weeks ago would have sounded insane…

For more information, visit this author on Facebook! www.facebook.com/denisespainwriting

9 798989 295128